The Colonel and the Bee

Patrick Canning

THE COLONEL AND THE BEE

FIRST EDITION SOFTCOVER
ISBN: 1622530241
ISBN-13: 978-1-62253-024-3

Editor: Lina Rivera
Interior Designer: Lane Diamond, with images by Briana Hetzog

www.EvolvedPub.com
Evolved Publishing LLC
Butler, Wisconsin, USA

Printed in Book Antiqua font.

DEDICATION

For travelers, explorers, and those who are kind.

-PART ONE-

SWITZERLAND

Chapter One

A light burned inside each house along the road, save for one. Most of the Swiss town's inhabitants were seated comfortably under the big top of our traveling circus. We'd held a show every night that week, despite advertising as "one night only." While this inaccuracy initially encouraged attendance, the profit margin inevitably waned, as those who wanted to see the show had now done so. Our money-hearted ringleader, Ziro, accepted that he'd squeezed all the juice he could, and relinquished, underlining "one night only" with black paint on each poster around town to emphasize that this time, he *really* meant it. As it often did, the sudden scarcity resulted in a sellout for the final performance, leaving most of the houses empty but warm by the glow of some dutiful pilot light.

A line of beacons with one broken link—the dark house, the one showing signs of disuse and waste. What had happened there? A hard and fast tragedy that had shocked the community, or the slow and quiet kind none ever spoke of? The Swiss, being a polite people, wouldn't have told a traveling acrobat either way. I knew only that if I'd been born in this town, the dark home would have been mine.

As I strolled the deserted street, waiting patiently for my portion of the show to begin, the singsong voice of The Human Thesaurus rang from inside the tent, delighting the audience with his wealth of wordage as he cycled through increasingly obscure synonyms for any word the audience suggested, all in Swiss-German, given our location. My conversations with the resident wordsmith on the long roads between shows had provided me a diction many considered outsized for an uneducated, thirteen-year-old circus performer, and a female to boot.

Gooseflesh bubbled upon my arms, and I knew the chilly gaze of Ziro's sentinels, the Mirrors, traced my steps. I could not see from where the Flemish twins watched, so I was careful not to stray too far, lest they be motivated to reacquire me, a process that rarely ended well for the fleeing performer. The brothers had grey eyes flecked with yellow, set into ashy skin only a shade lighter than the irises. The jugglers swore each twin could see through the other's eyes, but I did not believe as much. The Mirrors wore, as they always did, matching cloaks of powder blue and a peacock feather earring. They were entirely mute, and never showed the faintest shadow of a facial expression. A bejewelled dagger rested on each man's belt, rumored to have ended lives before.

I put aside the familiar sensation of unflinching surveillance, and inhaled deeply. Wealthy towns always possessed the best candles, and the night's breeze carried not the acrid and fatty signature of tallow, but something light and sweet—the expensive bayberry, or beeswax even.

One of the company horses, Charles, chewed morosely at a spare bit of hay scattered behind the big top. I ran my hand along his worn muzzle while my sight returned to the empty house. For the thousandth time, I was grateful to no longer dwell in such a place, even if Ziro's circus was hardly any rosier.

The thunder and grace of equestrian dance, the siren call of the calliope, the colourful nonsense of clowns and jugglers, the barely contained menace of big-toothed predators, the scream-inducing phantasmagoria—what child could resist such a menagerie of charm? I purposely recalled little of my previous life, except that setting off with the aft-mentioned characters sounded much more appealing. So I'd volunteered to join the company, stowing away in a costume chest until my dexterity and bravado earned me a permanent position in the show. I had escaped my deplorable upbringing but somehow still managed no improvement in my station.

"I summon *again*, The Amazing Beatrix," Ziro's voice flared inside the tent, waving away my cloud of thought.

Charles jostled at hearing the ribbon of anger in our master's voice. The horse and I were both well acquainted with the sting of his whip.

I departed the mistreated horse and cartwheeled through the tent flaps, up the gangway and into the centre of the big top, where my ringleader waited with concealed fury. His body was a block of flesh and bone, carved by a lazy sculptor with no eye for detail. His perfectly square shoulders were adorned, as always, with the golden epaulettes he felt signalled regality. To me, they looked more like the push brooms used to clean up after the animals. He wore a suit of black and white pinstripes, a relic of apparel from his early days as a clown. Clowns ranked only a hair below jugglers in my index of most disliked performers.

I snapped into an acrobatic pose as the roll of the snare finished in a cymbal splash, and the Swiss audience applauded politely.

Ziro's bulk angled precariously forward. "If I have to call your name twice again, I'll feed you to the lions," he whispered.

I knew the man well enough to understand this was no colloquialism.

"But we have no lions. You left the cage unlocked in Brussels last month," I reminded him, and even though he wouldn't dare whip me in front of a crowd, I quickly ascended the rope that hung between us.

Although he was shrewd, inventive, and driven, Ziro's most prominent feature, the one only revealed away from paying customers, was his cruelty. He had love for money alone, and anyone foolish enough to come between the two met with his merciless will, and often, his whip. The same whip that would likely find me tonight for my daydreaming.

I surveyed the night's crowd from the top of the rope—debutantes in ostentatious evening gowns, baronesses suggesting just-appropriate hints of hidden lace corsets, children eying popcorn, fruits, and other treats they couldn't risk eating over pristine outfits. I read people out of both boredom and necessity. I was slight, even for a girl of my age, and our troupe did not shy away from unsavoury towns. I never minded this, as the nefarious and unlawful often proved much more interesting than the moneyed. Tonight's crowd, sparkling with earls, dukes, and countesses to spare, was quite unremarkable indeed.

All but the man with flowers in his hat.

I saw him only a moment before he saw me.

A gentleman at first and even second glance, he wore a brilliant yellow waistcoat clasped tight over a crisp, cream dress shirt. High-waisted trousers anchored the ensemble, crowned by a white John Bull hat garnished with dandelions. I guessed him to be from Britain, or at least somewhere in the Isles. Below the brim of the hat peered a pleasant face accented by a smart moustache and a pair of strong eyes, all of identical chestnut colour. His powerful gaze made me feel transparent as glass, as if no amount of subterfuge or deflection could deter him from discovering all my deepest secrets.

"*Beatrix,*" Ziro hissed up the rope in a malicious tone, frightening even for him.

I would meet his whip that night, and he would put his ample back into it.

I looked back to the man in the dandelion hat, but his gaze had moved on. It seemed he had decided he knew all about me from just one look. A stranger he would remain; unknown but perfect in my image of who he might be.

A trapeze swung near, and I grasped it easily, gliding through the air to the amazement of the populous below. A hundred voices rose and fell in unison as I twirled and leapt from one trapeze to the next, all at fatal heights since Ziro insisted shows with safety nets drew fewer patrons. My act came as natural to me as inhale, exhale, leaving my mind to consider the itch of regret I now felt. I made a firm point of avoiding regret's acquaintance, it was no chuckaboo event concluded below. I took several bows from my high perch, and watched my principal players slip through the elegant crowd, no doubt bound for an even more exclusive engagement.

I slid down the rope. Perhaps I could follow—

Ziro's iron grip found my arm.

He beamed at the lingering crowd around us, but his voice was pure venom. "See to the calliope, Beatrix. Then, you and I have business. And do well to note that any more trouble from you tonight would be very, *very* unwise."

Chapter Two

Even with a heavy canvas cover, the calliope always managed to inhale terrific quantities of dirt, sharp pebbles, still-living insects, and the occasional dead mouse. Cleaning the instrument was the most unpopular task in the company, but none had to worry because Ziro had given me exclusive license, claiming my small hands were perfectly suited for the maze of pipes. I saw it for what it really was: a punishment for being "insolent" and "mouthy."

I hardly minded though because the best material for scrubbing the pipes was newspaper, which provided the best, and really only, opportunity for education. Ziro had always assumed I couldn't read, which had been partially true when I'd joined the circus. But I knew just enough to teach myself, and with the regular cleanings the calliope required, I soon earned proficiency through practice. Though our company travelled far and wide on the European continent, we were permitted no leisure days or excursions. Reading the newspapers allowed me a wider gaze into events happening beyond the reach of Ziro and his veil of ignorance.

To my delight, the papers inside the base of the calliope were both fairly recent and in English. I skipped bits about finance and politics, zeroing in on an article on crime. *International* crime! The story detailed a massacre in a place called Batavia, capital of the Dutch East Indies. The victims belonged to a famous family of treasure hunters, allegedly killed while on the hunt for a prize piece. Two members of a rival group of treasure hunters had been arrested in Britain and were now jailed, awaiting execution.

Treasure hunters! What a way to spend one's days. No doubt preferred to whippings and pipe cleaning.

The bench I read upon see-sawed as the German strongwoman, Fräulein Haas, sat on its opposite end.

"Don't let him see you reading. He's in a right state tonight," she warned.

"I suspect he has a bit more legal pickpocketing to do."

But I crawled under the calliope anyway to begin the torturous process of cleaning, Batavian massacres and mystery objects put to filthy metal.

Fräulein Haas began her nightly workout with the single iron dumbbell Ziro had purchased for her after complaining for weeks about the price. I couldn't have budged the weight with a running start, but Fräulein Haas displayed no sign of effort as she brought it up and down in patient curls. Then she stopped, as if realizing something.

"You mentioned the escaped lions again, didn't you?"

"It was nothing more than the truth," I said.

"Don't be obtuse, Beatrix. The man is quick to anger even without a reason. I'll never understand why you think it wise to give him one. Some dogs will always bark, I suppose."

I shrugged as best I could, up to my elbows in calliope whistle.

Approaching footsteps gave me pause, but it was only Jacques, the fire eater. Jacques had the dark skin of an African and the silky voice of a Parisian. He sauntered into the tent guzzling a pail of fresh milk to soothe the trauma of his performance.

"Ten torches tonight, Jacques. You are getting a little proud I think," I said, attacking a hardened clump of mud at the bottom of the largest pipe.

"I went for a personal record as I knew I would have zeis wonderful milk to smother ze flames. Ze Swiss 'ave always known 'ow to raise a cow." He drained the last of the milk then sighed contentedly, tossing aside the spent pail.

"Jacques, you brute, that pail was for us to share!" Fräulein Haas said as she switched the weight to her other hand.

"*Désolé*, Fräulein, but my scorched throat trumps your thirsty biceps."

"And what of our young acrobat?" Fräulein Haas clucked reproachfully at my thin frame. "Malnourished for so long. I fear it may have affected her growth."

I playfully waved her concern away.

"Perhaps I have been denied the leaves on the tallest branches, but I am quite adept at employing what I have."

To make my point, I pushed hard on the mud clump. Unfortunately, it showed no signs of giving, and my words failed to match action. Jacques kicked off the stubborn bit of mud and winked at me. I saluted my thanks and rolled away from the instrument. It was clean enough, and I'd a more compelling task to set about.

The magic lantern.

The lamp's coloured glass and slides of macabre imagery suffered the same filthy fate as the calliope, miraculously attracting the soot of the road despite being stored in a box. Just like cleaning the calliope, the maintenance of the lantern was my obligation alone, but this was by my own choice. The centrepiece of the phantasmagoria was my favorite curiosity in the entire circus, with its power to summon spirits and ghouls from the land of the dead. It was all smoke and mirrors of course, scientific machinery bent to thrill and manipulate the willing. I knew this, but let the box of light and color trick me because a departure was desired, and oftentimes, needed.

I blew the dust from the night's featured slide and shivered at the image on the red glass. The Spectre: a poorly postured skeleton beckoning the viewer with a bony finger and a murderous sneer of jagged teeth. The most damning feature a face could possess was not a scowl or a scream, but a wicked smile. I remembered the very same expression on a face much more real than any projected by the phantasmagoria—but no. I would subject myself to no toxic memories. The present proved challenging enough.

The Spectre was the only slide I genuinely feared. I quickly placed it with the other panes of colored glass at the base of the machine, then set about cleaning the lens and gears. The familiar task allowed my thoughts to range, and tonight, they ranged to the dandelion man.

He had been handsome, but not uncommonly so. He'd demonstrated no unique talent and made no impression from a direct action. Yet I was drawn by a quality, one that could be seen only by those who knew to look for it. I'd seen it from the top of the trapeze. I probably could've seen it from the top of a mountain. And yet if pressed to define it, I would fail. Here was the allure perhaps, the arousal of tremendous interest with no explanation as to why.

The startled meow of a tabby cat stopped my dreaming, for our company had no tabby cat.

The sound was a warning from one of the other performers, signalling our ringleader's ingress. Ziro was sharp when it came to matters of accounting, but never seemed to realize a phantom feline's mews announced his every approach.

His blocky form rounded the ocelot cage.

"Beatrix, come with me."

I drew myself in, delaying the inevitable beating. While I would never apologise or beg for mercy, I still harboured a strong dislike for torture.

Fräulein Haas set down her weight. Jacques rose from the cot he'd been lounging on and turned to face Ziro. At even a hint of insurrection, Ziro did what he always did: he called his sentries for help.

"Mirrors!"

A moment later, the men in blue cloaks slipped from either side of the ocelot cage, startling even the keen animal inside. Ammoniac and Javellisant were nearly as feral as the caged animal behind them, and it was extremely unwise to tease their involvement.

"I'll come." I stepped forward, wishing no harm upon my fellow performers.

Jacques and Fräulein Haas watched me go, helpless to intervene. It was my smart mouth and wandering attention that had summoned the whip this night—no reason my friends should be drawn into a predicament of my own creation.

Ziro and I wove through the cluster of sleeping tents, led by the mews of the phantom cat. Each performer we passed busied themselves with one task or another, returning to their card games the second we left. I could hear The Human Thesaurus' nightly practice and called out a suggestion.

"Danger!"

"Imperilment, crisis, jeopardy, risk, exposure..."

The jugglers, whom I'd always disliked, sent an obscene gesture in my direction. I was about to return it, along with some of my own synonyms for juggler, when Ziro's powerful grip pulled me forward. Trained acrobats rarely lose their balance, but my employer yanked with such force I fell straight into a puddle of cold mud.

"Get up. Wipe yourself clean," Ziro barked as if he hadn't been directly responsible for my fall.

Now came the whip, I was sure of it.

No blows found me. I looked up and saw the barred cage we normally transported the lions in, quite empty, as I had reminded Ziro earlier.

Shoemaker met tailor as the ringleader's heavy boot connected with my behind and I spilled into the cart.

"Burden the horses. I don't want to be late," Ziro said to the Mirrors. He squeezed into his traveling coach and snapped the door shut.

I watched through gnawed, metal bars as Javellisant affixed the abused horse Charles to my cage and saddled upon his back. Ammoniac put a horse to Ziro's coach, and we set off. While I knew nothing of our destination, I struggled to imagine how the development could be, in any way, to my benefit.

Chapter Three

Ziro's coach, little more than a weathered velvet box on wheels, bobbed side to side on the rough Swiss road. I had observed my employer's coach in travel many times, but never before had it possessed such a mocking quality. My transport jostled quite a bit as well, and with the unease brought about by the uncertainty of my predicament, I felt quite sick. Had I been fed a dinner, it may have returned at this moment.

Inspired either by the addition of bars to my perspective or my lingering regret regarding the dandelion man, nausea gave way to anger. I paced the enclosure, uttering grunts of displeasure that rang close to feline snarls; perhaps the spirits of the escaped lions still lived in their former prison. Why was it I who always seemed to elicit Ziro's wrath? None of the performers were treated well, but it was my behaviour that drew his attention, and consequently his whip, most often. I spoke out of turn occasionally, that was true, but I was pristine in my acrobatics and always drew some of the loudest applause of the show.

A small stone, disturbed by one of the coach's rear wheels, bounced between the bars and struck my cheek. I snatched the rock from the floor, ready to hurl it at Ziro's coach in frustration. But it was then we crested a hill, and the stone fell from my hand, forgotten.

On the picturesque mountain ahead, stood the largest manor I'd ever seen. The loud and tasteless architecture suggested ownership by someone very wealthy and very insecure. German gargoyles and Roman columns stood alongside too many rose gardens and a bronze statue of a man in a cape, a laughably serious expression upon his face. I'd have wagered my pitiful salary this was the proprietor.

We joined a number of expensive coaches parked around a Grecian fountain. A bevy of drivers and soldiers loitered, sharing cigarettes and flasks of liquor as they conversed in Swiss German.

A man I guessed to be the head butler, stepped from the ornamented front doors and descended the many steps down to the driveway. To my eternal disappointment, he wore no top hat. I was of the opinion that if one was wealthy enough to employ a butler, there must exist sufficient funds to ply that butler with a top hat.

"Welcome to Chartish Manor," the hatless butler said suspiciously as Ziro struggled out the small door of his coach. "Your title?"

"I am Ziro, operator of the circus Lord Chartish attended this evening. He personally requested my presence at this dinner."

The butler looked unconvinced.

Ziro's face flushed, and he gestured to my cage.

"I have brought entertainment."

"Ah yes, that is as well." The butler nodded as if a password had been given. "Bring her around back. I will arrange a place for you at the table if you are hasty about it. Dinner service is imminent. And please be so kind as to move your... transports somewhere more discreet." He nodded to Ziro's coach and my cage, out of place amongst the luxury coaches.

Ziro's face flushed even deeper and he bowed, nearly toppling over with the gesture ill-advised for a man of his proportions. He spun to address the Mirrors.

"Park around back. I'll come for her when we're ready."

Orders given, he sped after the butler, narrowly avoiding the closing front door.

We rounded the manor and parked near the busy kitchen where yellow squares of window were animated with harried servants and cooks, scrambling to plate the night's meal. Waves of flavour carried on the breeze, filling my head with visions of roasted duck spiced with tarragon, pumpkin soup with cinnamon walnuts, and sugary desserts too numerous to list.

The Mirrors sat side by side, waiting for Ziro's next command. The two were like magnets that could be separated for only brief moments in time before they pulled together once again. Stoic and stone-faced as always, they showed no sign that they too smelled the delicious meal being whisked away to those lucky enough to have secured a seat at the dinner table.

"If you let me out, I wager I can secure us a few of the lemon cakes on the ledge there." These words were met unsurprisingly with no response. "While I'm at it, I'll bring you the Blue Star Sphinx, and if there's time, the Crown Jewels."

Not a hint of a smile from either mouth.

The flutter of wings stirred my hair as a pair of birds zipped into the cage.

The black and white creatures regarded me with curious, beady eyes as they hopped around the wooden floor, nipping at tufts of lion mane caught in the splinters. I held out my finger for a perch, but neither took it. One let out a mournful cry, and the other attacked it playfully. I thought their breed somewhat strange for Switzerland as they were almost certainly seabirds. But they possessed flight just the same, and so made their easy departure, chasing each other off into the night. How I wished for the same casual power of escape.

Eventually, plates that had left heaping with food, returned empty. Ziro stumbled into the kitchen, nearly trampling an unfortunate woman balancing an armful of desserts.

"Watch it," he bellowed, chest stained with a carelessly consumed meal and splashes of red wine. Purple teeth and an unsteady sway indicated some of the wine had also found the tyrant's gullet. He beckoned drunkenly at the Mirrors. "Bring her to me!"

Javellisant unlocked my cage and helped me down. He handed me off to Ammoniac, who escorted me to the manor's rear door. While the twins were dangerous, I'd never known them to be needlessly brutal. They were simply dutiful, and so the cruel will of their master was sometimes exercised through them.

Ziro dragged me through the kitchen, squeezing my arm so tight it tingled in pain.

"These people are burdened with wealth beyond even what I dared imagine. You are to perform your floor routine, and this time you'll do so without distraction."

My arm was losing feeling, and I wrenched it from his grasp.

"I am perfectly capable—"

The ringleader's broad hand swept across my face. One or two of the passing kitchen staff raised an eyebrow but quickly returned to their tasks.

"Tonight is not the night for your viperous tongue. Do as I ask or by God I'll see you spend the rest of your life in that lion cage. Wait for me to introduce you, then enter and perform. Do *nothing* else."

Ziro brushed straight his tassels on each shoulder, then entered the dining room.

Rubbing the skin of my throbbing cheek, I peeked in after him. The refined guests of the dinner were seated around an astoundingly long table that bore clusters of post-meal coffee and brandy under a filthy haze of smoke. A wisp of a man in a garish violet cape sat at the head of the table, cigar in one hand, glass of brandy in the other, spilling liquid and ash in equal measure as he shouted self-importantly into adjacent conversations. Combed hair of white-blond and a bright red mouth that was too big for his face gave him a clownish appearance, but I guessed he'd never once met levity. The mirthless face matched the statue outside. Here sat Lord Chartish. I disliked him immediately. Perhaps unfair, but a strong instinct upon meeting a stranger is ignored at one's own peril. I had experienced a reaction just as powerful, in the obverse value, upon first seeing the dandelion fellow.

A murmur from down the hall pulled my attention. As if summoned by my thoughts, there stood the very gentleman! In the servants' quarters at the far end of the hallway, he was bent low with his arm around a maid of advanced age. On her face, I spied the expression that must have been mine: joy, elation, and disbelief. Who was this individual that carried with him such an immutable badge of good will?

He drew from his waistcoat a wax-stamped envelope and a coin purse swollen with a considerable amount of money. The maid hugged him, tears streaming down her face, and the warm embrace saw him facing me.

His eyes found mine.

I attempted a smile and quickly pretended to be interested in the dining room again. I hadn't meant to intrude on such a tender moment, but how could I have known what was to happen?

Out of the corner of my eye, I saw him hug the maid once more then stride in my direction. We were to meet. Though rare, life could prove wonderfully charitable without warning or sense.

"What have acrobatics done to your manners?" His tone was direct but not unfriendly.

"I beg your pardon, sir?"

"You are a trapeze artist and you have been caught eavesdropping. What is unclear about my question?"

I searched for words without success. A silence passed that was short in every way except how it felt. Guilt and despair racked my soul for what was really a minor transgression.

"I... I—"

The man's stance softened and he removed his hat.

"Please forgive me. This blockhead Chartish has gone and served a right terrible dinner even with enough resources at hand to fill the whole Alpine Range. The champagne is pure varnish! What's to become of the lively art of conversation when hams such as he are counted as hosts? Care for one?" He offered me one of the dandelions from his hat.

"Thank you, sir." I took it, and following his lead, popped it into my mouth.

"Perhaps not the most alluring flavour, but the goal here is nourishment, is it not?"

"A lamb shank corsage would do nicely next time."

My meekness tended to evaporate quicker than average, and anyway, here was a man I sensed had no use for meekness.

He raised an amused eyebrow.

"I find mutton a poor headdress," he responded.

A soothing pause transpired, as if we'd both discovered the other in on the same joke, a member of the same club. Little in life is more thrilling than meeting another of your ilk.

"You are here to perform?" he asked.

"I am."

"Tell me, does your guardian not feed you between performances?"

"I am no ward," I corrected with dark enthusiasm. "He is my employer, nothing more."

"You speak of him with toxicity. Are you mistreated?"

"I did not mean to complain," I said softly.

"That conclusion was a result of my detection, not your confession. I must say I doubt your words though."

"You what?" I said indignantly.

"You are a creature of wit. A tongue as sharp as yours dulls under mistreatment. I have known many of the persuasion."

"But you do not know me, sir."

He smiled.

"Indeed I don't."

Interrupting the forthcoming formal introduction, Ziro appeared from the dining room.

"I have called you twice! When we return, I swear I—" He noticed the yellow-vested man and cut off sharply. "I beg your pardon, sir. I did not see you. I apologise if she was being a nuisance."

"Far from such. I was the source of her delay. Accept my apology while I allow you to finish your sentence."

"My sentence?"

"Yes, you said when you return this evening you were going to do... something. Please finish your thought."

"Oh." Ziro drowned in himself as I had done a minute before. "I... I had meant to say we will be having a curt discussion on punctuality."

"Quite right. No doubt a lesson I could benefit from myself." The man held Ziro's gaze with purpose.

Ziro kept eye contact as long as he could then hung his head.

"I… I must take her to perform now."

"She is under your employ, not mine. Consign her as you wish, and as much as she permits, I suspect." The man smiled almost imperceptibly in my direction, then entered the dining room.

Ziro's courage returned opposite the vested man's departure.

"My whip will wear thin upon the flesh of your back. Astonish these nobles and I'll give you ten lashes less."

"Less what? I must know if there is value in the offer."

"Less any number I see fit!" Ziro's voice quivered, and he spit into my face. "I have had my fill of your insolence. You will put on a show because I command it. You need no other incentive."

He created a smile and re-entered the dining room.

I wiped his spit from my face and looked inside for the dandelion man. He had made his way to the far end of the table where he slipped into a seat across from a familiar pair: the General and his wife. One looked delighted at the dandelion man's arrival, the other less so. The dandelion man smiled gamely, regaling those nearest him with an effortlessly summoned anecdote. Although I did not know his name nor he mine, I felt I had a friend in the room.

I cartwheeled in and started to flip when I was shouted into submission.

"Wait, wait, wait. Stop, stop, stop. Let's have a look at you. Let us see what passes for formal entertainment." The caped host, Lord Chartish, abandoned his high-backed chair to inspect me personally. "Give us your name then. Hapsburg? Rothschild? Or perhaps Medici?" This earned a few chuckles from the table.

"I am The Amazing Beatrix," I announced with hollow showmanship accompanied by a half-hearted curtsey.

"The 'Amazing' is yet to be proven. I've suspicion about 'Beatrix' as well," Chartish mused to himself as he circled me. "You are short. You are thin. You have a body rather like a boy and short hair to match. Tell me, child, are you a boy?" His breath was thick with drink, and for the second time in a minute, I wiped spittle from my face.

"Surely even you know the sight of a woman, sir."

A soft scream escaped one of the debutants.

I had invited the ire of yet another petty man, a talent I wished to be rid of. Chartish glared at me in astonishment then grinned, bearing every single one of his hauntingly white teeth.

"You are at best a girl. That over there, that *woman*, is my fiancée." He directed my gaze to an attractive but vacant-looking woman seated near his empty chair, attempting with great difficulty to see her reflection in a salad fork. "*That* is a woman. Statuesque. Athenian. Do not think it is time that keeps you from those ends, for you will not grow to be anything more than you are now: small, shapeless, and servile."

"Fault!"

The dandelion man, previously engaged in deep conversation with the General's wife, now stood from his chair to address the host.

"You, sir, have forgotten common decency."

Chartish looked briefly scared before becoming indignant.

"Remind me of your title. I do not recall who you are."

"I am Colonel James Bacchus, and you have embarrassed yourself."

Colonel Bacchus? But I had heard of this man! A volitant interloper who soared amongst the clouds and birds, executing feats of great prowess and ingenuity in each place he touched down. I had believed the stories and their central figure only as legend. After all, no man could swim from Britain to France or outrun a cheetah, could he? And yet if any could, I was certain it was the very same man that now defended the honour of a lowly circus performer assailed by a person of status.

Chartish settled into a dangerous amusement.

"I have embarrassed myself," he mused. "Very interesting. Pray tell, how have I managed such a feat?"

"I am rarely an obstacle to the demolition of another's character when it's done in good fashion and the party is deserving. Neither of those conditions are met here. Lest this sound righteous, I fully acknowledge to falling prey to a social misstep from time to time myself, but that does not excuse me from disallowing the thoughtless words you've chosen. I should think the transgression is still salvageable by apology."

"Apologise?" Chartish exploded in disbelief. "To a commoner? In my own house? Surely you jest." Chartish relinquished his position of assault on me and strode to face Colonel Bacchus. "I don't recall extending an invitation to you this evening, *Colonel*. How did you manage entrance?"

"Manners can gain a great deal for the genuine individual. That's where you spoil yourself."

Chartish leaned close to Colonel Bacchus and sniffed loudly.

"Your odour is quite offensive. It is a stench unfamiliar to me."

Colonel Bacchus' disposition lightened.

"Ah, yes. That would be my lip balm. I was fortunate enough to traverse the Gobi Desert last month. The experience was rewarding, though dry air is a devil on the lips. The locals made for me a balm that is wonderfully soothing, but it is derived from urine of the yak, and as such, carries a distinct nasal signature some take issue with."

"Yak urine?" Chartish interjected.

"Quite right. You refuse an apology then?" Colonel Bacchus seamlessly moved back to the matter at hand, full stride in an exchange that outpaced Lord Chartish.

"I do indeed." Chartish managed, sounding only slightly unsure.

Something changed in Colonel Bacchus' chestnut eyes. It was as if Chartish's gaff had manifested into form, and that form was collected by the Colonel. He had secured the misdeed visited upon me as a debt of his own. I'd not known a kinder gesture in all my life.

"I've no wish to keep such company. I bid you all goodnight. Thank you for your hospitality, Lord Chartish." Colonel Bacchus dipped his white John Bull hat, shook hands with the men, nodded politely to each lady, lingered a half-moment longer on the General's wife, and before I could think enough to say or do anything, he'd gone from the room.

The men immediately went back about their conversations, but it seemed to take the ladies just a touch longer to resume hushed chatter.

"A scoundrel! A man in tremendous want of moral fibre," the General shouted to Chartish.

"He is unwelcome at Chartish Manor and that is the end of it." Lord Chartish recovered from the exchange and his manner regained confidence. "Now that exclusivity reigns once again in this house, let us have the entertainment. Perform for us, whatever your name was." Chartish took his seat and resumed smoking.

Ziro, mute during the entire ordeal, delivered a threatening glance in my direction.

Whatever your name was.

I cared for none in this room. At least one wished me bodily harm. And now the most interesting man to ever pass conversation with me had quit the party, and likely I would never see him nor his fantastic manner of dress again.

Whatever your name was.

It was time I showed some talent. Not for the dinner guests, not for Ziro, and not even for the departed stranger. I wanted to prove to myself that I had value.

Whatever your name was.

If I did what was in my head, there would be hell to pay. But why not? Hell was where I laid my head, and the flames could only get so hot. If they wanted a performance to remember, I would not be the one to deprive them of it.

"My name is Beatrix, and this is my show."

I arched backwards, hands meeting the cold marble floor as my feet left it. I crossed the expansive room, on my hands, until the tips of my toes touched the stone of a towering fireplace and I could retreat no more. I held the pose, my shirt firmly secured in my waistband. It would not come out, no matter the acrobatics performed, which was by design. Ziro's reputation would be ruined otherwise. I slowly arched back to my feet and pulled my shirt bottom free.

Ziro's eyes widened as he realized my intention. He coughed in alarm.

I ran at the table.

With a high skip, I oriented myself sideways into a series of dizzying cartwheels. The tips of my garment fluttered as I moved into backflips. One. Two. Ten in a row. Lord Chartish cowered into the back of his great throne as I leapt nimbly from his armrests to the crown of his chair to the chandelier high above the dinner table. The usual gasps of onlookers that traced my progress now exploded into applause as I waved from the spinning chandelier, casting a galaxy of twirling lights upon the entire dining room.

But this was not the finale.

Swinging my legs above my head, I curled them around a chandelier arm, relaxed my torso, and hung upside down letting the back of my blouse fell away, revealing the ghastly, whip-scarred flesh beneath.

Chapter Four

"I'll see you fall to your death. I'll see you burnt alive. I'll see you fed to the lions!"

I had only to raise an eyebrow to remind my dear ringleader of Brussels, the town that had gained several man-eaters last month whether they knew it or not. I guessed they did by now.

"I know they're gone! I'll see you hanged! Trampled! You think you showed those people something tonight? You don't know what a good whipping is."

The Mirrors rode parallel to one another at Ziro's order, so he could scream at me from the comfort of his coach. I had guaranteed the beating of a lifetime, but I had earned the looks on their faces: horror on the ladies', indignation on Chartish's, incomprehensible fury on Ziro's. Even some of the kitchen staff had peered into the dining room to witness the commotion, and although they were shocked, their expressions were ones of support and perhaps even envy.

The torches of our camp bobbed into view. Whatever violent fate Ziro held for me quickly approached.

I had seen Ziro's anger before. All the performers had. But my action on the chandelier had driven him into a total rage.

"You shall feel pain until you feel no more!" he roared, crashing around with such force that Ammoniac had to direct the horse to compensate. More of the plucky seabirds I'd seen before, fled from the vehicle's roof.

Perhaps too late, I realized this would be no beating with which I could simply employ a stiff upper lip and be done with. I finally heard truth in the threats of death that spilled ceaselessly from my employer's shuddering coach.

My only salvation lay in escape.

But how? I passed from one end of the cage to the other, looking for some sort of help from outside. My thin shoe pressed upon the small stone I'd forgotten on sight of Chartish Manor.

Was the idea ludicrous? Almost certainly. But the second hand ticked my fate, and the first idea was the best idea.

I stuck one arm between the bars, compressing the stone in my hand, allying it to my cause.

"Please," I begged. "*Please.*"

I slung the fateful stone as hard as I could.

Guided by my skill or by divine providence, the projectile found its mark, striking the horse that pulled Ziro's coach square on the left buttock. With a startled whinny, the stung beast galloped at full speed, veering away from the camp.

Javellisant leapt from our vehicle to Ziro's with incredible speed, trying to help his brother wrestle with the reins of the inspired horse. Their runaway coach quickly disappeared from view.

Confused by the sudden lack of input, my own horse trotted to a halt.

This was an outcome I had not considered, a hazard of action performed without due consideration.

"Charles!" I implored the static horse. "We are siblings of the same abuse. I can free us from bondage, but you must walk. I beg of you, please!"

Charles regarded me without haste. He blinked several times, turned forward… and began to walk.

"Yes. Yes!" I whispered for fear of influencing the horse's decision.

We soon reached the cluster of tents where there appeared no sign of Ziro or the Mirrors.

"Hello!" I cried out.

Several of my fellow artisans peeked out from their tents.

"Help me, please!"

Most tucked back inside, wanting no part of anything unusual. The cursed jugglers hadn't even roused from their tent, earning my scorn then and for always.

Fräulein Haas and Jacques were at the far end of the tents, but another round of pleas roused them at last.

"Beatrix? What has happened?" Fräulein Haas asked as they ran towards me.

"Ziro intends me a beating from which I might not recover. I set his coach astray, but he will soon return."

"We are with you, Beatrix," Jacques said, voice still hoarse from the show. "'ow may we assist?"

My eyes welled in gratitude.

"I mean to escape. For good. I'll take Charles and ride from this place."

"To where?" the strongwoman asked.

I was spared admitting I did not know as Ziro's approaching cries of vengeance echoed in the mountains.

"A concern of a lesser degree," I suggested. "Fräulein, can you bend these bars?"

"I can try."

"I will consume the torches to conceal your departure." Jacques added.

"Why not extinguish them in the mud?" I asked.

"I'll 'ave that personal record yet."

I clasped his hand.

"Thank you, Jacques."

"Good luck, Beatrix."

He kissed my hand and made for the torches.

Fräulein Haas spit into her hands and gripped two adjacent bars. Exhaling forcefully, she gritted her teeth and pried. The metal yawned and yielded. I slid through the narrow gap as the camp lights began to wink out one by one. It was my great fortune to have befriended such talented performers.

"Where will you go, Beatrix?" Fräulein Haas asked.

"I mean to gain the company of a certain man."

"A man?" She said it in a way I did not mean.

"Elevate your mind, Fräulein. I seek to know him as a peer. I do not know his whereabouts, but he has inspired me enough to seek them." I unhooked Charles from the cart then stopped. "I have endangered you. Your aid in my escape will be discovered or reported by some spineless juggler."

"So it will. Ziro may whip me, but my flesh is much more tanned than yours. If he gets too rough, I'll break him in half, the Mirrors' blades be damned."

Jacques and the Fräulein aside, there was one other thing I would miss from the circus.

"Back in a tick!" I dashed through the mud to one of the loaded wagons.

Throwing aside Arabian costumes, popping corn, and some of Jacques' performing torches, I finally located my treasure.

"The magic lantern?" Fräulein Haas said upon my return.

"I consider it severance for years of thankless service. I'll miss you, Fräulein."

"And I you, my child. I hope your search yields a more agreeable situation."

We embraced. She deposited me on Charles' back, and I rode off in the direction of Chartish Manor: my only lead to find the mustachioed man fabled to fly amongst the clouds.

I only hoped he hadn't flown off just yet.

Chapter Five

Lord Chartish and his guests had long since retired for the night, leaving Chartish Manor lively as a mortuary. Charles and I rounded the building and saw no light, heard not even a whisper.

Surely Colonel Bacchus had travelled a great distance already and, in his unceremonious departure, had left no indication of his destination. A hasty escape had delivered me, yet again, into a stalemate.

The tasty scent of roses drew Charles to one of Lord Chartish's gardens. I allowed the horse to eat the prize flowers while despair found me. My courage failed; I slid from Charles' back and lay helpless on the lawn, my tears joining the chilly midnight dew that dressed the grass. My apprehension suddenly felt inevitable. The Mirrors would be on my trail by now. Could I slink back to the circus and beg Ziro for a whipping that was not fatal? No. The impossibility was twofold: he would not take me back, and would never beg him for anything. I'd lie in this garden until the soil accepted me into its womb and the roses used me as their feed. The road ahead held no prospects, no arrangements, and was beset on all sides by the cool gaze of strangers. I was alone.

Red petals fell from Charles' mouth, and I turned my head to see what had caught his attention. We both watched a woman climb out a window on the second story.

She proved admirable strength and dexterity, leaping from one windowsill to another, peach nightgown fluttering wildly as she fell the last distance to the same grass I sat upon. Excited shouting and candlelight sprang up in the corner of the mansion the woman had just left. She got to her feet and sprinted in my direction, a white John Bull upon her head.

This was no woman.

"Colonel Bacchus!"

I sprang from my grave of desolation and gave the fleeing man a start.

"Good heavens, girl! I took you for a garden gnome. Is this your horse?"

"It is."

"High time we abandon this haven of ineptitude. Mount if you value your life!"

I scrambled onto Charles, and Colonel Bacchus swung up behind me.

"To where do we ride?" I asked.

A rifle discharged from a manor window, and we were showered in dirt.

"Away, young trapezist! We ride away!"

I heeled Charles and we were off.

Colonel Bacchus further specified above the bluster of wind and gunshots, "There is a lake just beyond this outcropping. Ride for the lake."

What mode of escape lay within a lake?

"I've heard tell of you!" I shouted over my shoulder.

"Rubbish no doubt," he said, brushing dirt from the nightgown's lace collar.

"They say you can fly. Have you forgotten your wings in the bed of the General's wife?"

"Most observant! If I had wings, they'd have been left behind in the ballroom I'd thought secluded, until the butler walked in halfway through and screamed louder than a twice-pinched monkey."

"I met two women in France that claimed to have met you. They each carried—"

"A small pistol, yes."

"But they too spoke of flying. How is it possible?"

"Did you not ask the French women?"

"They were too busy cursing your name and—" Enchantment arrested my speech.

Above a black Alpine lake floated a great wicker house, dressed with lanterned windows from its base up to its fourth story. The home hung from a colossal red balloon so large, the moon itself struggled to cast enough light upon its surface.

I had heard of conveyances such as these and even seen an illustration of one in Paris, but still I had doubted their actual existence. It was said they were lighter than air, which seemed to me an absurd notion. Now I was witness with my own eyes, and although it was the only one I'd ever seen, I knew it must've been the finest in existence.

"The Oxford Starladder," Colonel Bacchus said from behind me. "A welcome sight for those who call the sky home."

"It's... beautiful," I managed.

"She is indeed. After being away for any amount of time, my heart still pauses a beat upon seeing her again."

"But how is it possible?"

"Well, some subscribe wholly to Charlières, others, Montgolfières. Gas or heat, you see. I myself practice the Rozières system that employs both to—"

The whistle of a rifle shot interrupted the lesson. The General and his soldiers had taken up a position in some nearby pines and wasted no time in sharing their ammunition with us. No doubt remained as to the Colonel's activities in Chartish Manor.

"Our schedule does not now permit sentiment or instruction. On our way!" The Colonel heeled Charles and we were off down the gentle slope that met the lake.

"What of my horse?" I said as we reached the water's edge and dismounted.

"My dear, these Alps are a horse's paradise. Ample fine grasses and butterflies to chase for days. We should all be so lucky."

I held Charles' muzzle in my hands and kissed him, my fellow refugee from a brutal system.

"Not putting me on, are you?" I asked Colonel Bacchus.

"I tell no false stories. I say, speak truth always and with brevity! Come now and loose the poor beast before a bullet finds the three of us."

I let fall the animal's saddle, and, tearing off one of the buckled straps, slung the magic lantern across my back like a bandolier. With a pat on the rear, Charles bounded off, his aqueous twin running in inverse before the original broke from the lake and vanished into the wild green beyond.

"Into the water!" The Colonel directed me.

I dove in without delay, and a thousand needles of cold pierced my body, removing my breath as successfully as the Oxford Starladder had done moments before.

"Double-time now!" The Colonel leapt from the shore and soared over my head, lady's nightgown and all, into the icy water. He let out a cry of surprise then began to swim towards a rope that rose taut from the centre of the lake.

By the time we reached the spot, my hands were so numb I could scarcely make a fist, much less grasp a rope. We both clawed fruitlessly at our means of exit.

The gunfire rang closer, and I could now see two light blue cloaks fluttering down the hill. Ziro and the Mirrors had indeed found me.

"My hands are frozen," I cried out. "I've no grip!"

"Do you know pat-a-cake?" the Colonel asked.

"I d—do," I shivered.

"Pump those matchstick legs of yours and keep your hands above the water line. Here we go!"

Although the singing was unnecessary, together we slapped our hands in rhythm, shouting: "Pat-a-cake, pat-a-cake, baker's man. Bake me a cake as fast as you can. Pat it, roll it, and mark it with a B. Put it in the oven for baby and me."

The soldiers had reached the shore. Their shots surely would have been true had they not depleted so many flasks earlier in the evening. But we couldn't rely on poor aim forever, as even a drunken soldier finds his mark eventually.

"Patty cake, patty cake, baker's man. Bake me a cake as fast as you can. Roll it up, roll it up, and throw it in a pan!"

The Mirrors cut like shark fins through the lake crowded with drunken soldiers who squeezed off wild shots from their rifles amid efforts to avoid drowning.

"Patty cake, patty cake, baker's man. Bake me a cake as fast as you can. Roll it up, roll it up. Put it in a pan andtossit in the ovenasfastasyoucan!" With an authoritative slap, we concluded the thawing of our hands.

"Grasp without delay!" the Colonel shoved the rope into my hands. "I'll unseat our anchor."

He tucked his hands into the sleeves of the nightgown and swam down, leaving his white hat to float on the surface.

"Colonel Bacchus!" I gasped.

The rope shuttered. I squeezed the line tight just as it raked upward with tremendous force, burning even my well-worn palms.

Freed from her mooring, the Oxford Starladder rose up at an angle. I looked below my trembling feet to behold the Colonel rising majestically out of the water and into his hat. He stood upon a hook that had moored us to the lake, waving his John Bull in valediction to our frustrated pursuers: the drunk soldiers, the red-faced General, the even redder-faced Ziro, and the twin wraiths that had gotten close enough to cut a slash in the Colonel's nightgown.

"Climb if you wish to see another morning's light!" the Colonel shouted up the rope.

"We have eluded them. We are escaped," I said, clutching tight to the rope.

"See beyond your direct predicament. Our path will dash us to pieces."

I followed his gaze. We were caught in a healthy Swiss wind driving us straight towards a cliff face.

"There is a leather strap that hangs below the envelope—"

"The envelope?"

"The balloon, young performer, the balloon! You must pull it to gain us altitude. Now climb! Climb, damn you," he cheered.

I scrambled up the remaining length of rope with shaking hands as the lingering freeze of the lake was exacerbated by the very wind that sought to destroy us. How had we so angered nature?

Upon reaching the wicker of the basket, I looked down. Never in my life had I seen the ground pass by so quickly; all below stretched into blurred lines of dark colour.

I climbed across the bottom of the basket. Had I chosen any profession other than acrobat, I think I should have lost either my grip or my nerve and plummeted to certain death below. But I was strong in finger and will, and easily made the side of the basket. From there, I clambered up the thatch-work wall, past windows coloured with the light of Moroccan lanterns and arrows buried deep in the wicker, tails fletched with the rainbow feathers of some tropical bird. It was safe to assume the Oxford Starladder had travelled beyond Switzerland. At last I reached a staircase that wound round the craft's exterior, and I was permitted to sprint the remaining distance.

Upon gaining the top deck, I rushed to the thick leather strap that hung exactly where the Colonel had said. The balloon above eclipsed the moon, giving the red fabric a rubicund glow that delayed my action with its charm. Regaining focus, I heaved down upon the strap and was blasted to the ground by a force of volcanic air.

"Higher!" the Colonel called from somewhere within the basket. "Higher, you incorrigible gymnast!"

I could hardly believe it. His voice was not thick with worry or even fear. It was jovial. The madman enjoyed this.

Springing to my feet, I again pulled on the leather, this time prepared for the stifling ceiling of heat that fell upon me. The basket pushed against my feet. We were gaining altitude, but was it enough?

No.

The Oxford Starladder had risen but still stayed on target to smash into the approaching mountain.

"The cavalry has arrived!" The Colonel sprang from a spiral staircase in the middle of the deck and joined me at the leather strap. "On three. Actually, better make it two. One, two!"

We pulled on the strap until I feared it would bear no more force and break apart in our hands. The flame above our heads erupted into a pillar of angry light, illuminating the brilliant crimson of the balloon so that it was all I could see, and the world was but a shimmering ruby. The basket pulled roughly to keep up with the balloon, then in a shock, tipped forward. The Colonel and I spilled into the waist-high wall of the deck but were saved from being ejected as the basket swung back to equilibrium.

A herd of stones tumbled down the mountain behind us. The basket had struck it, but only enough to disrupt a bit of rock and snow. We were, at long last, properly escaped.

The Colonel collapsed onto a thick leather chair, exasperated with pleasure.

"Close shaves are rather invigorating, are they not? Turned out to be a rather fine dinner party after all."

I opened my mouth to speak but was cut off by a frightening chorus of bird calls that enveloped us from all sides. The noise was haunting, yet beautiful, and rose to a deafening racket as what must have been a hundred birds fled from hidden roosts in the basket to circle the craft in a frantic ring of black and white bodies.

"There, look." The Colonel indicated the sky beyond the ring where two more of the birds approached in the moonlight.

One landed upon his outstretched arm, and I took closer stock of the animal's features. It was definitely some sort of seabird—an elongated beak paired with a compact, oval body. The Colonel stroked the bird's chest and it let out a forlorn note that reminded me of a dog left out to the cold.

"Manx shearwaters." The Colonel plucked a note from the bird's leg and the relieved animal flew out into the circle. "They have something of a bad reputation for their devilish cry, but they are loyal, self-reliant, and can home like few other species. These two have just come from Belgium."

"Belgium! But how could they find you so readily?"

The Colonel kicked a dark grey stone next to his chair. Set into the rock was an antique-looking compass.

"The rock is a magnet. They seek it out." His voice trailed off as he became lost in whatever news the note brought.

I refrained from interrupting as I observed his disposition traverse from jest to solemnity. Then he recalled my presence.

"The order of the evening has been altered from recreation to obligation. You may stay here for the night, but you must be off in the morning. There is a room on the third floor you may rest in—the Nimble Hare. I will leave a carry of provisions for your departure."

"Nimble Hare? But where are you going? What news has the Manx brought?"

"Bad, I'm afraid."

"No matter your path, I must come with."

His attention found me, and he shook his head with resignation.

"Out of the question. This ship's destinations are far too dangerous. I will grant you escape but not permanent passage."

I moved to protest, but the man in the peach nightgown departed down the spiral staircase.

The panic I'd felt in the rose garden returned. Here I thought I'd gained an ally and perhaps even a place to lie my head. It was clear now these were luxuries that would not simply be gifted, and if the order of the morning was one of expulsion, I had only that night to make my case.

Chapter Six

I descended the twisting staircase the Colonel had taken. Judging by sound, he had taken to some part of the fourth floor, but I continued my descent per his instruction.

The third floor held the colourful lights I'd seen on my harried climb out of the lake: Moroccan lanterns ancient and gorgeous, lighting one hallway in leaf green, another in glacial blue, a third in rich gold, and the last in a royal violet.

I traced my fingertips along the walls of the green-lit hallway. The wicker felt thick and sturdy, hung with scientific sketches of plants, an ornate Cuckoo clock, and many other curiosities I forced myself to take no note of. Were the Ox really to be nothing more than a wonderful memory, perhaps I could ease the sting by lessening the powers of detail.

The floor was oriented as a cross, with bedroom doors set into the inside corners. Above each was a display of taxidermy: a frog lying on its back underneath a distended belly, lazily stretching its tongue for a fly; a pair of mongooses, one boosting the other over a low stone wall; a showy praying mantis, green and pink limbs stretched high in a grand display; and a rabbit bounding over a fallen branch. At least the Nimble Hare mystery was solved.

A soft bed filled one corner of the room, at its side, a lamp to read by. I ducked out of the strap that held my magic lantern and set it on the ground. The wooden showcase behind me held a set of handsome swords, some of which had been disrupted by our collision with the mountainside. I restored them to their showcase and traced my fingers across intricate symbols in their metal hilts I guessed to be Chinese. The showcase itself was accented with carvings of Norse gods. Yes, it was certainly safe to assume the Oxford Starladder well-travelled. While Lord Chartish's international stylings had been careless and garish, the Ox's pieces felt collected, not simply bought. These keepsakes were common, and all the more impressive for it. My attempt to avoid falling in love with the Ox had failed almost immediately.

I moved a small leather chest from the bed and laid my head upon the pillow, gazing into my sole possession. The magic lantern had survived its unexpected dip in the lake. The Spectre's red glass was slightly askew, so I withdrew the slide and quickly returned it to its proper place. Often I had snuck the magic lantern into my tent at night where I would light it under the covers and sleep with the company of creatures yellow of eye and black of horn. But never The Spectre. The demon's smiling expression always summoned the memory of being unwanted, something I needed no reminding of. Now I was faced with a new unwelcome, and to depart this station would be intolerable.

I bound from the bed. This was an opportunity I'd never seen before and would never see again. Colonel Bacchus fascinated me. I was not sure I *liked* him, but by God he was interesting.

Yet he insisted I could not stay, and what had I to offer? He didn't impress me as a man easily entertained by cartwheels and big tent theatrics. It appeared he lived his life in a manner even more death defying than my own.

What could I offer then... except myself? He did have an appetite for women.

"And am I not a woman myself?" I said aloud.

I rifled through a clothes dresser. Inside lay a flowing blouse, moss green in colour, much too large for me. But my intentions did not require a glove fit. I removed my clothes and hung the blouse about my body.

My mind was thick and my fingers tingled as I climbed the steps of the spiral staircase. We'd a hypnotist in the circus, and while I'd never believed the effect, I was sure this was the advertised sensation. Candelabra in one hand and excess of dress in the other, I stepped from the staircase and found Colonel Bacchus inside a cluttered navigational room. He stood immersed in concentration over an abundance of maps, tracing routes with his finger, murmuring in disapproval, and starting again. Still in my trance of desperation, I framed myself in the doorway until he looked up.

I allowed the generous dress to fall a bit as it wanted so badly to do. Head hung tight to my chest, I attempted to flutter my eyelashes as I'd seen burlesque dancers do. My stupor abandoned me at this critical moment, and embarrassment hit as cold as the shock of the Swiss lake. This man had the refined females of Chartish Manor dizzy with lust. He could've seduced any woman in the room—likely the world. Chartish was a bastard, but perhaps he was right. I was no Athenian, no paradigm of physical beauty.

Colonel Bacchus had still said nothing, and I somehow managed to raise my chin.

"Colonel Bacchus, if—"

"Lose the thought and do not find it again," he speedily returned the dress to my shoulders, swaddling my neck with the surplus. "You'll catch a death of cold walking around this way." He turned from me and clasped his arms behind himself, tucking them into the small of his back while he paced in deep thought. Then he stopped and looked at me. "I pity your situation, but understand I've no use for an employee."

"I do not want your pity," I said, suddenly annoyed.

"I have no desire to be a wet nurse either."

"And I have no use for one!" I cried, now fully aggravated.

He resumed pacing, arms locked in their position of deep contemplation. He began to shake his head and I feared an undesired decision was coming.

"What news did the Manx bring?" I asked quickly.

"I seek a dangerous criminal. Some agents of mine may have a lead in Belgium."

"I will help you find this criminal."

"I will assume you do not possess the tracking techniques of the American Indian nor the psychic powers of the Eastern mystic? The question then becomes, what skill do you have to offer?"

The question was not put to me coldly, but I responded with great enthusiasm. "I saved our lives only moments ago. If not for me, you would be dashed upon the side of the mountain or shot through in the rose garden of Chartish Manor!"

He ceased pacing and stared at me for a time before answering.

"What is your name?"

"Beatrix."

"Beatrix what?"

"Just Beatrix."

"You have no family name?"

"I do not know it. You may call me The Amazing Beatrix if it's more comfortable."

"I have neither the desire nor the lung space required to use such a ludicrous moniker. How does Bee strike you?"

"I've been called worse by better people."

"I doubt the latter." His eyes narrowed in amusement, then his arms released. "I apologise for my debt of introduction. My name is—"

"Colonel Bacchus. I've heard of you, remember. They say you traverse continents in a day's time, draped in doting cherubs and ribbons of white cloud."

"The timetable may be off, and I can't speak to the nude infants, but I suppose we do tow a bit of cumulonimbus every so often. Anything else you've heard is likely understated rumours of debauchery, which cannot stand in place of a proper introduction. I am Colonel James Bacchus, citizen explorer of this marvellous world and tenacious solver of its inhabitants' many problems. Friends simply call me, Colonel."

He removed his hat and bowed in humble introduction.

"Does this mean I can stay?" I hazarded.

"You may help me find the man I seek. If you cease to do so, you will cease my company. If you prove utility and worth, you have a ticket. But hear this: I am not responsible for your safety or peace of mind. This ship has a purpose. You are not my guest and I am not your employer, guardian, or steward. You will be leagues from mistreatment, but understand that the Ox is, by necessity, a meritocracy. If you consign to travel upon this ship, you must do so as an equal."

He held out a hand.

I resisted the urge to jump and embrace him. As had been made abundantly clear, this would not be a traveling ticket won by inappropriate affection. I met his grip and we carried out a sound handshake.

"The illusion of a free ride could prove disastrous to your worldview. Your first flying lesson begins tomorrow, in the small hours. Goodnight, Bee."

He turned his attention back to the maps. I'd gained his company for a while longer at least.

I quickly retired from the map room and returned to the Nimble Hare. With passage granted, I allowed my heart and eyes to open fully and accept the Oxford Starladder as I nuzzled into the bed's bountiful sheets and quilts. There was work to be done, but for the time, I was warm and safe. A fox in her buried den. An owl in her lofted nest. Better yet, I had discovered a clear purpose and aim, even if only for a time. I would help find the criminal sought—that was the chip I'd bargained with after all. But too there was this enigma pressed into flesh, adorned with cap and flower, dropped straight into my path. Did he fly to avoid definition? Well I now flew with him. If I'd any ability to read others, here was my ultimate test. I would know the man. I would know him true.

-PART TWO-
BELGIUM

Chapter Seven

I was awoken the next morning by a shock of cold upon my cheek. I rolled nimbly from the bed to behold a drip of frigid water coming from the ceiling. Had we crashed in the night? Was the Ox submerged? The open window beside the bed showed a dark sky, quickly nixing this hysterical theory. I raced up the spiral staircase to discover the source of the drip and found the Colonel brewing coffee in the Ox's kitchen, directly above the Nimble Hare.

His chestnut hair was freshly combed, the peach nightgown replaced by clean-pressed pants and shirt of brilliant white. On the table lay his John Bull, now home to two yellow daisies. His waistcoat was again yellow but slightly different than the first I'd seen him in. It matched the colour of the flowers exactly. How expansive his wardrobe must be to match the hue of every bit of flora. At his feet lay a large chunk of ice.

"Ah, Bee. Good morning. I hope you aren't put off by the ice, but I find it useful for affecting a brisk start to the day."

"Where did you find ice?" I asked.

"Plucked it from a lake we crossed near an hour ago. I thought a slow drip through the floor would allow you enough time for rest and, of course, also put an end to it. Since you are indeed awake and appear revitalized, I will assume I was correct. Before we make the deck, would you like a coffee?"

"Have you any tea?" I asked.

The Colonel gave a staccato laugh as he poured his coffee. "Why, Bee! Tea is for the indecisive, hard pressed to take a position on which way to comb their hair in the morning. A more apathetic beverage is hard to come across. Coffee begs you to take it somewhere new. A welcome traveling partner, an astute mind sharpener, and a trustworthy enema you can set your watch to."

"Very well put, Colonel. Just the same, have you any tea?"

The Colonel sighed.

"In the box here."

He produced a small tin and slid it across the smooth wooden countertop. I opened it to find a healthy store of tea leaves, some of which smelled of lavender. I inhaled fully and smiled in olfactory ecstasy.

"If tea is to be drunk, I find lavender to be one of the rare acceptable flavours," the Colonel said, still spurned by my insistence on such an indifferent drink.

I scooped some of the lavender into an infuser and set it in a mug of hot water before we climbed to the deck. Our cups steamed furiously in the brisk air of a morning barely lit by a sun still below the horizon. Several Manx floated up from their nests below and lazily played amongst the ropes of the great red envelope. Still dressed only in my performance tights and blouse, I began to shiver.

"You'll find outerwear in the chest there."

The Colonel nodded to a wooden chest along one of the low walls of the deck. He set our mugs and his hat on a two-chaired table adorned with a bowl of sugar cubes. The great leather chairs accompanying the table were wind-worn and deeply creased. If furniture could be wise, these would be village elders.

I pulled the pelt of some huge black animal from the chest and shuffled back to the Colonel in my woodland disguise.

"There are no accolades or demerits in this instruction," he began. "With regard to flying, there are safe landings, and there are wrecks, with hardly an in-between. I think it's rather more fun that way."

"I'm listening," I assured him from beneath the overbearing cloak.

"The balloon will obey two commands: up or down. To gain direction, you must find a correct lane of wind. Take us up a touch, and I suspect we'll drift northwest."

He ceased speaking and left me to action.

"How do I know the direction?"

"A capital first question. Do you know how to use a compass?"

"Yes."

My eyes went to the brass compass set into the magnetic rock at our feet. The compass' tarnished surface suggested it was definitely aged—a clasp on the side looked about ready to fall off. The indicator turned constantly in a slow spin. Either we had traversed some spectral boundary, or the instrument had broken.

"Well I don't know how to make use of a broken one," I said, confounded by the restless needle.

"One for significance, one for function," he announced. "That one there's quite useless for navigation, a result of the magnetite I felt would make a handsome mount for it. I presume the wandering needle has some metaphorical significance I'm not nearly clever enough to identify. The instrument you seek is here."

He gestured to a glass orb mounted atop a pillar of elmwood. The elaborate compass inside might have been made from the wares of a king's finest watchmaker: rotating rings of declination and position moved in steady concert above calligraphed letters of cardinal direction engraved into the azure base of the sphere. Delicate stencils of moon phases, constellations, and wind positions passed over one another in a slow mechanical dance.

"Marvelous," I breathed.

"But how does it work?" he said, anticipating my question.

I was then enlightened on matters of magnetic north and true north, on why crescent moons made for the best traveling partners but were bad luck for a game of Old Maid, on what times of the year Orion's patch of sky was temperamental and how his mood could be overcome. I also learned how to make a polish from Manx guano and sugar that kept the orb's glass invisibly clear.

"The trick is in finding the sugar, as I'm a fiend for it in my coffee and any remainder is often thieved by the stowaway!"

His pronouncement ended in a shout, and for a moment, I thought he meant to attack me. He leapt forcefully across the deck, landing near the breakfast table where a small rodent scurried away with a cube of sugar in its mouth. The Colonel's outstretched hand could not find the animal before it disappeared into a gap in the basket.

"Blast!" He brushed off his waistcoat and noted my lack of reaction. "You've no aversion to rats?"

"I came across enough in the circus to form an opinion. I actually find them to be some of the more amiable of creatures considered vermin."

"*That* is Jasper, a packrat. I've nothing against his kind except for their proclivity to dash off with anything small or shiny. We've no more marbles to play with and the ship's store of salad forks and cufflinks are forever at risk. Everyone of substance needs a foil, it's just my great misfortune to be paired with one that can escape so readily. Ah, tea's ready."

He withdrew the infuser and handed me my mug. I thanked him and shed the animal pelt as golden waves of direct sunlight reached us at last.

The tea tasted delicious, and I gratefully drank most of it down before the Colonel had even finished preparing his coffee. I watched as the man built a crystalline pyramid of sugar in his cup, nineteen cubes in total. He stirred the structure into the black liquid until it eroded into a brown slosh.

"There we are."

"You take no milk?" I asked, half in jest.

The Colonel huffed.

"Imbibe the mammary ghost slime of thoughtless gluttons bested by a pasture fence? I've far better things to do with my time than ingest the excrement of udders. Surely you know me better than that by now."

"This coming from a man who by his own admission employs yak urine on his face?"

"A fresh coat this morning, you may notice," he said through shiny lips. "Now then, if we're quite through discussing the finer points of diuretic embellishments, I do believe we're about to shake hands with the pines."

A fast scratching noise began to repeat somewhere at the bottom of the basket as we descended into a forest. I yanked the burner strap and we jerked up into the clear sky once more.

The Colonel eased my pull on the thick leather cord and our ascent evened out.

"Despite the demands of last night's departure, a gentle touch is almost always advisable. Finesse will see you arrive safely."

The burner strap above our heads was easy to identify and know the function of, but it was only one of many whose appearances were deceptively similar, like the ropey canopy of a great leather jungle. The Colonel gave me a once-over at breakneck speed, and I did my best to remember which was which. The braided valve line vented the top of the envelope, and a secondary looped valve line vented the smaller balloon of helium *inside* the main balloon. Twisted ballast lines released bags of sand for quick lift, the bags' individual weight corresponding to the thickness of the cord attached. Most dangerous of all was the ripping line, which connected to the ripping panel: a perforated strip of canvas on the main balloon pulled only for a quick landing when the craft was not more than a few metres from the ground. Pulling the ripping line at any significant height meant certain death for all aboard.

"The name of the game is buoyancy, of course. Less than a degree of temperature informs our ascending or descending. Weight is of similar importance, so I like to keep a close eye on it. I pegged you at about six and a half stone?"

I nodded, impressed, and remarked, "It's a brave man who estimates a woman's weight aloud."

"Only if he does so without accuracy," the Colonel returned. Then he reconsidered. "Although that too can invite trouble... In any case, six and a half stone was the total weight of the ballasts I dropped. With regard to altitude, I prefer to travel in the neighbourhood of approximately five hundred metres, depending on the required direction of travel, naturally. You'd do well to remember the helium cools more quickly at night. That should suffice for now. I abhor formalized instruction. Comes dangerously close to the greatest of all presumptions: giving advice."

"But I've still got so many questions," I protested.

"Flying the Ox is much more akin to playing an instrument than operating a machine. Approach the challenge less formally, do so with confidence, and the craft's perfect obedience will be your reward."

I lost sight of the burner strap and by accident pulled a vent on the main balloon. We began to rotate and descend with great rapidity. The Colonel allowed me to find the correct cord on my own, and I did so just in time as the Ox nearly scraped a rolling pasture hill, startling a herd of brown Belgian cows enough to sour their milk.

Taking care to avoid the ripping line, I continued to bring the Ox up, searching for the northwest wind. To my chagrin, I sent us southeast, and it took a deft intervention from the Colonel to set us right. Applying the correct pressure on the correct combination of cords in the correct sequence did indeed give him the appearance of an accomplished maestro.

"Skill comes with practice, and northwest can be elusive. North*east* can be downright tempestuous," he said as if recalling a talented snooker rival.

I readied another question, but the Colonel anticipated me. He held up a gentle hand to stay the incoming query, motioned with both hands downward, indicating I should relax, then gestured to the edge of the Ox.

So worried I'd been about that morning's lesson, I'd hardly taken a moment to observe our environment. I joined the Colonel at the railing, and became lightheaded with wonder. The full effect of flight had been disguised by darkness the previous night, and now, in the maturing light of dawn, I beheld a world transformed by perspective: rivers and mountains were maps come to life, trees were seas of leaves that shimmered emerald in the breeze, even birds flew at a height far below the Ox, moving like schools of fish in currents of wind.

"Toast my bloomin' eyebrows," I mumbled, forgoing any attempt at eloquence. "I didn't know... I couldn't have imagined..."

"Wonderful, isn't it? From this height, we're permitted to see plainly the orchestrations of daily life, rank with crisscrossing motives and the clutter of needless haste. Up here in the rarefied air we are weightless in cool æther, unspoiled by the odour and noise of man's desires far below."

We stood side by side, watching the scene in silence, until something in the distance stole the Colonel's gaze.

"There. Antwerp on the horizon. Drink your leaf juice if you must."

By now, all of the Manx were flying in a loose halo about the Ox, gently displacing the Belgian mist we floated in as they dove and twisted as birds in play.

"They have such charm and spirit," I said.

"They detect my excitement. This visit could prove fruitful in our search for the criminal. He's been most elusive thus far."

"Do you know the murdered party?"

The Colonel's face fell a note, but he recovered quickly.

"I'm interested in the criminal."

"To bring him to justice?" I gulped my tea. "For this or a past transgression?"

"There is plenty to choose from. It is enough for you to know I seek an audience with the man."

"He has committed other crimes?"

"Certainly."

"Is he dangerous?"

"*Most* certainly."

I finished my tea as the green vegetation and black soil of tilled fields shifted to the red brick and grey stone of buildings. Antwerp's harbour introduced itself to the nose long before the eyes.

The Colonel inhaled deeply.

"Have you been?" he asked.

I shook my head.

"A bastion of crime and seafood, how I adore this city. I apologise as it's unlikely we'll have time for a proper tour. Perhaps a return under less harried circumstances. Unfurl those ropes there, won't you?"

The spiderweb of roadways below passed ever faster as we descended. I let drop a collection of heavy ropes over the side of the Ox as the Colonel set her down in a rather regal park. Despite the posh surroundings, there was an air of danger. Apparently, the Colonel felt it too.

"No chance we're deflating here," he said. "Down the steps with you. Help secure us."

I stepped from a door at the bottom of the basket and onto the grass to find a stout, friendly-looking couple approaching the Ox.

The Colonel called down from the roof.

"Thelma and George, this is Bee. Bee, you are meeting Thelma and George, the Newlyweds. Pleasantries to follow, no doubt, but for now marry us to the ground."

George tipped a Scottish cap, Thelma nodded a warm greeting, and the three of us set about hammering the Ox's stakes into the lawn. I found the work easy, as it was not unlike setting up the big top.

The Colonel joined us on the ground and was immediately assaulted by Thelma.

"She's not of proper age! You've gone too far this time, Colonel!" Her scolding finger backed him up a stair or two.

"Thelma, your outrage is well-intended but ill-informed. Is your regard for me really so wanting? She is a fellow passenger, not a conquest."

Thelma looked at me, and her anger melted.

"Oh. Oh, I see! Lovely to meet you, my dear!" She rushed forward and embraced me tightly. "We haven't had true company on the Ox for some time now."

"What about that three-penny upright in Holland? The large one?" George mimed a big stomach and waddled back and forth.

"Tarts don't count, George!" Thelma scolded. "I mean a lady of refinement who stays for more than a night!"

"Well, how's I supposed to know what ya mean?"

Thick Scottish accents delivered their words back and forth with great volume and intensity but not unkindness. They spoke like a married couple.

"You are newlyweds?" I asked, somewhat dubiously as they did not appear to be, in any accurate sense of the word, young.

The Colonel stepped off the stairs and joined us.

"They married long ago. I call them such because they still act like newlyweds."

I had taken the pair as siblings at first, their heights and dispositions so neatly matched. When the Colonel had spoken of his agents in Antwerp, cheerful Scots of advanced age was not what I had imagined. They were smartly dressed in unremarkable clothes, well-worn but tidy. George wore a green tartan blazer and a matching tam o' shanter with a great ball of red yarn at its centre. Thelma's jumper, the colour of faded camel hair, was crowded by a half-dozen pockets packed with train tickets, bits of yarn, and other practical minutiae.

I liked them immediately and immensely.

"Where's the scene then?" the Colonel asked.

George unwrapped a paper from his breast pocket and handed it over.

"Le Grilleon Aveugle. Translates more or less to The Cross-Eyed Cricket. Shoddy place with a painting of a cricket next to the door. Bunch o' sailors inside who don't look to have tasted the sun for some time. An' they're already half up the pole with drink, so be careful. That there's a map and the amount I think the police'll take."

The Colonel raised an eyebrow at the price but didn't balk.

"How enterprising of them. This is an estimate?"

"They were bloody hard to pin down. One's all but inconsolable about some marital troubles or such. Other one seems a bit thick in the head."

"Their hunger for francs seems healthy enough. Very well. If you'd be so kind as to fix us up again. The usual expendables should do. And if you can manage to secure some jenever and the requirements for a good waterzooi, I would be immensely grateful. I'll see to the fish."

"Right-o," George said, understanding directions I found most confusing.

The Colonel stepped into the Ox and returned with a rapier and a fold of francs he tucked into a vest pocket. The thin sword entered a sheath on his belt.

"James," Thelma spoke up, looking at the Colonel with increased sincerity. "We're very sorry."

The Colonel nodded curtly.

"Thank you. Bee, you're with me." He strode off, and I jumped to follow.

What had just transpired I couldn't be sure, but this was not the time to press.

"You consider no firearms?" I asked instead, studying his rapier.

"They are unsporting, fit only for ladies whose principal aim is self-defence."

This sounded to me an attitude likely to find him shot through with an unused sword in hand, but I said no more on the topic.

"Are we really to leave the balloon up in such a way?" I asked, trailing after him while returning a sunny wave from Thelma.

"Fuel permitting, I have found it prudent to always prepare for a quick exit. Most times it is not needed, but the additional effort is forgiven by the times it is. Our recent foray in Switzerland, for example. Keep up now, they won't hold the scene forever."

"How *is* the Ox fuelled?" I dodged a merchant's horse and coach as it sped by, the driver and his animal harbouring little concern for the welfare of pedestrians.

"A supremely inflammable gas they call hydrogen, and another, helium, which does not burn but is rather expensive. One can quite easily obtain these miraculous elemental substances by dissolving metals in acid. I've a network of amateur chemists who inherently deal in the practice, or have been otherwise persuaded to do so by my subsidy in the past. My merry band of alchemists."

I pulled him out of the path of a team of horses that thundered straight across our intended path.

"Cheers," he replied, hardly altering his step before the explanation resumed. "My symphony of lift is more efficient than any brazier of coal alone, but I of course employ a burner as well. Common sense dictates I use helium in between hydrogen and the burner to avoid becoming a firework. We are very much in debt to the Montgolfier Brothers, as well as Mister Cavendish, Archimedes, and so on. There's a bit of literature on the subject in the Ox's library."

"The Ox has a library?"

"Of course she does."

"But what of the weight?"

"Ignorance weighs far more than knowledge. A man of my profession relies on information and education quite often."

Our surroundings, once the luxurious flats and cheery vendors bordering the picturesque park, had twisted into crooked lines of streets buttressed with shadowy architecture. I suspected moral fibre became more scarce the closer one drew to The Cross-Eyed Cricket.

"Colonel, what is your profession exactly?"

The Colonel deliberated on what I had assumed was a simple question.

"These days I would self-report as a problem solver. I'm rather fond of employing intellect and ingenuity in concentrated bursts so the burden of existence that rests upon my shoulders, and the shoulders of those I encounter, is lessened."

"Crowded guild meetings for that?"

"A rare occupation, to be certain. But don't forget, you've more or less signed up for the same job. Steady yourself. I believe we have arrived."

The ramshackle building that housed The Cross-Eyed Cricket looked primed to collapse at the slightest suggestion of wind. The bar itself was somehow in even worse shape, nestled at the base of the structure like a rotten oyster that refused to be shucked from its battered shell. There were no windows and no signage, save for a weathered painting of a blind cricket, just as George had said. Two police officers guarded the entrance, one standing in a slouched posture, his lip quivering terribly.

"Good morning, chaps!" The Colonel gestured to the two of us, "I am Colonel Bacchus and this is my consociate, Bee." He offered a slight bow of introduction I quickly matched. "We are at your service. Now then, what's the order of the day?"

The troubled-looking officer stared at the flowers tucked into the Colonel's hat and broke into tears.

"Daisy! Daisy," he wailed.

His partner clapped him on the back.

"Pardon him, sir. Lukas here is having a bit of trouble with the misses. She, eh... well, her name's Daisy."

"Don't say her name, Felix. Don't anyone say her name!" Lukas got out between sobs.

"We are trustworthy confidants," the Colonel reassured him. "And furthermore, we may be able to aid in your predicament. What are the particulars?"

I had not envisioned travelling all this way to console police suffering marital strife, but I paid close attention. Unlike Ziro, the Colonel likely possessed many useful wisdoms I could gain by.

"She... she... she..." Lukas tried and failed to start three times. He nodded at Felix and buried his head in his hands.

"Lukas' wife is from... er... where is it again, Lukas?"

"Ghent!"

"That's right. Ghent. They went home to visit her family last month, and this morning, he comes to find out she's had something of... an adventure with one of the men there during their visit."

The setup piqued the Colonel's interest. I must admit my listening skills improved as well. A part of me wondered if the indiscriminate Colonel had been the partner in Lukas' wife's adventures. But he'd been in the Gobi. Hadn't he?

"I see," the Colonel said sympathetically. "Is the identity of the man known?"

"That's just the problem," Felix said. "Well, sort of."

"The barber!" Lukas shrieked from behind his tear-soaked hands.

"Yes, it was the barber," Felix repeated in a much more reasonable tone. "Poor Lukas overheard it was the barber but doesn't know who the man is. The residents of Ghent are quite reserved. Not likely they'll give up one of their own."

"Why, this is no problem at all!" The Colonel announced happily. The three of us looked at him, Lukas with hesitant anger. "It is not difficult to locate the cobbler or butcher either."

"My, she has been busy," I jested carelessly.

"What do you mean?" Lukas grabbed the Colonel's vest in desperation.

"Mind yourself!" I pulled the officer's collar and pried him from the Colonel. All three men looked surprised by my strength. Men always were. Did they think it was ladylike manners that kept me on the trapeze all those years?

"No need to be incensed." The Colonel placed a calming hand on my shoulder. Felix relaxed in turn while Lukas shook with impatient curiosity. "I simply mean to say there exists a method for identifying profession."

"How? How do I find this man?" Lukas begged.

The Colonel put his arm around Lukas and explained.

"The cobbler will be known by wearing the finest shoes, and the butcher's dinner table will always know the finest cuts of meat. The barber—"

"Will have the finest haircut!" Lukas interjected.

"No. His position is unique. He will be known by his terrible hair, for he has none to properly cut it for him."

"Oh sir. Oh sir, you are correct!" Lukas' face lit up as if he'd discovered a cure for Antwerp's powerful fish smell. "My gratitude belongs to you!" He kissed the Colonel on the cheek and ran down the alley, undoubtedly on a path to confront either the man in question or some poor bloke guilty of nothing more than poorly cut hair.

The Colonel turned to the remaining officer.

"Now then, Felix. I intuit you are too clever to have been made a cuckold in such a pileous riddle. Thus, allow me to instead aid in putting your undoubtedly faithful wife into a new pair of shoes." He pressed half the fold of banknotes into Felix's hand and we were on our way.

Chapter Eight

"There is an odour," Felix warned as we shuffled down a short staircase to the basement bar.

I thought this an obvious comment, considering the entire city had an odour, but I was soon to miss the sour smell of Antwerp's harbour. The scent in The Cross-Eyed Cricket was that of a deceased body. I'd not come across it before but knew it right away through some ancient, intrinsic knowledge. I suspect all people do, upon the experience.

My vision took a moment longer to make any headway. In the low-burning lamplight, I could see several sailors at the far end of the bar, huddled over their drinks like protective mother hens. The gargoyle of a bartender scowled at our presence and made no mystery of it. I had the feeling new arrivals weren't a common or welcome sight in The Cross-Eyed Cricket.

"Over there." Felix pointed to the darkest corner of the bar, where I could just make out the shape of a body crumpled beside a low table.

The Colonel absently handed me a yellow daisy from his hat.

"Chocolate daisy. It is fragrant," he said and approached the corner, absorbing the scene with a roaming gaze. He crouched close to the prone figure. "Was he robbed?"

Felix kept his voice low.

"There was apparently a rather large sum of money present. It was... acquired by some other patrons after the murderer fled."

"The supposed murderer took none of the money?"

"Apparently not."

The sailors watched our party openly, and a cheerless chorus of wrinkled faces they were. Undoubtedly some of them had pockets filled with newly acquired cash that would soon be spent at The Cross-Eyed Cricket or similarly dilapidated establishments. Drinking their money away, they seemed unconcerned with the recently-made cadaver smell mingling with the stench of the harbour.

I myself felt quite concerned. I breathed in the scent of my flower and was glad to have it. It truly smelled of chocolate. The Colonel's prudent planning was welcome, but now I wondered. Did he have extensive experience with decomposing bodies? In what capacity?

The Colonel carefully rolled the body over, exposing the dead man's snow-white face. I would've guessed him in his sixties or seventies, certainly on the thick end of a hundred years. Strapped across the face was a dirtied, white eye patch. The visible eye was extinguished, betraying no expression. Old scars striped the nose and forehead, with one ear missing almost entirely. A white cane, broken in half, lay against the wall. I tried to decide which wars he might be a veteran of. All of them from the look of it. The mouth however had frozen into a slight but unmistakable smirk. He had died smiling.

I observed the Colonel's reaction as best I could: the mustache was level, the eyes intense. Shock? Recognition? Was this man known to him? My captain revealed little.

The Colonel plucked the other chocolate daisy from his hat, removed the stem, and tucked the flower into his moustache. He leaned whisper-close, examined the entire body head to toe, then stood and approached the bartender.

"Were you present at the murder?"

The man said something in French.

"He said he doesn't speak English," Felix translated.

"He certainly did," the Colonel put forth evenly, still looking at the bartender. "I say, there's a rather large spider on your shoulder."

The barman jumped and swatted at his shoulder. Then he calmed and glared at the Colonel.

"I had nothing to do with those men, and I took none of the money."

"How fortunate for us you've remembered your English lessons," I said.

"I've no wish to cooperate with any authorities, *girl,*" he said to me. "Can't see how it'd be to my benefit."

Daisy still in his moustache, the Colonel leaned close to the barman and spoke conspiratorially.

"We represent no agency or law. We conduct ourselves exclusively in curiosity. I do not suspect you of any wrongdoing and have no interest in the missing currency. Now, if you would be so kind as to pour me the dead man's drink." The Colonel placed several bills on the bar, surely more than the drink was worth.

The barman's sunken eyes narrowed, but he produced a glass and filled it with clear liquor.

"And?" the Colonel asked.

"There was a fruit as well. He'd brought it with him."

"Small and green?"

"Yes. But not a lime. I don't know what it was." The bartender reached for the money, but the Colonel's hand sprung forward and arrested his arm to the wood.

"Who drank with him?"

The bartender tried to wrestle his hand free to no avail. Some of the sailors shifted in their seats.

I reminded myself where the exit was.

"I wish only to know his audience," the Colonel said calmly, keeping his eyes locked to the bartender's.

"Two men."

"The three of them arrived together?"

"The dead man waited for them."

"The two other men, did they arrive together?"

Patience tested.

"No."

"Did either of them have red hair?"

Patience waning.

"No."

"But there was a third man, wasn't there? And he had red hair, didn't he?"

Patience gone.

"*If you know, why do you ask?*" The bartender said darkly.

"Thank you." The Colonel released the bartender, who rubbed his wrist before snatching up the money.

"If you would be so kind as to draw attention," the Colonel whispered to me on his way back to the corner. "Any measure of your showmanship is likely to do the trick."

"Colonel, I think we should—"

"We are far nimbler than this lot, and my light fingers do not like an audience. Just take care not to stray too far from the exit."

I nodded.

Felix eyed us both with increasing interest. The cooperation we had purchased was spending itself in a hurry. No matter. If malice meant to find me, it would find me dancing. I ran through a list of possible demonstrations, took stock of my surroundings, and before I was entirely ready, began speaking.

"Gentlemen! A moment of your time."

I leapt to the bar easily, widening a few eyes.

"For those who search for spectacle and pine for pageantry, I am pleased to announce the arrival of a show of incredible wonders." The practiced pitch came much more easily knowing my efforts would not further enrich Ziro. "Sights you've not seen before. Exhibitions not to be believed by those foolish enough to miss them. Watch Fräulein Haas the German strongwoman lift an anvil with a single finger. Behold Jacques the Fire Eater from the great plains of Africa as he quenches an unbelievable twenty torches with an iron throat. But save your applause for the acrobatic, the fantastic, the bombastic, The Amazing Beatrix!" I posed and held for applause.

One of the sailors belched.

Hoping my small frame would compensate for the low basement ceiling, I tucked into a backflip onto one of the tables. My toes grazed the smoke-stained ceiling above, but I managed well enough. Some of the frowns did not deepen. I considered this progress with the sailors, but Felix had still only half-turned to me.

Pulling two chairs so they were back-to-back with an arm's length in between, I carefully lifted my feet to the ceiling and stood by my hands on the chairs. Then I plucked a snifter from the bar using my toes and juggled it with my feet. On display was my darkest secret: I could juggle, and worse, I sometimes enjoyed it.

Some of the sailors grunted sounds resembling approval. Felix stepped in my direction to get a better look. I alone had eyes on the Colonel as he drained the contents of the dead man's drink into a thin vial he corked with haste and tucked underneath his John Bull.

My arms began to shake from exertion. The pose was not unreasonable, but I never had cause to hold it for such an extended period.

The Colonel patted the dead man's clothing, stopping at the armpit of the blazer I could now see had a slight bump. He whisked a penknife from his vest, ripped the seam of a false pocket, and extracted something he deposited underhat. After collecting the fractured cane as well, he nodded to me.

The sailors' impressed groans built to a cheer as I gratefully pushed off into a backflip, catching the snifter as I bowed.

"Hear hear! The Amazing Beatrix!" the Colonel announced as he tugged me towards the exit.

The barman, suspicious to the end, hobbled over to the body. He fingered the ripped pocket in alarm.

"They've found more money! *Voleurs*!" he cried and pointed a gnarled finger in our direction.

The Colonel shoved me to the door.

"Leg it!"

We burst into the alley, followed closely by a thoroughly-riled bartender, a police officer that had rediscovered his duty of apprehension, and a tidal wave of money-hungry sailors who proved most expeditious when the carrot was orange enough.

Keeping pace with one another, the Colonel and I dodged the horses and carts of Antwerp that continued to bramble about with no concern for bipedal life.

"Have they no traffic laws in this godforsaken town!" the Colonel cried out as we were nearly flattened by a Clydesdale.

"The park is this way," I said, pointing in a direction opposite of where the Colonel ran.

"Our path must be indirect so as to confound our pursuers."

"You seem to find yourself the subject of a foot chase quite often," I noted as we darted into a busy fish market.

"Two in as many days is excessive for me."

We twisted past stalls of spoiled fish and eclectic trinkets with an air of having been stolen. Just as my breath began to fail, the Colonel slowed.

"Our elusion has been successful I think."

I flicked the daisy from his moustache and we walked slowly enough to shed the attention of the fishmongers and their customers.

"At least you're to experience this city's markets. Some of the finest around," he said.

"What do you carry in your hat?" I asked.

He tilted the John Bull and let fall the vial and a fold of paper, both of which were quickly pocketed.

"Clues, dear Bee. How I adore clues."

"What does the note say?"

"Our investigations will have to wait. There are more important matters at hand."

"Have we been found?" I spun around to fend off any attacking sailors, but there were none. Instead, the Colonel had been drawn to a fish vendor.

"My good man, is that burbot?" he asked.

A vendor behind a trove of ugly thin fish nodded.

"Burbot, *oui*, burbot."

The Colonel handed over some francs and wrapped the fish himself.

"Don't mind the intrusion, old chap, but we're dealing with a considerable amount of united action. Loitering is ill-advised."

The vendor shrugged it off, happily counting his francs.

"For our waterzooi." The Colonel tucked the wrapped fish under his arm and we made for the park, just across the street.

"What in blazes is waterzooi?" I asked.

"A superb Belgian dish. It will make for a meal you'll not soon forget."

Running for our very lives from the scene of a murder and this man's mind was on supper.

Our feet crossed onto the grass of the park, a successful escape imminent, when a voice arrested our progress.

"It appears we have something in common, Colonel Bacchus."

A dark-skinned man, squat and portly, spoke from his perch on a park bench. His clothes were dark, his manner confident.

"We both pay the deputies of this town. But I am the Directorate of International Crime: their employer and manager. Your relationship is much less clear to me."

Unflapped, the Colonel approached the round man like an old acquaintance.

"They were most accommodating. Well-instructed and disciplined. May I ask how you came to know my name?"

"You are the famous Colonel Bacchus, are you not? Identifiable by smart dress, a moustache of substantial gauge, and a flying contraption that must be seen to be believed." He nodded in the direction of the Ox, which had drawn a healthy crowd of astonished onlookers.

"A generous reputation I endeavour to someday earn," the Colonel said. "How may I address you, sir?"

The squat man stood, gaining almost no height in the process.

"My name is Sharif." He wore the traditional Arabic headdress called a keffiyeh and a thick scarf, both of a fetching, deep maroon. Perhaps the city was more international than I realized.

"Monsieur Sharif, we are glad to have visited your well-policed precinct, but I am afraid we are in need of a hasty departure. Perhaps we can enjoy a lengthier conversation on some future date?"

"Perhaps through the bars of a jail cell? You have agents in my town and you arrived before the blood was dry, in a manner of speaking. These facts are of tremendous interest to me."

"Do you guess me to be a man capable of such baseness?"

Sharif studied the Colonel.

"I do."

The Colonel was not put off.

"I have spoken without accuracy. Do you think me guilty of this particular crime?"

Sharif took an agonizing length of time before concluding, "No, I think not."

"Of course not. Any constable capable of rising to a rank such as yours can recognise as much."

"Flattery will get you nowhere with me, Colonel. And your possible innocence in the act does not excuse nor explain your knowledge that some misdeed was to occur."

Shouts of recognition came from the direction of the fish market. Our recent acquaintances of The Cross-Eyed Cricket had located their prey.

Sharif took notice as well.

"My deputy I can control. Merchant sailors however are known to be much more unwieldy."

"What is it you want?"

"Information."

"I seek one of the men involved in the murder."

"He is either your target or your conspirator. In either case, I must insist on joining your investigation."

The Colonel's mouth went flat in indecision. Allow a presumptuous lawman into the bosom of his beloved Ox, or suffer the will of a greedy mob and an ensuing imprisonment?

"Don't mark too much time, Colonel Bacchus," Sharif advised.

"Be quick about it then," the Colonel said at last, and we resumed our path in haste, joined by the Belgian Directorate of International Crime.

The Colonel was definitely right about one thing. To see the Oxford Starladder was to see her always for the first time. The proud red balloon shone brightly in the midday sun, positively dwarfing the Belgian park below where the Newlyweds were showing her off to a group of curious children.

"Look lively, chaps! Thelma, loose the stakes. George, on the burner," the Colonel cried, plucking children from the Ox and skilfully tossing them into the arms of shocked nannies.

The Newlyweds sprang into familiar action, George's tam o' shanter bobbing up and down as he ascended the outside staircase while Thelma yanked out each anchor with practiced efficiency.

Sharif and I made the staircase just as the basket began to ascend. We both helped Thelma on board as the angry mob of sailors grasped fruitlessly at her heels. The nannies of Antwerp shielded young ears as the sailors let loose a cavalcade of Belgian profanities aimed skyward at the shrinking basket.

"Known you all of an hour and already I'm in your debt, Beatrix," Thelma said.

"Think nothing of it. We've all your anchor-loosing skills to thank for the flight we now enjoy. This is Mister Sharif," I said.

"Thelma," Sharif nodded. "And Beatrix. A pleasure to meet you both."

I was impressed he had taken note of our names, even in our ballyhoo of quitting the park. Most observant.

He looked nervously over the edge of the stairs as Antwerp fell farther and farther away.

"May I ask if there is a more suitable location to continue our introductions?"

The three of us made the deck, George and Sharif were introduced, and we all rose into a calm blue sky each knowing the other's name.

"What is our heading?" I asked loudly, taking a place at the burner. The Newlyweds looked impressed, as I hoped they would.

"South southwest," the Colonel answered. "We make for a lighthouse at Gibraltar. Mind the crown line. It's been in a bit of a state lately." He disappeared down the spiral staircase.

The impressed looks faltered when I lost control of the envelope and Thelma had to whisper in my ear which was the cord I sought. The Ox would not be conquered so easily. But I gave myself little grief in the moment; my mind was awash with the bright lights of joy.

"Is he off to work the case?" I asked George of the Colonel's departure.

George smiled.

"Far more important. He's off to start supper."

Chapter Nine

By late afternoon, we had hitched a ride on a healthy wind over the sun-warmed vineyards of Eastern France. I suggested flying low to pluck a few bunches for dinner, but the Colonel chastised me, declaring it an idea fitting only of Jasper the packrat. He, the Colonel that is, holed up in the kitchen, preparing our supper using the burbot he'd bought in the market. Sharif announced he'd some thinking to do regarding the murder. He gladly accepted a hookah from the Colonel, and was soon nestled into a corner of the top deck under an umbrella, pensive clouds of smoke wafting out in regular intervals. Determining our new addition's true nature and motives was difficult, so I reserved judgement on his character for the time being. I happily furnished him with a reserve supply of coals, seeking to distinguish myself as a reliable hand on deck and not a mere passenger.

George felt he'd been dragging about after keeping watch outside The Cross-Eyed Cricket all night and gratefully retired to the third floor to check his eyelids for holes. Thelma, insisting my circus tights looked about as comfortable as unmentionables made from porcupine hide, took in a blouse left behind by the so-called tart from Holland to my less substantial dimensions. She argued she could sew me an entirely new garment that didn't have such a chequered past, but I was grateful to have anything at all. And anyway, the Holland woman's blouse had a pattern of tiny windmills I found supremely charming. I was only too happy to toss aside my circus tights once and for all.

Perhaps I was the only newcomer to such international games of cat and mouse, but my new companions behaved as if we were on holiday rather than on the trail of a criminal. I inquired again about the items taken from The Cross-Eyed Cricket, but the Colonel insisted a discussion of the investigation was best suited for dinnertime and sent me away so he could focus on chopping the celery just so since, "A waterzooi with poorly cut celery is only permissible at an establishment of no repute, like a pig trough, or Chartish Manor!"

"Don't mind him," Thelma guided me away from the kitchen. "Gets a bit fussy when he's cooking. How'd you like a more proper introduction to the Ox?"

"Oh, Thelma, that'd be wonderful."

I followed her up the staircase.

"This is the Cloud Deck, but I suspect you've seen this well enough. A bit smoky at the moment too, isn't it? We'll see ourselves down the staircase. This is the central spiral staircase, the iron's a bit heavy for the captain's taste, but it makes for a good spine of the ship. The other zig-zags up the outside of the basket, a bit longer but consider the views, what ya might call the scenic route. Here's the fourth floor. Back into the kitchen we go. Don't mind us, Colonel, just having a look about. You see our rather robust oven here in the corner. All the countertops are tight-grain wood tough as my mother-in-law. She's from Glasgow, so enough said there. All the knives one could ever need and much better secured than those dastardly swords in the Nimble Hare. Oh, that's your room, isn't it? Well do be careful. You'll notice this wall alive with many an herb or spice. Thanks to the green thumb of our—oh alright, no need to harrumph, Colonel. We'll get out of your way. Here, dearie, have a sprig of mint before we go."

There was no focus or theme to the selection of books in the library. The Ox could provide a bit of insight on just about any topic desired, provided you were willing to search for it. The shelves were neat and organised, lined with cordage to keep their contents in place, but the room's corners were jumbled towers of literature and reference. Even the floor was bricked with hardcovers, some packed so tightly one would need an iron crow to leverage them free.

"Moving on... here's the dining room. Truth be told, it's rarely used, since we often eat on deck. But in the event of rain or the odd swarm a' bats, Borneo's positively black-skied with bats, this room has its purpose. There are only the four chairs, so if we dine here soon, one of us will have to settle for a barrel. I nominate Sharif. Bit odd, isn't he?"

A giant drafting table blanketed in dozens of maps dominated the navigation room. Walls were crammed with countless shelves and drawers overflowing with sextants, dioptra, and magnifying glasses.

The ceiling blazed with colour as the sunlight streaming through an open window exploded through the ruby glass of a dozen Moroccan lanterns gently rocking in the breeze. I had failed to notice most of these details the first night, so distracted I had been with the attempt to horse trade my flesh for conveyance. Now I could see how truly wonderful the space was. If one needed inspiration to explore, they had only to step into this room and their wanderlust would be forever enlivened.

"This chart here's the Beaufort scale. Measures wind conditions. Zero is calm, my personal favourite, then all the way up to twelve, hurricane force, which I could do without ever meeting again."

We took the spiral down to the third floor and Thelma lowered her voice in consideration for her napping husband.

"Bedrooms, a 'course. George and I take up in the Intriguing Mongooses here." She regarded the closed door underneath the pair of mischievous mammals. "George is our resident taxidermist. You can ask him the meaning of each of these, but I don't think ye'll get much by way of an answer. He says they're *artsy pieces*, and as such, open to individual interpretation. The Digesting Frog's been given to Antwerp's top lawman. The Colonel lays his head here in the Ostentatious Mantis: showy but refined, and an occasional annoyance."

A few skips down the spiral and we entered the Nursery.

"Really the Colonel should tell you about this one, but he's up to his elbows in Belgian stew at the moment. As ya know, our captain's a wizard of floriculture. The pretty little plants turn his gears something fierce. When we're not pursuing other orders of business, the Ox serves as a transport for floral specimens, some of which are known, some I suspect have yet to be categorized."

The crowded greenhouse felt warm and humid. Thelma explained the Dutch lights: windows specifically designed to focus the sun while retaining moisture.

"The bedrooms get a touch muggy from time to time, but the Nursery is the Colonel's baby, a 'course."

She pointed out one corner reserved for pragmatic plants that were always kept aboard. A small cinchona tree that produced malaria-treating quinine in its bark, a batch of yarrow herbs that could aid in stemming the flow of blood from a wound.

"Ask the Colonel at your own peril. He can speak endlessly on which tree barks lessen the sting of a snake bite, which mosses can be smoked to inebriation when liquor isn't at hand, which floral accent is advised for the coronation of a duke versus that of a baron… And here, the lowly cabbage. Main ingredient in the Colonel's hangover tea, alongside garlic, liquorice, and cloves, all grown here in the Nursery as well. The smell's been known to clear the Manx nests."

Thelma gestured to the ceiling.

"The Nursery doesn't actually connect to the floor above, except for the corner posts a' course. There's a gap set into the weave just large enough for the birds to get through. In this way, their nests help heat the Nursery, but the birds can easily reach the outside world by climbing over the partition. They more often spend their days in the nests that ring the overhang of the Cloud Deck though, much more easily found by fresh air."

A scampering in the ceiling riled the Manx a touch. Thelma tracked the sound with her eyes.

"Jasper's on the move. Maybe Sharif's dropped a coal."

"How does he get about?" I asked, recalling the packrat's escape from the Colonel that morning. "Jasper, I mean."

"The Ox's built with cavity walls. So there's a space between 'em, ya see. Helps keep the heat in more easily. The exterior walls," Thelma slapped her hand against one, "are singular, so that we don't all cook ourselves to death. Because of this, and encouraged by Jasper's hidden caches of buttons and Manx feathers, the deeper inside the Ox you are, the warmer it is. Some have said this allows one to feel the Ox's heart, which I think rather beautiful, don't you? On we go."

The bottom floor, called the Bulkhead, focused entirely on utility. Fuel for the burner, packs for hiking, weapons, foodstuffs, casks of water and wine, and an army of sounding balloons used for a preview of the winds before setting aloft. Like the Nursery, this floor eschewed rooms and hallways for an open storehouse feel, with a large trapdoor near the base of the spiral staircase.

"That'll sum her up for the moment," Thelma concluded. "Though a 'course the Ox is always known to surprise. Plenty a' hidden spice stores, shortcuts through floors, handy bric-a-brac stuffed throughout. It's a tortured soul that tries to quantify it all. Oh, I hope I haven't just done that."

The Colonel arrived harried on the spiral staircase.

"Ah, Thelma, there you are. I am a bit strung up. The waterzooi is nearly finished and the fox tureen is proving most elusive."

"I believe it's behind the slavers," Thelma said.

"Below the ramekins?"

"No, the ones—oh I'll see to it. 'Bout time I roused George anyway."

"A Herculean task when it comes to the man who sleeps deep as the winter bear. You are a saint amongst us." The Colonel turned his attention to me. "Do you approve?"

"Why, it's wonderful!" I exclaimed, leaning out a window to examine the base of the Ox. Planters of dirt ringed the foundation of the basket, out of which grew the thick, pale bamboo the structure was made of. "You grow your own bamboo?"

"Ah yes, one of my finer ideas. It allows us a nearly endless supply for repairs, and you'll notice as well some of the stalks grow directly into the frame. The Ox is as strong as they come. I normally despise a correcting ass, but the material is rattan, not bamboo. I find it less temperamental. It also affords this sour fruit. The Manx adore them." He plucked a nutlike fruit from one of the stalks. "The fruit is passable as a citrus, but I value it for the resin that can be extracted." He directed me to a nearby table where a pile of fractured fruits sat next to a mound of red powder. "It's called dragon's blood. I use it to colour the envelope. It makes for a rather lovely digestif as well."

"Why did you inquire about a green fruit at the tavern in Antwerp?"

He smiled. "Keen memory. I believe the fruit of interest to be marula. Native to the south of Africa, where the dead man hailed from."

"Then you do know the deceased."

He nodded reverently but pressed on.

"The fruity anecdote serves to strengthen my guesswork. I will speak more of it at dinner, when I present my theory on the whole." He turned, then paused. "May I confide in you?"

"Certainly!" I struggled and failed to keep the eagerness from my speech.

"I wish you to keep a close eye on Sharif." The Colonel folded his arms behind his back and began to pace. "As I explained to our constable friends, a town's barber is identified by a poor haircut. Similarly, I harbour an inherent distrust of any top policeman, for there is none above him to provide incentive to follow the law. I have known fine constables to be sure, but I don't know if Sharif will number amongst them. He worries the Manx as well. That's more than enough for me."

"As a new passenger myself, I have little room to criticize, but why take him aboard? Could you not have employed your rapier as a means for our escape?"

"Likely, but do not be fooled. Our lawman in residence is merely a clue dressed as a man. Just as he correctly deduced our excessive knowledge of the murder, he too shows signs of involvement beyond mere investigation. Now, I must return to the kitchen to finish preparing the waterzooi. Please keep any surveillance concealed for the time being." He began to climb the stairs then stopped. "Thank you for your keen sense. The observant are always welcome on the Ox, especially as we now navigate a maze of deceit and murder, one that will no doubt twist and turn for some time to come."

I nodded firmly, with the eagerness of a soldier who'd not yet been to war. I prayed this reflected conviction and not naiveté, and reminded myself that one usually outlasted the other.

Chapter Ten

Fräulein Haas once told me the Germans had a way of thinking about people that roughly translated to each individual being a beer. The overall brew might be simple or complex but almost always a drink was dominated by a few choice ingredients that give it distinct character. Jacques chimed in that the French had a similar view, using wine instead of beer. Fräulein Haas called him a fancy pants and told him to shut up. I missed them already.

I suspect the Colonel's brew would've been the following: one litre aeronautics, one litre floriculture, a twist of chivalry, two sprigs of sensual mischief, and of course, nineteen cubes of sugar. Add to the recipe, a spoonful of supper aficionado. To call the Colonel a culinary stickler would be wrong. He had strong opinions regarding food but was infinitely more entranced by the *ritual* of dinner—a way to take stock of the day's events, to hear of the trials bested or lost by friends and loved ones, and to remember that to a certain extent we were all in it together. This was how the Newlyweds told it as we sat with Sharif at a round table brought up to the deck for dinner.

Sharif followed with a yarn about a jewel caper he had foiled in Amsterdam several years ago. I felt ashamed to have no thrilling anecdote to offer in turn. Weeping tales of neglect and abuse were hardly interesting dinner preamble, but I was spared an embarrassing lack of contribution as the Colonel summited the spiral staircase. The aforementioned fox tureen, cracked along one side, exhaled waves of wonderfully fragrant broth flush with hearty amounts of fish and vegetables. The unified flavors swaddled my nose and I suddenly became very hungry.

"Waterzooi, a marvellous gift from the people of Belgium," the Colonel said. "My interpretation, with the principal ingredients expertly selected by George, thank you George, contains a fine burbot and the correct amount of parsley. That's the trick, isn't it? I find most versions of the dish to be criminally under-seasoned when it comes to parsley. In any case, let us wash our necks first."

A glass of the spirit known as jenever accompanied each bowl except for Sharif's, as he did not drink. The glasses had been filled to the brim and, per the Colonel's example, we each leaned in to take the first sip directly from the table. A tickling burn came with the liquor, which actually tasted quite good after the fact.

The Colonel ladled out generous portions of his waterzooi and broke several loaves of bread baked in the kitchen below our very feet. It was far and away the finest meal I'd ever tasted, and I was glad of our captain's devotion to a fine supper.

I was about to relay my gratitude, when Sharif initiated his own desired topic.

"You knew the dead man, did you not?"

The question came pointedly, but the Colonel was not at all dislodged, and took his time finishing another sip of jenever.

"Not personally. Rather, a man I looked up to. He had something of a famous reputation."

"As what?" Sharif asked.

"A peddler of riddles. I believe him to be a man by the name of Noel Ebbing. Are you familiar, Mister Sharif?"

"Yes, perhaps," Sharif mused thoughtfully, as if searching his mind's vast store of past suspects.

The Colonel pulled a pipe carved in the shape of a bird from his white waistcoat.

"A well-practiced dealer in the highest echelons of desperately sought goods. Gold, jewellery, vases, all the nonsense royals and hangers-on busy themselves with." The Colonel lit his pipe and kept it well-attended between helpings of waterzooi. "He is loved for the quality of his wares but despised for the methods by which they are sold. Elaborate riddles, treasure maps, and the like. I've never quite sought his wares myself, but I've always admired his style a great deal."

"You're a treasure hunter," I said with whispered astonishment. The closest I'd come to a real treasure hunter were the newspapers that cleaned the calliope. Now I dined with several of these mythological creatures, and what was more, I counted myself in their party.

Colonel Bacchus puffed his pipe.

"I have been pulled into that sphere on occasion, but as I said, I have not actively sought rare goods for my own gain. I prefer the indulgences of exploration, which sometimes run in parallel."

"You say you admired this Ebbing man, Colonel Bacchus?" Sharif resumed his interrogation.

"The admiration lives on." The Colonel lit a cigarette for Sharif, and the detective sucked it down in nearly a single puff. While our captain had considerately kept his pipe smoke on the periphery, Sharif allowed the ash and smoke from his cigarette to collect above our table in the calm evening air. I waved a cloud away from my stew and sent it back in Sharif's direction.

"But why would he employ such a bizarre method?" I asked.

The Colonel pulled a snowdrop flower from the band of his John Bull, replenished since our activities in Antwerp. The delicate white sepals cut through the stubborn cigarette smoke as the Colonel twirled the stem in thoughtful meditation.

"The reasons for his *bizarre method* are several-fold. First, it gave him time to distance himself from the buying party while they attempted to solve the puzzle and locate the item desired. Some accused him of selling false maps that lead nowhere, riddles with no answer was a common charge. In his method of sale, he had plausible deniability. Buyers purchased only the instructions, not a guarantee to find the actual item."

"I know you respect the man, James, but how's that any way to run a business?" George shouted. "How'd he get customers?"

Jasper sped out of a hole, nipped a piece of fallen bread crust, and disappeared once again.

"Because most of the time the maps were true," the Colonel responded. "Ebbing did enjoy misleading people, though. He was known to re-sell old riddles or leave some sort of false-treasure where the genuine article should be. Unfortunately, wanting to kill the man was nothing exotic, so a general suspect list would be something of a global census. I have studied some of the riddles solved before and found them to be most challenging. Many of the resting spots of the treasures were often wildly inaccessible. If the buyer failed to gain what they sought, Ebbing could always say they simply failed to solve the riddle."

"As George said, I know he was a hero of yours, James, but what tricksy rubbish!" Thelma concluded. "I'd have no patience for such nonsense. If the money paid is of substance, then so too should be the goods bought."

"It is not wise to speak ill of the dead," Sharif inserted.

The Colonel shot a narrow-eyed glance at Jasper, returned for another crumb of bread.

"Lucky for Ebbing, he was in possession of many rare items and, as such, he could play games as he wished."

"Apparently, he dealt with someone who didn't want to play," Sharif observed. "What else do you know?"

"Little of any value. That is why we fly for Gibraltar. I know a man there of exceptional intelligence and contextual ability." He dabbed his mouth with a napkin then vented the balloon.

The Ox began a gentle descent that mirrored the setting sun as we drifted into a stronger echelon of wind.

The Colonel's enigmatic nature was a tease to me, a faucet kept at a deliberate drip. I could tolerate the rate of flow, but Sharif's face suggested a man dying of thirst, and if the Colonel wouldn't let information pour… I wondered how long the lawman's polite manner would survive.

Chapter Eleven

Dish washing on the Ox was assigned on a rotating basis, and although I heartily volunteered for the task, it was the Newlyweds' turn. I insisted on carrying down the last of the plates and was able to witness the tender scene of George washing and Thelma drying. "Newlyweds" fit the pair quite nicely.

I made it back on deck in time to see the last of the sunset. Splashes of orange and purple dyeing the bottom of a thousand clouds we'd passed through. As the Ox sailed through this virgin æther, I wondered how I had come into such fortune. My situation had been so undesirable only a day ago, and now I called home this miraculous vehicle where I shared incredible food with astonishing company. It was true our acquisition in Antwerp had done little to warm my heart with his clouds of smoke and rather pointed questions, but he was not without his quiet wisdoms, and his dedication to the task was beyond question. He had already returned to the hookah under the umbrella where he likely reminisced about a past apprehension or fantasized about the one he now sought. A chubby hand waved me a polite goodnight from behind the curtain of shaded smoke. I returned it, then made my way down to the map room, where the Colonel worked our route.

"May I join you?"

He nodded. "Have a go at the glass here."

I took control of a magnifier that resembled a large bead of dew. The glass slid smoothly across the south of France as I attempted to locate our position.

"We've been following a river for some time," I observed.

The Colonel nodded.

"I would say... the Saône?"

"Superb navigation!" The Colonel swung his fist in enthusiasm. "We are indeed following the Saône, which will take us to..."

I slid the glass bead further south.

"Why to the Rhone of course, then past the mountains into Spain."

"First rate."

"When can we expect to make Gibraltar?"

"Exact time is a dangerous lure to chase in a craft like this, but I would wager no more than a few days. We will be making a stop first in the north of Spain, in a town called Jaca."

"What for?"

"Because," he took a snowdrop from his hat and gave it to me, "sometimes things should be appreciated simply because they are beautiful."

"Why do I feel you're only telling part of the truth?"

This earned a wry smile from the captain.

"I knew I liked you, Bee. I stand by my previous statement, *however*... there are additional truths. I love the snowdrop for its subtle beauty. But it also possesses antidotal properties to some poisons, lest you or I unknowingly came into contact with any unsavoury agent lingering in The Cross-Eyed Cricket. Fortunately, we both appear to be operating normally."

"You suspect Ebbing was poisoned?"

"I saw no wounds or blood loss. I have witnessed poisonings before unfortunately. It leaves something of a unique skin pallor that brings a morbid recognition. We are not always fortunate in the things we can recognise, are we?"

"I can identify a dozen different types of animal droppings," I said. "Specializing in big cats of course."

"We're each with our burdens then."

"You still haven't answered my question, Colonel. You spoke of additional truths?"

My persistence summoned another grin.

"A treasure hunter resides in Jaca. A poor excuse for a man that may have had cause to purchase the fatal riddle from Ebbing." The Colonel rolled up the map of France. "And anyway, I've always found the Aragon slice of Spain to have the jammiest bits of jam. Regarding the females, you understand."

"Then you mean to visit as a gadabout."

"Priorities need not always be exclusive. Our Jacan detour may eliminate two birds with one stone, though don't let the Manx hear you tell it that way."

"Perhaps unsvoury agents linger in places outside The Cross-Eyed Cricket," I observed.

"The seduction of a fine woman is an art, Bee. It's the philistine who directs Da Vinci not to paint."

-PART THREE-
SPAIN

Chapter Twelve

A walled citadel in the shape of a star marked the centre of Jaca. The walls had probably been erected to prevent invasion from the French or Portuguese, or perhaps even Genghis Kahn if he were quite lost. Now though, the intruder came from above, and he was neither French nor Portuguese, nor a Mongol warlord as much as I was aware.

While the Colonel's history was clear as mud to me, his immediate intentions were more easily guessed. Our captain's activities with the General's wife were not to be an isolated incident, and I wondered if all the mothers of Jaca, in a simultaneous moment, had the inexplicable instinct to keep close watch over their elder daughters that night.

The Manx ventured out ahead of us and were met by waves of brown sparrows that spilled from the citadel walls. At first, I thought the birds to be fighting, but after a time it became clear they were soaring in harmony. I was jealous of them, of all birds really, as they seemed to share a special collective consciousness. None were left to flag or fall behind, but would get picked up in the motion of the others in an unbroken chain of support.

"The Manx're havin' no trouble assimilatin'," George observed, his hands tangled in yarn as Thelma knit a new scarf to replace the tattered and stained one about Sharif's neck.

"Smell that?" The Colonel inhaled deeply over the Cloud Deck's railing. "The Spanish have such a skill with saffron. That sweet hay note always reminds me of the Ox and vice versa. A wonderful turnaround to find oneself in." He straightened a saffron crocus in his hat, the flower of wide violet petals and long red stigmas from which saffron came. "I suspect this little number may look quite pitiful to the Jacan connoisseurs, but the Nursery does as well as she can."

Although I found the whole affair a touch ridiculous, I had to credit the Colonel's dedication to formal dress. The purple waistcoat and red cufflinks coupled with his cap's floral flourish were nothing less than poetry of attire. Some might say my wardrobe, comprised entirely of one windmill-patterned blouse left behind by an unsavoury woman, provided me scant room to judge.

"Now then," the Colonel said, giving his cufflinks a shine, "I'm off for beverages and revelry at the finest establishments Jaca has to offer. Any are welcome to join, although be forewarned, my intention is to woo and I could therefore make for distracted company."

"You're a hedonist," I charged, causing Thelma to miss a stitch in laughter.

"Heavens no," the Colonel said. "Hedonists are without ambition or introspection. I make an effort at both. Hedonists do however throw the best parties, and so I make a point of keeping their company." He attended to his moustache, greasing it with something black and oily. "All must decide in what manner they will live their life deficiently. No one philosophy is perfect and all encompassing. Some sacrifice liberty, others compassion, others reason. Hedonists do away with the unpleasant, and so, fine night-time companions they make. I've nothing against a fast woman, provided she's slow enough to be caught."

"Is that... shoe polish?" I asked of his moustache grease.

"Lord Kimber's Shoe Tonic," he specified. "Available only in London and only at exorbitant prices. Worth every sovereign though. Now, any takers?"

"I've no desire to play bloodhound on your fox hunt," I announced. "But I have even less desire to refuse a visit to a city unknown to me."

"We're deep into this scarf, love," Thelma said to the Colonel.

George held up his shackles of yarn. "Aye, I believe it's to be a relaxing evening on deck for us... and the remainder of the jenever."

"You as well, Mister Sharif?" I asked. The detective, sloth in body but nimble in mind, set down a sizable volume titled *Scribes of the Alexandrians.*

"I've no wish to allow too much air into this investigation. I will join you."

The Colonel nodded without emotion then turned back to the Newlyweds.

"You two are blankets wet enough to smother a fire at the Royal Opera House. I will take it as a predilection for jenever and leisure, which I can hardly admonish, and not a comment on my character." The Colonel sprayed his lapel with a liberal amount of cologne.

Thelma waved the Colonel's friendly teasing and pungent cloud away from her face.

"Ya smell like an undercooked ham, James."

"Alluring in this part of the continent, I assure you. *Buenas noches,* Newlyweds. We'll see to the envelope."

The Ox landed softly on Spanish soil.

Down below, the Colonel and I pulled a line to set the deflating envelope over the side of the Ox like a count's cape, allowing the Newlyweds to remain unsmothered by the heavy canvas.

"Look alive," George called out. He tossed the finished scarf off the Cloud Deck, and it fluttered down into Sharif's waiting arms.

"*Shukraan,* Thelma," Sharif's thank-you floated up in the warm, clear air.

"Yer welcome, dear," Thelma shouted back.

The three of us walked a road of orange dirt towards the walls of Jaca as stars introduced themselves into a blackening sky above.

"Can you restrain yourself long enough that we might make some investigations on the criminal?" I said.

The Colonel laughed.

"You must have known many talents in the circus ring, but even us theatrical laymen are capable of spinning two plates at once."

"You spoke of a true treasure hunter as a citizen here," I said carefully, not knowing if Sharif should be privy to the disclosure.

"A rotten apple in an orchard of good. Do not let his residence signal a lack of standards in these parts, for we enter a superlative upon superlative. Spain is amongst the finest countries and Jaca is amongst her finest cities. Though I haven't visited in some time, I've no doubt—" We passed through a gate in Jaca's proud walls and found ourselves in a minor square, dominated by a towering bronze statue of a man holding a long sword above his head. "Oh dear," the Colonel mumbled softly. "Beware the still-living man who sees fit to monumentalize himself."

The last such offender was the repugnant Lord Chartish, and I contributed a grunt of firm agreement.

Marching footsteps sounded on the cobblestone behind us, and I spun to face the form of Noel Ebbing bearing down upon me. This was rather curious as I knew him to be a dead man.

A moment later, I was relieved to understand that the figure was composed not of reanimated flesh, but straw. An eye-patch and walking cane were affixed to the rather authentic effigy.

The crowd carrying the effigy passed us without consideration. The Colonel immediately pulled Sharif and me in tow of the procession. It was in this formation we witnessed the mild horrors of Jaca.

Mounds of garbage lined every visible alley. A putrid smell that had been masked by the fields of aromatic crocus beyond the walls found us with relish. The sights were even more rotten. We were an audience to no less than two flagrant robberies, carried out by perpetrators that looked entirely unconcerned with retribution or arrest. Children scurried about in filthy, roaming bands, making repeated attempts to steal food from hostile vendors.

Shouts of furious conviction from our marching party continued as we snaked our way to the centre of town. The looks that met us from the rest of Jaca were ones of terror. The faces of curious children lucky enough to have a home, floated away from shuttered windows as they were withdrawn by vigilant mothers. The men of the town, leaning protectively in doorframes or gathered in huddles along shadowed walls, regarded our passage with weary but unchallenging glances. The entire village appeared afflicted with some phantom sickness.

Then we met the cause.

Atop a torch-ringed dais in the town's largest plaza, stood the subject of the statue at the town's entrance.

"That's the offender," the Colonel said. "San Miguel."

In nearly the exact same pose as his metallic doppelganger, San Miguel raised a theatrical hand to halt the parade. He beckoned for the effigy to be brought forward.

Cloistered citizens watched in silent fear from windows around the plaza.

The parade party placed the effigy on the dais and stepped back. San Miguel sauntered around the form, an amber-hilted sword leaned upon the shoulder of his star and moon robes.

"Here we have, at last, that wily charlatan who dangled many a sparkling prize before men more worthy than he."

The Colonel harrumphed loudly, and I backhanded his midsection for silence.

"But I bring tidings of tremendous fortune. The purveyor of dead ends has himself taken his last breath."

Our mob delivered cries of support.

San Miguel issued a wild battle cry and brought the sword around in a swooping arc to chop the effigy in half. But the blade only made it halfway through the stomach before lodging firmly in the straw. San Miguel's celestial cloak rippled as he attempted to withdraw the blade, but his strength proved insufficient. He eventually surrendered and threw hands in the air as if he had intended to do so all along.

"There it shall remain!" San Miguel stepped away from the figure to confused but ardent applause from his supporters. He threw his arms around the straw neck and wrenched the head off.

I was surprised to see the Colonel, normally astute at shielding his emotions, looking quite somber. Perhaps mistreatment of an effigy did not earn the same intervention I had so benefited from, but public defacement of someone he admired, even just a reproduction, had stolen his normally unassailable vitality.

San Miguel threw the head to the ground and kicked it until the bound straw fell apart. He stood, breathing heavily, then withdrew a rod from his waistband.

"Shall we see who truly commands power in this realm?"

The supporters cheered.

"That's a snake he's got there," I said, squinting.

I knew what San Miguel was about to do because I knew the trick. A performer from the Subcontinent had toured with the circus for a time and had given me the secret. The Egyptian Cobra, when pressed just so below the head, becomes rigid and motionless.

San Miguel tossed the rod to the ground. The cruel shock of the action, as it always did, brought the snake back to consciousness. This impressed the crowd, even those beyond the mob.

"See, I control the great Egyptian Cobra just as I shall control Egypt's finest jewel! Furthermore—"

His speech arrested as I climbed onto the dais. I knew not if San Miguel was a murderer, but if the boorish man wished to disparage the dead and dishearten my friend, his mistake came in doing it in front of me.

I performed a mockingly exaggerated sweep of my arms as I carefully grasped the cobra. I pressed below the animal's head and turned in a slow circle, showing the animal's stiffness.

"From the realm of the common illusion, witness my mediocre power!" I tossed the snake, more gently than San Miguel had done, and upon contacting the stone of the square, it once again sprang to life. San Miguel's supporters looked horrified and angry but those in the windows murmured with interest, some even laughed.

San Miguel regarded me with flushed incredulity. I'd pulled the ripping line on his planned moment of greatness. Noting their leader's discomfort, San Miguel's supporters quickly resumed their march to distract the citizens of Jaca. I met the Colonel's bright eyes, a smirk below his mustache. My moment of triumph was cut short as I was chased off the dais by the an understandably agitated Egyptian Cobra.

Chapter Thirteen

"Why bell the cat in such a way!" Sharif roared as we quickly left the town, our departure encouraged by jeers from San Miguel's reactionary patrons.

"The man's an ass," was all I said, hustling along the cobblestones.

"You think you've robbed him of some power?" Sharif spat.

"Perhaps diluted it, yes!"

"For whose benefit?" Sharif persisted. "Certainly not ours."

"How about the citizens of the town?" I said.

"What do we owe them? If they are to be led astray by a man as unremarkable as San Miguel, then I say let them! Compromising our exclusivity—"

"He already knew of Ebbing, and further, what the piece is," I said. "Egypt's finest jewel, that's what he said."

"But he knew nothing of our competition," Sharif said. "Believe me, girl, I've been at this game much longer than a few days. Any advantage, however small, is invaluable, and you have just disposed with one of ours. I recognized the Colonel in Antwerp just as San Miguel recognized him after your trick. You may not be known, but your captain *is*."

Sharif made to jam his finger into my chest, but the Colonel swiftly stood between us.

"We are home," he said plainly.

"And what of you, Colonel? Mute and inactive?"

The Colonel was not baited into emotion.

"Mister Sharif, there is a time for thought and a time for action. I'm comfortable with my choices this evening. Perhaps you are dissatisfied with your own?"

Sharif looked from the Colonel to me and back again. He grumbled something unpleasant in Arabic and stormed aboard.

"A most biting temper," the Colonel observed with narrowed eyes. "My warning of the man is confirmed."

"Do you think I was wrong in my action?"

"In this company, you answer only to yourself," was all he said.

I stepped onto the Ox, disappointed at the lack of approbation. No footfalls rang on the steps behind me. The Colonel headed back to Jaca. I should have known better. The captain's nighttime ambitions were unfulfilled.

"Persistent in your passions. That's what the armed women in France said of you."

"The Derringer Sisters! I pray I don't come across any tonight." He held up a gloved hand in departure.

Armed or not, the wise mothers of Jaca had locked up their daughters for the night, and hopefully vice versa.

Chapter Fourteen

So steady was the Ox's flight in good weather that upon the break of morning, I had to peek out the Nimble Hare's window to confirm we were in fact, aloft. I opened my door to find the one below the Ostentatious Mantis still closed. The fox hunt must have been successful, and some wooed Jacan woman had yet to rise for the day.

Wanting to distance myself from the entire production, I skipped up to the kitchen for a cup of tea. The cutting board was stacked with a growing heap of lemon pastries. Thelma pulled a fresh batch out of the oven.

"Didn't wake you, did I?" She asked.

"No," I said. "I slept wonderfully."

"Dinner's always the topic but let's not forget the humble breakfast. Stick a few of these to your ribs." She passed me a tray of cooling pastries and I took one. It was, of course, delicious.

"Thelma, may I ask you something?"

"Ask away, ma dear," she said as she stirred a bowl of yet more future pastry.

"The Colonel's... dealings with women."

"Ah," she acknowledged.

"Who are the Derringer Sisters?"

"Membership rivals the population of Luxembourg I'm sure. With such a robust influx of companions, the Colonel needed to devise a system by which he could rid himself of these temporary guests. Otherwise I doubt even the mighty Ox could lift from the ground."

"And you approve of the system?" I steeped some lavender tea.

"What these ladies choose to do below the waist is their own business and certainly none of mine. I *do* ensure that they are treated well while aboard. After their night of interaction, the lady is permitted to wake upon her leisure, at which point she is delivered a breakfast cooked by the Colonel. After breakfast, the Ox is landed somewhere safe and the lady is given a small leather chest."

"I found such a chest on my very own bed the first night. The rogue meant to treat me like a common four-poster conquest!"

"Try not to be offended, dearie." Thelma patted my arm. "The chest is strictly provisions for survival. Two day's food and water, a compass, a local map, a modest amount of that country's currency, a cigar, matches, and a book of poetry written by..." Thelma blushed. "By me. Nice to have an outlet for me work, though I'm exclusive to the sexually adventurous women of the world."

"I'd no idea you were a poet," I said.

Thelma blushed deeper.

"If you fancy reading about foggy moors and what a marvellous chap George is, ya might like it. Last in the kit a 'course is the Derringer pistol. The Colonel had the pistols custom made and they're really quite beautiful, a pair of Manx inlaid into the handle. Anyway, this practice went on for some time and eventually these women realized there were others with these pistols and a book singing the praises of some Scottish bloke named George, all gifted after a single night on the fabled Oxford Starladder. Some were fine with this outcome. They kept the experience as a treasured memory and moved on. The dissatisfied ones began to band together and form groups that eventually came to be known as the Derringer Sisters. They have chapters all across Europe and elsewhere. I've heard of a burgeoning New Delhi branch as well."

"The Colonel has no doubt altered his arming methods then?" I asked.

Thelma shook her head.

"The Derringer Sisters are, as far as I know, the only thing he fears, but he insists the pistol is essential for a companion's safety. He puts that above even a group of internationally organised, spurned women who seek to meet him again with the expressed intention of putting a bullet in his arse."

I ate my sixth or seventh lemon pastry and reached for another.

"Can't tell how I feel about it all."

"He insists that many of them have never left the town they were born in and claims bringing them aboard gives them a chance to see the world, if only for a time," Thelma said.

"You believe these words?" I asked.

"I do in fact, although I certainly understand the feelings of the Derringer Sisters and why they exist. I think it a nice balance to the system of irreverent coupling the Colonel so loves to practice."

"Does he even speak Spanish?" I asked.

Thelma shook her head.

"Not much past *buenos dias,* but then, women can understand a well-given compliment in any language."

"Hmm," I demurred mildly. "Think I'll nip down to the Nursery before he comes to make that breakfast."

"Take a few more pastries with ya," Thelma encouraged as she slotted in a new batch. I did not disobey, tucking several onto my tea saucer.

The moist air of the Nursery was already warm with morning sunlight that illuminated the canvas of green, accented with the proud colors of so many flowers.

I was drawn to the lowly dandelions. My journey had begun with them after all. I nipped one of the yellow crowns and dropped it into my tea. The robust little flower might not have been a tremendous meal, but it contributed a delicious note to the drink. Abreast of the dandelions were the chocolate daisies that had spared my nose in The Cross-Eyed Cricket, the stark white of snowdrops and rich purple of the saffron crocus not far off. Recognition may not have always been desirable when it came to signs of poisoning or different kinds of animal waste, but in this case, it was splendid.

A niggling thought I had been suppressing insisted consideration at last: *had I overestimated the Colonel?* Was he a man, as Ziro would have put it, who was all tent and no circus? One who speaks but does not act, who promises and does not deliver? Was the criminal yarn just a lure to lead women into the bedroom? But he'd resisted my feeble attempt at seduction without a second thought. Why then, had he taken me on at all?

Jasper nicked one of my lemon pastries and sped into a hole in the wicker. I went to where he'd disappeared with his citrus prize, pushing through a fan of staghorn fern. Jasper was the Colonel's foil, not mine, I had no interest in pursuing a hungry animal.

Instead, I was interested in the book tucked against the wall, behind the purple and green leaves of a spiderwort plant. The thin journal was bound in green leather, greatly wilted from its humid surroundings. Faded gold lettering spelled out the title, *Manifest Philopatry.*

Curiosity and decency sparred within my mind. Decency told me this book was private and had been concealed for a purpose. Curiosity promised intrigue and enlightenment.

Curiosity made the stronger argument.

I checked the staircase to ensure no others were awake, then opened the book.

It held eighteen names, each accompanied by a physical description, occupation, and location. Some of the locations had been scratched out, others circled with enthusiasm. They were spread across the European and African continents—a few were even in the Orient. The top of the list was faded, difficult to make out in some parts. I could see though that all entries were accompanied by an X. All but one.

Christopher
(red hair, criminal)
~~*Batavia?*~~
~~*Maulgate Prison?*~~
~~*Antwerp?*~~

I quickly restored the journal to its place behind the curtain of spiderwort, wishing I'd never found it.

Was my captain some sort of bounty hunter? A murderer for sport or pay? He had publicly professed a disdain for manslaughter but was rather secretive and carried with him an arsenal of weapons. What sins had this Christopher visited upon the Colonel to become a target? What had the others? The professions on the list were of baker and lawyer and other common trades. Men and women alike. Did their corpses trace the wake of the Ox?

My stomach fell, due not to these fluttering suspicions, but a rather drastic change in altitude.

Through a twisted nest of hibiscus encroaching on one of the Nursery's windows, I observed the Spanish countryside rising to meet us. The Ox touched down and almost immediately rose again into the air.

Left aground was a beautiful Spanish woman, a saffron crocus in her hair, a leather chest in her hands.

Had I fled the clutches of an abusive ringleader only to gain the company of a well-groomed and prolific murderer? Perhaps I'd traded one environment of discord for another, albeit one with much more pleasant scenery and cuisine.

I had wanted to know the Colonel as a matter of my own curiosity and contest. Now it could be that my very safety depended on separating those who meant me no harm from those who practiced deeds far more nefarious than advertised.

-PART FOUR-

GIBRALTAR

Chapter Fifteen

The tiny country at the foot of Europe was enveloped in a fog so thick, I could hardly see my hand held out at arm's length.

"Just some uninvited stratus. The clouds are teasing us." The Colonel emerged from elsewhere on deck, swirling his hand in the moist air. He knew his cloud classifications fairly well but would more often refer to them by their taste on the tongue or how much dew they left on the rear end of a female conquest. He inhaled deeply. "Ah, I've come across this blend before. You might think the saline taste would dry the lungs, but I've found it has the opposite effect. If you've a mind to sing a ballad, now's the time."

After the shock of the *Manifest Philopatry*, I had kept my distance from the man, though in careful measure so as not to rouse suspicion. Fortunate for me, the Colonel was distracted with what we had discovered in Jaca: news of Ebbing's demise had absolutely travelled faster than the Ox, and conjecture was healthy that the riddler's final masterpiece was now unfolding. Excitement amongst the people was thick, but details were thin. What was the hidden treasure? The citizens of Jaca could not agree on that, and if the Colonel knew, he did not say. An Egyptian treasure? A description so simple was useless as the Egyptians were a people of many treasures.

Sharif joined us on deck, cheerfully whistling a charming Arabic folk song. Either he possessed a natural talent for the act, or the Colonel had been right about the benefits of the misty æther. The detective seemed uncommonly chipper at the prospect of the lighthouse keeper catalysing our progress in the mystery.

Unlike his ultimate intentions, the Colonel's flying skill was above question, and he navigated the whiteout with ease. After an hour of sightless flight, he checked his pocket watch and vented the envelope. We dropped through the forest of cloud, pulling a trail of mist on one corner.

The peninsula below was utterly without vegetation, populated only by huge boulders of grey and white. A trail wound through the rock formations, ending at a mighty pillar of sandstone at the edge of the continent—the lighthouse, a lonely sentinel against would-be shipwrecks. Easily the tallest structure I'd ever laid eyes on, the lighthouse stood as an unmistakable punctuation for Europe and her Basque stepchild. Even from this distance I could see mounds of sea salt caking each line in the masonry, a defiant icing left by decades of relentless ocean air.

The Colonel joined me at the railing to take the sight in.

"Here lies our next juncture: the Lighthouse at Europa Point. She's the largest in the world. Operated by a mad man, insane in a good way, whom I love dearly."

The entire flock of Manx shearwaters gushed out below us, speeding straight for the frothy ocean. Though their screeches were ones of joy, were I not familiar with the Manx I should have been frightened by their howling calls.

"Your birds!" I cried.

"The Manx are seafarers and adore any opportunity to fish. They will return."

"How are they trained so well?"

"I have raised them for generations. Always liked the Manx. I believe I am the first person to train the species to home, which I am rather proud of. I have also taught them to defecate into the soil of the Nursery, which I am equally proud of. Seabird guano is positively crackling with nutrients." The Colonel gestured to a shepherd's crook of bluebells on his John Bull that looked quite well-fed. "Devil birds indeed," the Colonel huffed, watching his beloved flock spread above the angry waves.

"The great engine behind all your floral panache is quite literally bird shit," I said.

"So it is!" The Colonel seemed delighted with my observation. He brushed some wrinkles from his waistcoat, the same rich blue of the flowers in his hat.

We set down near the base of the massive lighthouse, from which burst a rather excited individual waving at us in greeting.

"James! Hello!" he said, nearly tripping in his haste as he approached the Ox's exterior staircase. Large, restless eyes inventoried us from beneath a wild nest of snow-white hair. His skin was quite dark, suggesting a Mediterranean or even African heritage. The proximity was certainly correct for either. "I haven't flummoxed the date, have I?" he yelled at the Colonel with worry.

"Not at all. I come with regard to another concern. Well, there are parallels, I suppose, but the date in question has not passed."

Sharif and I exchanged confused glances as the two greeted with a warm handshake.

"Ah bluebells, my favourite!" The man plucked the arch of bluebells from the Colonel's hat without preamble and admired it closely. The two of them must have been rather well acquainted, for the Colonel showed no ill reaction to the unsolicited harvest.

"George, Thelma, how do you do!" The white-haired man wrung both hands and then seemed startled by Sharif and me. "But you have new additions! My name is Billingsly. Absolutely thrilled to be meeting you!"

"I am Beatrix, and this is Sharif," I said, adding for some reason, "He is a man of the law."

"And Bee is my cohort," the Colonel said proudly.

Billingsly cupped his hands around his ears. "Sorry once again? I've suffered hearing loss from many unexpected chemical reactions."

"Explosions," the Colonel clarified.

I repeated our names, and Billingsly nodded in greeting.

"Wonderful, wonderful to know you. By God, let's get inside, lest the fog chill us to an early death. Good weather for singing though, isn't it?"

We followed Billingsly through the small door and found ourselves in a great city of paper. Here was the equivalent of the Ox's literary collection, writ large into the expansive confines of a structure unconcerned with weight. Billingsly led us through the maze of written word to a staircase that ran along the shell of the tower.

"Look there. Some book lice," the Colonel said loudly and winked at me.

Billingsly was undeterred in his progress.

"Button up, James. We've matters far too pressing than to waste time on your instigations."

I saw none of the referenced pests but instead found a ragged grey goat contentedly chewing paper out of an equally ragged book jacket.

"A goat!" I blurted, half in surprise half in an effort to be heard. I tried to free the literature from the animal's mouth, but it tugged back, proving the greater desire.

Billingsly glanced over his shoulder and waved my concern off.

"Not to worry, young lady. In an inexplicable curiosity, he eats only the lesser works. You'll notice my collection of Milton is quite untouched whereas the meal he's enjoying now is a guide to anatomy that not only spells appendix incorrectly but locates it somewhere near the heel of the left foot."

I released the book, and the goat haughtily resumed its meal. I made a face at the nuisance and hurried after the group.

The second tier proved even more interesting than the first, crowded with equipment and machinery I did not know the exact function of but looked to be scientific. There was enough glassware to satisfy the windows of the largest basilica, filled with liquids in various stages of distillation or vaporization, several bubbling quite violently. Blue electricity crackled along the surface of a giant slab of metal. Animals in cages tittered excitedly at our presence, as pops of black smoke presented themselves worringly above a heated tin cauldron. The air itself was thick with a quality of instability.

"Anything need attending to here, Billingsly?" Thelma said.

"How's that? Oh, the experiments. They're quite alright, quite alright."

The rest of us hurried up the stairs as the cauldron that seemed primed to erupt was little more than an arm's length away.

The third tier ended the trend of increasing spectacle, for here were Billingsly's living quarters: a tiny kitchen with a tiny bed. The cabinets were mostly bare, the bed was made, both frosted with the dust of disuse. I surmised our host did most of his sleeping in the laboratory or the dunes of literature below.

Billingsly repurposed empty supply crates for seats as we crowded into the kitchen.

"You must disclose the purpose of your visit before my mind tears itself to shreds in violent curiosity!"

He freed some coffee from the crate I sat on, set it to brew, and joined us, battling back the thick plumes of hair he seemed constantly at odds with. The man didn't so much sit, as temporarily confine his fidgeting to one location, hands cupped to ears to amplify his guests' speech.

"I am after a criminal," the Colonel said. "It is terribly important I find him as soon as possible. George and Thelma were able to locate him in Antwerp while I attended to some business in Switzerland. The criminal involved himself in a murder the night before I arrived."

A boom issued from the second floor, loud enough that even Billingsly heard, but he waved off our concern as he set out five mismatched mugs for our coffee.

"I am afraid I may deplete your sugar stores," the Colonel said. "I can draw from the Ox's supply—"

Billingsly waved again.

"I don't drink coffee. Puts me on edge."

I thought of the exhausting man's poor heart and concluded a dose of caffeine would likely kill him.

"This criminal, is he part of—"

"Yes," the Colonel cut Billingsly off before he could reveal more.

"What's all this?" I said, hazarding intrusion. I couldn't imagine the Colonel meant to keep anything from the Newlyweds and hoped it was Sharif that was untrustworthy and not I.

"Billingsly has helped me with a project whose breadth is too large to divulge without delaying the conversation... any further." The Colonel poured everyone coffee, his own atop a nineteen-cube mountain of sugar.

I stared with manufactured interest at my coffee. I'd gambled and been rebuked. A misplay. At least the Colonel wasn't cross, or he did not let on as much.

"Our man fled the scene, possibly in league with others. We know little, but I was able to acquire some elements of interest," the Colonel said.

"You have clues?" A wide-eyed Billingsly nearly toppled off his chair in his eagerness.

The Colonel produced the vial of liquid and the piece of parchment. Sharif's eyes bulged nearly as large as Billingsly's as he let escape something between a cough and gasp.

Billingsly flattened the paper and all closed in to study it.

At the Treble of the *fare see*
Caught at the point where the *rite* and *vile* Joyless, and the snips find Less
where the Lord comes to Instill on Lakes of Columns so grand
Deaf *dyes* a *mail, Knew* and Drink
Predator to *hymn* and be Silent to the Remain of the Daughter
Single within your Buried and *meat* the Part
the Active you will have Divided
at the Pro of Future Pulling Many

"But this must be an Ebbing!" Billingsly said.

I winced a touch. The man's enthusiasm for Ebbing meant the knowledge of his demise would be painful.

"My thought as well. Billingsly, I'm sorry to tell you it is he who has been murdered," the Colonel said loudly but with gentility, walking the thin line between audibility and consideration for the lighthouse keeper's feelings.

Billingsly's face fell in a heart-breaking display of grief. His gaze grew distant as he pulled absently at tufts of snowy white hair.

"All my life I've studied the man's work after the fact. Now it is that one of his riddles finds me still-unsolved, but it comes with news of his passing."

"What is verso?" I asked, trying to distract Billingsly's emotional state.

"Once more?" Billingsly said, cupping his ear nearest to me.

"Verso. What does it mean?"

The opportunity to inform brought him slightly back to centre.

"Recto and verso refer to sides of a paper. Front and back, left and right, that sort of thing. It would appear we have only half of the riddle."

Sharif slammed the table in exasperation.

"Half the riddle? All this for a regular duck egg! The snipe hunt of a dead man!"

"Mister Sharif," Thelma chided. "Mind that temper."

Billingsly, ignoring or perhaps not hearing the lawman's outburst, collected the vial and disappeared down the staircase.

"I shall test for toxicity," he echoed up from the laboratory.

"He is of singular mind, you may have noticed," the Colonel said. "I myself think I'll join the Manx in their costal feast. I remember this area to be flush with a wonderful culture of oysters. Paired with some exquisite garlic I acquired in Jaca, I think they will make for a fine supper."

The Colonel tipped his hat and left. Had his eyes lingered on me a moment longer than natural? Was my inquiry into his secret *project* to become an issue? The man welcomed curiosity except when he was the thing being explored. I might be wise to keep a tighter tongue.

"I'll see that this nutter Billingsly doesn't muck up the investigation," Sharif said. "If you should hear an explosion, be sure to throw water on me first." Then he too was gone.

"Strange fellow," George remarked. I guessed he meant Sharif, although the observation would have been accurate for any of the three men that had left.

Chapter Sixteen

Billingsly placed as much import on liquor as he did knowledge, evidenced by a wine cellar as large as the library. That night we dined on the Ox's roof, where the Colonel's fresh-caught oysters were paired with a steely Galician wine. The Colonel had to pull Billingsly, quite literally, from his laboratory. An already insatiable drive for deduction inflamed by the death of a hero had turned Billingsly into a machine. He mumbled possible solutions and theories to Ebbing's riddle as often as he breathed.

The Colonel successfully calmed Billingsly down and made him receptive to communication by arranging for a cache of strong drink to be placed within the lighthouse keeper's reach, starting with the wine.

"Liquor brings the gods." The Colonel clapped his friend on the shoulder and raised a glass of chilled wine. "If ye seek an audience with voices timeless and wise, you need only to pull a cork."

"The creed of any well-loved host," George toasted.

"And many a drunkard," Thelma added.

"This wine is an absolute ambrosia. Truly exemplary of the magic of consumables," the Colonel observed.

"Don't sell me a dog. Magic does not exist," Billingsly grumbled absently as he swallowed a mouthful of oyster.

"Shame on you, Billingsly," the Colonel said. "Of course it does."

"Uh oh, parrot and monkey time," George whispered to me.

"Shame on *you,* Colonel," Billingsly returned. "I considered you a man with all his buttons on. Both of us have benefited from the bounty of numbers and letters so many times. You insult them by speaking of something as inane as magic."

The Colonel drank the rest of his wine and refilled any wanting glasses.

"Do not think I speak of magic in the same way as our Spanish charlatan of low to no repute, San Miguel," he nodded to Sharif and I, then returned to our host. "Come now, Billingsly, what have you been doing here besides robbing the barber? You observe life, do you not? What is magic? Magic is a preview to knowledge. Something we understand the result but not the process of. We take existing knowledge and apply it where it does not belong, and so it is predictably insufficient. At that point, real information, yet known or understood, becomes magic, a placeholder that stands in until it is replaced by genuine knowledge."

"There is that which is impossible," Billingsly contended.

"I am of the belief that nothing is impossible. Truly. Imagination comes first, understanding later. Magic is the interim. We can conceive of things long before we understand how they work. Magic is the light that guides the path to knowledge. Breakfast, lunch, and dinner. Imagination, magic, and understanding."

"Then since dinner is the ultimate meal of the day," I joined in, "is it then assumed you believe knowledge to be the ultimate goal?"

"No," the Colonel said cheerily as the wine began to take hold of his disposition. "I rather enjoy supper, but I do not see it as the inevitable destination of all things. Do not forget that the next day brings another breakfast, another lunch, and so on. Above all others, I admire those who seek knowledge with thoughts based upon logic, provided they do not adopt a closed mind. It is a tightrope act, which you can occupationally appreciate the difficulty of, Bee."

"That's your wisdom for the night then? Breakfast is imagination?" Thelma asked, pushing away her plate of spent oysters.

"If I am forced to give a bit of wisdom for the night..." The Colonel searched the stores of his mind. "Experience as much as your situation allows, as much as won't see you dead or locked up."

"This is the advice of a gentleman?" Sharif huffed.

In every conversational dartboard, the Colonel always seemed to find himself the bullseye. Inquiries, both friendly and not, appeared designed to pin the man down to an ideology or even mere opinion. I, of course, was guilty of this very aim, but he was quite adept at evading classification and moreover seemed to enjoy it as a sport.

"When you have to make as many decisions as I do, strong opinions are essential. Confidence covers the spread from time to time. With such tremendous conviction, it's a wonder I'm not wrong more often. If I gave the impression of advice, I apologize. A gentleman never gives advice. Normally my hosting skills are above such amateurism. I can mix a drink better than an Irishman, deal cards better than a Gypsy, and outmanoeuvre even the most skilled pelican."

"Oh give it a rest, James. We're, all of us, well aware of your mode of living." Thelma said. "I'm much more interested in what Billingsly's been doing. Your hearing's a bit worse I must say."

"My what? Oh yes, my hearing. Well that's an easy explanation! A chap's recently gone and invented something he calls ni-tro-glycerine. Devastatingly clever, but a bit nasty too. I've been working with it quite frequently. Small amounts of course," he reassured unreassuringly, then read our expressions. "Worry not, *most* of my work is in the written word as the chemistry is exceedingly complex. But enough of this high-minded chatter. Play us some mandolin, won't you, James?"

I tried my best to keep pace as the well-acquainted group moved quickly from one topic to the next.

Our captain nodded in compliance to the request. He disappeared down the spiral staircase, from which a moment later came a barrage of fiddling. The Colonel stepped up the stairs ferociously playing the instrument as if his proficiency had been called into question instead of directly requested. I must say he was not very skilled in the instrument, but he did not seem to mind in the slightest.

The music, as music often does, inspired the drinkers to drink more and faster. Wine gave way to a hidden bottle of jenever, and jenever gave way to a liqueur called pacharán: a stinging potable Billingsly made himself in the lighthouse. In no time, Billingsly, the Colonel, and the Newlyweds were well past drunk. I did not care for alcohol that evening, and Sharif declined as always, greedily gulping down a lion's share of the oysters, his mood still darkened by news of an incomplete riddle. Billingsly's liqueur was so potent I became light headed upon catching the scent of his breath after he had taken a generous swig, and I nearly became drunk by association.

The mandolin settled to a plunky wandering melody as the Colonel told tale of his adventures in the Gobi, where it sounded like he had taken several days' walk through the sands. Exactly why was anyone's guess.

"Deserts are beautiful, but they do make me a touch restless. No greenery to occupy the mind. Much the same here! Would it kill you to plant a sapling or two?" he charged Billingsly.

"Serves you right for neglecting geology," Billingsly said. "Know the value of a rock and you'll never be restless again. The world is ply with enough igneous to satisfy a lifetime of curiosity." He beckoned for the bottle of pacharán and George obliged, passing it over my head.

"Not untrue, o' wise man, not untrue," the Colonel said to Billingsly. "But my heart belongs to another field of study. We can agree, at least, that it is the fool who studies animals."

"Why's that?" I said.

"Look in nearly any wilderness on earth and behold thousands of plants. By that same vista, you could count yourself lucky to see one or two animals. It is the sadist that devotes his time and study to such sparse things. The plant does not shrink from touch, and each contains a multitude of inspiring secrets." His fingers danced clumsily upon the mandolin strings. "A bear kills with tooth and claw. There is little to discover there. But I could, for instance, name you a dozen plants that can kill just as quickly as the bear. And they are not stop and go like beasts. Plants always have an aim, and they are always working towards it."

"Best not to let the Manx hear your true feelin's," Thelma said, eyelids drooping.

"There are exceptions of course. And before any point out these things are also true for Billingsly's beloved rocks, let me remind you I am a mortal man and incompatible with a geologic timeline. Enough about my fascinations, let the point stand that the Gobi is a land of tremendous desolation. I found nothing of fur nor leaf, and I left without my criminal."

"Christopher is his name, is it not?" I said.

The mandolin stopped.

I had waited all day to slip this runner into the race, and thought now a good time, with the night's drinking providing quality cover. Utter silence on the Cloud Deck indicated I'd done this with all the tact of a bloody rhinocerous, and my discovery and unauthorized reading of the *Manifest Philopatry* was now obvious. *Curse your errant tongue!* I chided myself.

The Colonel unearthed a new bottle of pacharán and poured himself a full glass.

"So, we enjoy the company of more than one detective tonight. It would seem you have a colleague in Bee, Sharif."

I immediately regretted making my play while the Colonel was under the influence of drink. Not only had it failed to disguise my inquiry, I was now to deal with the careless words of a drunk. Careless, and perhaps more truthful.

"I met you as an eavesdropper," the Colonel said, "so I suppose this much was to be expected."

"You met me as an acrobat," I corrected him nervously.

He took a rather large pull of the pacharán straight from the bottle, then leaned close, so that the side of his John Bull pushed against my hair.

"I admire curiosity, dear, but you would do well to keep out of my affairs. Is that clear?"

Billingsly let out a cry of triumph, mercifully breaking the tension. The near-deaf lighthouse keeper had employed spent oyster shells to his ears and was thrilled with the results.

"Don't be so hard on her, James. You are a difficult fellow to know at times," he said.

The others looked confused as, unassisted by shellfish amplification, they had not been privy to our exchange.

Thelma shakily stood.

"Is 'e minding 'is manners, Beatrix? James! What've you said to 'er?"

"It's alright," I said. "Really I'm fine. Just a touch tired. Goodnight, all."

I made my way towards the stairs as George and Billingsly launched into a spirited debate about Fresnel lenses being preposterous. The Colonel joined in, but I felt an icy gaze upon my back that almost certainly belonged to him. I do not consider myself sensitive to harsh words, but mild condemnation from the Colonel felt worse than the vilest treatment from Ziro. I cared for him and hoped he cared for me in turn. Vulnerability such as this was new to me. It surprised me, the capacity with which my emotions could be influenced, and not just by the Colonel. I wanted the admiration of George and Thelma as well. I wished them to be proud of me. Even Billingsly seemed of genuine character and deserving of my admiration. Sharif's opinion I was less concerned with.

Passing into my bedroom, I found that one of Jasper's stockpiles in the ceiling had fallen through the cracks. I picked up swivel bar cufflinks, a playing card, coins of exotic currencies, dominos, and a box of matches. I placed all but the matches near a hole in the wall so the Ox's denizen thief would have little trouble reclaiming his treasure. The Colonel had warned about leaving matches lying around lest Jasper turn the Ox into a prime bit of tinder, so those were relegated to a drawer in the nightstand.

The fog outside had thinned and settled low to the ground, flowing over itself in pillowy folds lit by the nearby lighthouse. I extracted the magic lantern from beneath my bed and lit the limelight within. I sought the lamp's warmth but also the opportunity to see my spirits upon the fog. Fog and smoke were always preferred to a flat surface, as they allowed the ghouls to dance and approach, making the illusion all the more real. The only question was which slide would I employ. There was the stalking lion, the dead-eyed ghoul, the screeching cat, the half-open coffin, the bandit with a dagger, and the Spectre.

I inserted the lion slide. The great predator flashed golden against the wall of the Nimble Hare. I moved to the window, allowing the terrible animal to race to the ground below, where it rolled on the animated surface of fog.

Screams of fright came from two men lurking at the base of the Ox.

I was about to sound an alarm when a voice above did the job for me.

"Aha! Who's this?" the Colonel announced.

The Ox trembled as a grease erupted on the Cloud Deck.

"Ee's taken the riddle!" George slurred.

I screamed as a man fell past my window. He crashed upon the ground below and limped off into the fog with his waiting companions, chattering excitedly in Spanish.

"After them!" Sharif bellowed. The Ox again shook as the fat detective bounded down her outside stairs with incredible speed for someone leagues from lithe. The Colonel, Billingsly, and the Newlyweds spilled down the staircase after him, stone drunk.

"Which way'd they go?" Thelma said.

"Can 'ardly see the tip a' my nose in this fog," George announced as he swatted at the haze in vain.

The light in the lighthouse chose that moment to go out, and the remote peninsula plunged into darkness, the Ox's lanterns creating a tiny island of light.

"Billingsly old boy, you've neglected the lamp again," the Colonel charged.

"Ahoy," I shouted and tossed two extra lanterns from the Nimble Hare down to George. Then I crawled out my window and scaled down the Ox with expert nimbleness, even with the magic lantern in one hand.

"Many thanks for the illumination, acrobat," the Colonel said. Apparently our quarrel had been set aside in the event of the midnight burglary. "Let's have a light please, George."

George tossed him one of the lanterns. The Colonel lit it and regarded the Newlyweds.

"If you two can assist the pliable Billingsly here in relighting the beacon, I think we should all benefit by the revealing sights it may afford. I'm after Sharif and the miscreants."

"Stay with the Ox, dear," Thelma shouted to me as all parties dispersed.

Stay with the Ox? Thelma surely meant well, but she was the fool amongst us if she thought I would cloister myself behind the walls of rattan.

Led by my fiercely maned lion, I plunged into the fog. My search had no informed direction, so I tried to cover as much ground as possible. What would they say when it was the sprout amongst them who found the thieves? The rocks below my feet were moist with seaspray and I slowed my pace lest I fall headfirst into the rough waters beyond.

Several minutes went by with no sign of the thieves, nor Sharif, nor the Colonel. And why hadn't the lighthouse returned to life? My lion became less opaque, then flickered out of existence. Only now did I realize the fog had soaked straight through my windmill dress, and although there was little wind, the night had grown strikingly cold. Should I cry out? What if I drew the thieves? No, even worse than that, I would look as a child. I would be no babe in the woods.

A crash stung my ears and I fell to the gravel in fear. What could bring a clamour of such magnitude? Had one of Billingsly's ill-tended experiments finally become reactive to the point of detonation? Had I heard the lighthouse falling down on itself? What had become of George and Thelma...

Day came in an instant as the lighthouse blazed to life, the torch of some unseen god. The fog inherited an amber glow, and visibility increased from nix to nix-plus-a-small-increment. I had strayed a good distance and was indeed quite close to the perilous coastline.

Gravel crunched underfoot behind me. A hand protruded from the golden haze, in its grip a gun, pointed straight at my chest. These bandits wouldn't stop at the riddle—they meant to rob me of my life as well. The figure continued to advance and revealed not a Spanish criminal, but Sharif.

"Sharif?" My voice choked in the impossibly damp air.

"Put it down," he shouted.

I set down the magic lantern.

"For heaven's sake, Beatrix, *move!*"

Sharif shoved me aside. His gun had not been sighted on me, but the trio of bandits holed up in the costal rocks behind me. I had nearly walked straight into them.

Two of the Spaniards looked scared out of their wits, but the third kept his head high in defiance and spit at our feet. He held the stolen parchment.

"I said put it down," Sharif repeated, and he took a step closer. The cold blaze in his eyes told me he meant to kill these men.

I sprang to my feet and carefully crossed the gap between our two parties.

I held my hand out for the riddle. The bold Spaniard's eyes met mine. His were brave and unyielding, but surely he had no wish to die.

"He will shoot. Do you understand? He will kill you," I said, imploring with my open hand for him to return the riddle.

With contemptible slowness, he placed the paper in my hand.

"There, I've got it," I announced.

"Bring it here," Sharif said.

I delivered the riddle. Sharif checked it over to make sure there had been no trickery. Satisfied, he raised his gun once again.

"No!" I cried, but it was to no avail. Sharif fired.

The Spaniards dove deeper into the cluster of boulders that sparked with Sharif's bullets.

A man of substantial height wearing a bluebell-coloured vest fell from atop the same cluster of boulders. The Colonel got to his feet, soaking wet, dozens of wine corks spilling from his pockets.

"Holster that excitement," he shouted. "You've the riddle in hand!" The Colonel shook his hat, dislodging yet more corks. "My goodness, I doubt even our group could've consumed this much wine. Where've all these blasted corks come from?"

"What's happened to you?" I asked.

The Colonel's chest heaved in exhaustion below a reddened face.

"Lost my footing and fell clear into the drink. Things were touch and go for a time."

"I'm well within my rights to shoot these men, Colonel." Sharif still bristled with furious energy.

"You most certainly are not," the Colonel declared. "Stay your correct anger, lest it spoil to bloodlust."

Sharif lowered his gun.

"Were it not for me, they'd be neatly escaped," he asserted.

"The apprehension has been made. We will see them back to the lighthouse. On your feet, lads. *Vamonos.*"

The trio of men, now all thoroughly frightened, crawled from their refuge, each keeping a wary eye on Sharif. Having myself witnessed the transformation of a once reserved lawman into a bloodthirsty avenger, I could hardly blame them.

Chapter Seventeen

We repurposed the lighthouse's wine cellar into a jail for the Spaniards. The hatch was hardly bolted when Billingsly yelped like he'd left the tea kettle on. He threw the hatch open and bounded into the cellar, snatching a corkscrew away from the Spaniards just as they were about to enjoy some of his wine.

It was all for naught though, as the Colonel soon used some of the very same wine to extract information from the men. The bottles served first as a show of good will, then as a lubricant for the expulsion of secrets.

"They got on at Jaca, hid in the Bulkhead." The Colonel stepped from the wine cellar and I slotted the bolt. The uninhibited singing of the drunk Spaniards reached us in muted tones. "I should've noticed the difference in weight just as I should've expected some adhesive trouble from that town."

It was only just past the small hours of the morning, and the drinkers in our group grappled with formidable hangovers. The Colonel had brewed some of his noxious cabbage tea that the Newlyweds and Billingsly politely but firmly declined in favour of black coffee.

Thelma's balance wavered and George helped her to a seat atop a stack of books.

"Mercy, I'm still a bit fishy about the gills. Oh, I'm afraid I must look quite a fright. Not you though dearie." Thelma reached out and pinched one of my cheeks. "Pretty as a basket of oranges."

George patted his wife on the back before taking a seat himself.

"Me head's ringin' like a church bell."

"Our compliments for the pacharán, Billingsly. A masterclass in potency," the Colonel said.

Billingsly executed a small bow and nearly toppled over. None but the Colonel had yet escaped the pacharán's effect. I credited our captain's sobriety to his dip in the ocean and the pot of cabbage tea, which smelled strong enough to raise the dead. He took a sip of the hellish brew and rested on a stack of atlases. A row over, the grey goat was halfway through a book of nursery rhymes spiced with language not meant for children. I gave the bothersome beast another ugly look. It bleated, spilling a few shreds of paper, and I bleated right back.

"If you please, Colonel, what of the scoundrels in my wine cellar?" Billingsly asked.

"Patience, my good man. Allow me a moment to colour my yarn. You recall last night I spoke of the man called San Miguel, governor of Jaca?"

Billingsly nodded.

"Though dastardly and uncouth, the governor is no fool. He knew something of Ebbing's final riddle, knew of our interest, and judged us worthy to follow. The men below our feet were sent to learn what we know and to abscond with anything of value. When the riddle had been revealed and we were all plied with strong drink, they set about the plot. If San Miguel secures Ebbing's ultimate prize, which is sure to be fantastic, and presents it to his constituency with what will surely be tremendous theatricality, I should think he'll have bought a lifetime of compliance."

"Unfortunately for him, his thieves hadn't counted on my keen eye that found them like crabs amongst the rocks, scuttling in fear of my pistol," Sharif boasted.

"Certainly they hadn't. But their seaside cloister wasn't motivated by your pistol." The Colonel turned proudly to me. "It seems our resident acrobat is one of many talents, for these men hid from a phantasmal lion commanded by a tamer in a windmill dress."

"Good show, Beatrix!" George congratulated with a swing of the arm, accidentally toppling off his book stack.

"Good show indeed." The Colonel gave me a smiling wink.

"What's the difference who's done what?" Sharif threw his hands up. "We had nothing, had that subtracted, and are only now back to nothing! What good is half a riddle? We've come to seek the wisdom of an oracle who can't see past his own damned hair!"

Billingsly ignored the man. His focus had been drawn to the bottom of the riddle.

"My word, I nearly missed it. I dared not hope, but here it is." His attention returned to us. "You said the governor spoke of the finest treasure of Egypt."

"There are too many to count," Sharif said.

"But the *finest*. What would you say?"

"Not the Blue Star Sphinx?" the Colonel said.

Billingsly displayed the parchment. There, below the riddle and nearly the exact hue of the paper, was the outline of what looked like a cat.

"The Blue Star Sphinx," Billingsly announced.

The group was awed, including me. But I had to admit I knew of the piece only as legend.

"Do you mean to tell me it's actually real?" I asked.

Billingsly looked positively delighted.

"The Blue Star Sphinx's sapphire was found, perhaps unsurprisingly, in Ratnapura, Sri Lanka. The City of Gems they call it."

"Why would the Sri Lankan's choose a Sphinx shape?" I wondered.

"This piece was carved by no Sri Lankan," Billingsly said. "The story goes that two Egyptian craftsmen, having heard of the sapphire's discovery, travelled to Ratnapura, where, after demonstrating their unmatched skill in sculpture, were given the commission to shape the gem."

"You mean to tell me they crossed an entire continent just to carve a blue rock?" Thelma challenged.

Billingsly shook his head vigorously. "The Sphinx's sapphire is rare in triplicate. First, in that it exhibits asterism, an optical phenomenon that resembles a diamond star within the main gem. Second, it is of the cat's eye variety of asterism, also known as chatoyancy, dominated by a long vertical slit. And third, the sapphire exhibits twin chatoyancy. Two cat's eye asterisms, perfectly oriented. The Egyptians were well aware this was a precious stone amongst precious stones. A standard ornamental piece, no matter the expertise, would not do. So they fashioned it into a heart scarab." Billingsly looked around for an effect and found none.

"What'sat?" George asked.

"Heart scarabs were amulets used by ancient Egyptians to ensure the heart did not become separated in the afterlife. Memory, emotion, dreams—they believed all these things to be recorded in the heart. As such, the heart would be weighed upon death to determine acceptance into the afterlife. The scarabs contained inscriptions, instructing the heart not to betray its owner." Billingsly beamed with excitement. "Now, Ebbing traveled to Ratnapura as a young man. He slowly accrued all the jewels he could, and instead of hording his purchases, he spent his time giving them away through map and riddle. It seems, at some point, he acquired the Sphinx."

"How wealthy the original creators must have been," I fantasized.

"Not in the least. Not for long anyway," Sharif said darkly, assuming the mantle of explanation. "Soon after the carving was done, someone tried to steal the Sphinx. The gem's original founder and both the craftsmen were killed. A well-known thief was himself found dead just days later. So began the Sphinx's collection of souls. Those who possess it seem not to do so for long. It seems even the great Noel Ebbing was no match."

"Does everyone but me know the piece's whole story?" I asked.

Billingsly hunted amongst the esoteric organization of his books and plucked a tome called *Treasure of the Ages*. He flipped to a page on the Blue Star Sphinx and excitedly thrust it at me.

In keeping with its international makeup, the winged creature sketched on the page more closely resembled the sphinx of Grecian legend. Long wings lay flush with a torso whose long neck ended in a dreadful smirking face.

"*The Blue Star Sphinx*," I read aloud, "*is an object whose rarity is eclipsed only by it's danger. Many consider the piece cursed, manipulative, and excessively wicked*. How's an inanimate object supposed to be *excessively wicked*?"

"It is coveted by treasure hunters and sinners alike," Billingsly said. "The first group after the stone's immense value, the second believing in its redemptive power. The Colonel and I are great admirers of Ebbing." Billingsly's attention turned to the detective. "How are you so acquainted, Mister Sharif?"

Sharif was spared an inquisition as the lighthouse door burst open, rattling hard against the stone wall behind it. A figure stepped into the doorway to address us, a line of sailors at his back.

"Lo, it seems we've drawn the ire of the entire town of Jaca," the Colonel said.

I, however, took the man's almond skin and erratic hand gestures to suggest Italian descent.

"Who keeps 'de light 'ouse!" he demanded. Definitely Italian.

"I do," Billingsly said, oyster shells about his ears.

The Italian rushed at him, swinging his arms wildly.

The Colonel intercepted the man.

"Slow yourself, sir, or suffer retribution!"

The Italian collapsed onto his knees and sobbed fat tears onto the stone floor.

"My cork, 'ets all lost!"

The inactive lighthouse. The loud crash in the small hours. The sea littered with cork. I didn't need Billingsly to explain what had happened. Nor did the Colonel.

"The oversight of the dark lamp is my fault entirely," he said. "Visit blame upon me and me alone." The Colonel sat the inconsolable man in a chair. "Now then, tell us your woes. Perhaps we can put some disrupted pieces back together."

"I'm a merchant, bound for Napoli. We came in this morning... I couldn't see..."

"Tell of your wares. The cork."

"Fresh from Portugal. I was to sell it in Napoli. Now it is ruined!"

"Surely if any cargo can stand to be tossed into water, it's cork."

"You do not know the buyers in Napoli," the Italian growled. "They are greedy. They'll use any excuse to pay half price or less."

"What is your price?"

The merchant's sobs stopped.

"My p-price?"

"Yes, man, tell me the price of your stock."

The merchant whispered the price, tears returning to his face as he quantified his misfortune aloud.

"Turn off the tap, old boy. I should like to purchase the entire stock for one and a half times the value to account for the damage to your vessel as well as the inconvenience visited upon you," the Colonel said.

The merchant sat speechless, but only for a moment.

"But some has been lost to sea."

"If your men help collect what yet floats, I will pay cash on the barrelhead."

The merchant stuttered then looked to our faces for any sign of trickery or deceit. Finding none, he resumed crying, this time in joy. He hugged the Colonel and wrung his hand, shouting words of gratitude.

"You are a man of true virtue, *signore*!"

The Colonel brushed a pool of seawater from one of the man's broad shoulders.

"Virgin words spoken in regard to me."

"Oh, but you are, *signore*! *Grazie*. Thank you!" He ran outside and shouted the news to his men, some of whom were gathering the spilled cork from the surf. A cheer arose from the coastline and by the day's end the white gravel of Gibraltar was home to a pyramid of the small cylinders of springy wood. The sailors had rescued about seventy percent of the original stock by their own rough estimate, and it was a large stock indeed. An impatient Jasper sped out of the Ox to snatch a few samples for his collection.

The Italians attached a heavy canvas skirt to the base of the Ox and filled it with the thousands of newly-bought corks. The canvas came from the sails of a boat wrecked on the coast a few weeks earlier when Billingsly learned about something called an electromagnet and neglected the lamp while trying to construct one of his own. Whoever appointed Billingsly lighthouse keeper must have been thicker than pudding, and I made a decision that should I ever find myself at sea in bad weather, I would stay leagues away from Gibraltar.

The Colonel presented the money promised. It was in several different currencies, but the ship's accountant confirmed the total after some scribbling in a ledger.

As the Italian's hand moved to scoop the pile of money, the Colonel stopped him.

"Just one last thing, old chap."

The Italian's eyes flashed fearful as if the deal had been too good to be true.

"I should like to have your name, so I know whom I am paying. I myself, am Colonel James Bacchus."

"Oh! How rude of me. My name is Augostino. I am from Sicily!" Augostino wrung the Colonel's hand.

"Ah, Sicily. All nations hold some place in my heart, though I admit the Sicilian property has not always been ample. It would appear a correction is in order. It is my great fortune to know you, Augostino. If you'll permit an abridged interaction, we've a schedule to keep."

"Of course, of course! We too should like to pass through the strait before nightfall, not to question the abilities of your lighthouse keeper."

"His abilities should be in nothing but question. I wish you speed in your repairs and the remainder of your travels." The Colonel bowed low.

Augostino returned the gesture with interest and set off to join his men, who had nearly finished patching the damage to their hull. They bailed out the seawater in buckets passed from hand to hand, a cheerful work song on their lips. Their spirits were high following the Colonel's purchase, not to mention the steady supply of pacharán I had provided them.

The Colonel gathered our party in the lighthouse.

I sat between the Newlyweds, the two of them refreshed after sleeping off their drunkenness while the cork had been gathered.

"I'm swearing drink off for the rest of my days," Thelma pledged.

"I'll put odds against that," George offered with a wink to me.

Sharif plopped down nearby and the Colonel began.

"Sharif, although spoken in an uncouth manner, your words regarding this investigation's lack of progress were not entirely untrue. We're overdue for some legwork." Sharif made no sign of apology, and the Colonel continued. "We're richer in information than when we arrived. We know the object dangled at the end of Ebbing's line and, although cryptic, we have a description of where it might be found. I've made an exact reproduction of the riddle, which I should've bloody done in the first place." He handed Billingsly the original parchment. "Billingsly, you've this riddle to stew upon, and we've other leads to follow. Christopher's immediate trail is cold, so we will fly farther into his past for our next instruction. Thank you for your hospitality."

Christopher.

Will all the goings on, I'd nearly forgotten the name and the turmoil it had caused. Regret found my heart.

Just before I took to the Ox, Billingsly pulled me aside.

"Our dear Colonel may have a soft heart for the Spaniards, but keep your wits, Beatrix. Before their thievery on the Ox, they stole some of my work on nitroglycerine. Very, very dangerous information. I doubt you can retrieve it, but just the same, it's a fool who trusts the blatant thief."

"Why are you telling me?"

"I've told James, but you've got your head on. I'd feel better knowing you're watching over my friends."

"I will," I beamed, feeling prouder than I had in… perhaps ever.

I climbed the Ox's staircase and we set towards the sky, our departure taking a bit longer than usual. The Spaniards and cork couldn't weigh *that* much, could they?

I leaned over the railing to see Billingsly waving goodbye from under his storm of white hair.

"Goodbye, Beatrix," he called.

"Goodbye, Billingsly. And for heaven's sake, keep the bloomin' flame lit!"

"He's told you of his missing work then?"

The Colonel stood behind me.

"Yes," I said.

"A prudent warning, but I must disagree. It was not the Jacans who've stolen his essential work."

"Who then?" I asked.

"Sharif."

"Sharif? How do you know?" My eyes darted to the squat man being shown proper burner operation technique by George.

"As you have no doubt noticed, our traveling companion is an inquisitive of the highest order. Yet when it came to the nitroglycerine, a subject of extreme interest to any with a pulse, he was mute and his interest couldn't be persuaded. Has his beloved curiosity departed, or is there something else at play? Mind the Jacans if you must, but mind our lawman all the more."

I nodded and watched our departure from the Lighthouse at Europa Point.

We'd gained the Jacan thieves as passengers despite Sharif's protests, Augostino and his men had gained a small fortune, and Billingsly had gained the riddle and a pair of Manx, should he make any further breakthroughs. We'd also mercifully acquired some focus in our investigation. Christopher was after the Blue Star Sphinx. And we were after Christopher.

Find one, and we would likely find the other, though I doubted either discovery would come without cost.

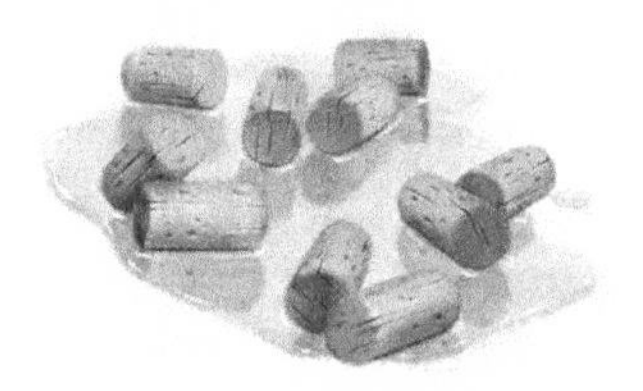

Chapter Eighteen

The Newlyweds and I were locked in a fierce round of the Chinese tile game Mahjong when a choice riot from the kitchen below disrupted our play. The row was one-sided as Sharif's nearly hysterical shouts met with the even-keel of the Colonel's responses. Sharif's heavy boots clanked down the spiral staircase, followed by the slamming of a door.

A minute later, our captain stepped on deck with the flawed fox tureen steaming with pungent soup.

"Mulligatawny!" George jumped to his feet and joined the Colonel at a table where the two of them wasted no time in devouring spoonfuls of a thick, yellow broth.

"Fine by me," I said of George's departure. "He was winning."

"You'll have to excuse the boys," Thelma said as she poured a bowl for me and herself with much greater composure than our counterparts. "They go to absolute smithereens over this ridiculous Indian soup. Mind you, it is good, but you'll not catch me proclaiming it the pinnacle of cookery. Alright, James, out with it. What's got our *beloved* Sharif so wasp-stung?" She winked away any sincerity on beloved.

"Oh, that," the Colonel said between spoonfuls of Mulligatawny. "We've two quick detours before reaching Maulgate Prison in Britain. The excitable detective below our feet went to pieces rather quickly upon learning this. A man of queer reactions, don't you think?"

"I give him no more credence than the thieves in the Bulkhead," I said coolly.

"Well said, as our first appointment is a trip back to Jaca. I tried to console our resident constable with the plain fact we shall not even be touching Spanish soil. And that is the truth. But he howled like a petulant sow and refused to assist."

"What's the second detour?" I asked.

"Ah, that shall remain a surprise I think. Hopefully that secrecy does not endanger the helping hands I must request for our first detour in Jaca."

"I'll help," I said immediately.

"Us as well," George said, adding "a 'course" as if insulted his and Thelma's participation was ever in question.

"It warms me deep to know I've put in with such a hearty crew. Here is our undertaking."

Smoking a post-Mulligatawny pipe, the Colonel told us more of the beleaguered town of Jaca.

"Magicians and false prophets alike give me gooseflesh. When the two are found in one man who holds a seat of power and walks his route with a sword he claims fell from the heavens, well that's enough to give me indigestion. I've been inside many a cloud and never have I come across weapons of forged steel in their bellies."

"Perhaps they yield trophies only to the deserving," George teased.

"I make no claim to virtue, that's for certain, but as this reason-sieged town is on our path, let us tip the scales back to the other side. San Miguel is poisoning a once great city. The men in our very Bulkhead have proved quite reasonable when treated well. San Miguel would've seen them dead just to get his prize."

"And Sharif would've seen them dead for even less," I added.

"Yes, well, that's a beast yet to be wrestled. San Miguel is presiding over his roost and consequently hatching sloth, ignorance, and ineptitude of provincial proportions. My return to Jaca the other night did not inspire hope in my soul, though it did produce a rather limber-"

"James!" Thelma cut him off. "I don't like that kind a talk in front a Beatrix."

"I'm no prude!" I wailed.

"Ain't that ye can't handle it, Bee," George poured himself some more soup. "There's a place for that kind a talk and it ain't over Mahjong and Mulligatawny. Suitable diction, James, let's have it."

I rolled my eyes. The Newlyweds veered into parental territory at times, and I was unlikely to talk them out of it. But it happened seldom, and further, I sometimes appreciated it.

The Colonel navigated the unfamiliar restrictions as best he could.

"It would be to the world's discredit to allow these artisans of ham and saffron and… horizontal contortion, to wither and die. Just try to find a decent meal or… boudoir protagonist for a hundred kilometres in any direction beyond Jaca's walls."

"Boudoir protagonist?" Thelma looked at George, who shrugged.

"I like food, and I like women!" the Colonel chopped his hand into his palm in exasperation. "Jaca is a haven of finery for both, greatly endangered by a no-account governor."

"Who may be guilty of Ebbing's slaying as well," Thelma pointed out.

The Colonel shook his head.

"I asked my Jacan companion if she could account for San Miguel's whereabouts the day of the murder. He was dead centre of a parade, thrown in his own honor. He is certainly guilty, but it is of being an ass, not a murderer."

"All agreed, but you still haven't told us the plan," I said.

The Colonel focused once again.

"No need to reinvent the wheel. To best this Saint we shall take a page out of the book of another. Saint Nicholas."

"Father Christmas?" I laughed.

"The very same. His habit of dressing like the British Infantry and practices of animal husbandry we can do without. Ditto the list of good and bad children. What arrogance to pass judgement on the world's juvenile populace! What bizarre Polar standard informs these decisions? Where's the transparency!"

"Colonel! What's he to do with your plan?" I said.

"Yes, well, it's his method of chimneal infiltration we're after."

"Chimneal?" George questioned as he tilted his bowl to pool the last bit of soup.

"The practical means by which he deposits goods, unseen, and of principal importance, unharassed." The Colonel made jumping movements with one hand. "Roof, to roof, to roof."

"What're the Jacans to do with toys?" Thelma asked.

"*Tsk tsk.* You lot have neglected the Bulkhead. The Ox flies not by magic, but by the powers of chemistry and the fortitude of man!" The Colonel kicked the magnet-set compass in his excitement, and the poor instrument rattled with what sounded like broken parts. "Our stores of hydrogen and helium were replenished by our ally Billingsly, but generous too he was in the donation of hundreds of books. I nearly cleaned out his stock of Spanish language material. The keen traveller will have noticed our dear Ox is much heavier now than before our stay at the lighthouse, and not only from the addition of cork and a few mischievous Spaniards."

I privately chastised myself for failing to solve this riddle. I had claimed great powers of observation to gain passage on the Ox. Hopefully the others had not lost faith in that proclamation.

"The Ox is bursting at the seams, full as after a Boxing Day feast. Time we expelled the remainder onto Jaca."

Thelma's face soured at the analogy, but the Colonel was unperturbed.

"Bundles of five should do the trick, tightly bound, covering as diverse a range of knowledge as possible. Ignorance is the common flag of the savage and the exploited alike. It must be assailed at every opportunity. What say you?"

"Let's sully the bastard," came George's war cry.

Thelma slapped his arm on account of the language, but she too looked resolute.

"Aye, this man could do with a spoonful of humility. I think it's high time the governor found cold weather."

I had no curses or idioms to add so I simply nodded my allegiance, grabbed the fox tureen, and made for the Bulkhead to feed our resident Jacans.

"The loudest words of all," the Colonel commended. "Right good form!"

Chapter Nineteen

As the crimson sun set that evening beyond Jaca, another red orb rose.

Armed with bundles of books primed to inspire and enlighten, the Ox and her long shadow glided silently over fields of saffron crocus that ringed the town.

True to his word, Sharif offered no assistance. Circus folk like myself despise a loafer, and this blatant absenteeism during a physical task added to my ever-expanding dislike for the man.

The would-be-thieves, however, proved most reliable after several days of wine, curried onion soup, and fair treatment. We dropped them off a ways from the town to avoid charges of collusion should our operation fail.

For the rest of us, excluding Sharif, the time for action had come. The sun was properly set, the books properly bound. George stood positioned at the burner. The Colonel, Thelma, and I huddled around the hatch in the Bulkhead.

Our first bundle struck the stone rim of the first chimney. The twine holding the bundle burst, and while most of the books fell into the chimney, one tumbled down the roof tiles and struck a passing man square on the head. This may have been a non-issue with some of the smaller books, but this particular book was *Dante's Inferno*, unabridged.

Whisper-shouting apologies to the dizzy Spaniard, we continued on to the next home, and again, hitting the mark proved to be rather difficult from our height.

"This won't do," the Colonel said.

He tied a tow line round his waist and lowered himself through the hatch and onto the next Jacan roof. Thelma and I had hardly any time to react before he softly called up to us for a new bundle.

Thelma devised a primitive pulley with two hooks, by which we could lower the bundles. As each new freight of books was lowered, the unloaded hook would travel back up for new freight.

George peered down the centre of the spiral staircase to witness our terrific efficiency.

"Capital work, ladies," he said while tending to the controls. The basket kept at a mostly even height as we drifted from one row of houses to the next, but an exact flightpath was of course impossible.

The Colonel sprinted across the next rooftop in order to reach the chimney before he was yanked by Ox-tether into the air and onto the next roof. Perhaps not quite as graceful as Father Christmas, but at least the packages were now finding their marks.

That night in Jaca, it rained tales of gothic horror and scientific essays alike. A menagerie of wordage compiled in innumerable ways to free the shackled and bloom the wilted. If a chimney was active with flame, an extra bundle would be given to the neighbours in hopes the Spaniards would share with one another. In a moment of unfortunate timing, one Jaca resident lit their fire in the same instant the Colonel dropped his bundle. The addition of paper kindling sent the fire below into a blaze, and although the fire was extinguished, the commotion was enough to rouse the neighbourhood. This, coupled with a growing number of residents discovering their own bundles, caused a tremendous excitement that rippled throughout the citadel.

"Nearly done. Stay the course," the Colonel called up to us in full voice as there was no longer any point in attempting furtiveness.

Thelma attached the last bundle while I watched a man in sun and moon robes shove through the crowds with reckless fury. Something glinted orange on his belt as he leapt from a cart onto a balcony and climbed up onto a nearby roof. It was the amber hilt of San Miguel's sword. The governor was upon us!

"Colonel! Mind your rear!" I cried out.

The Colonel spun around just in time to dodge San Miguel's blade. The broad sword sliced clean through the line, severing our captain's connection to his ship.

It was impossible that the governor knew exactly what we were doing, but he was clever enough to recognise *something* was happening, and any unapproved change in the town of Jaca was liable to be bad for him. Thus, the attempts at dismemberment.

Another swipe from San Miguel was dodged by the Colonel, but this time it cost him his balance. Our captain skated upon dislodged tiles that careened over the roof's edge. He twisted at the last moment, grabbing the overhang and arresting a fatal plunge.

"George!" I cried up the staircase. "You've got to slow us down."

"I can't," his reply came back. Of course he couldn't. Lateral influence was not within the Ox's power.

I scampered down the severed tow line and onto the long rooftop that held the combatants. As I ran towards the Colonel and San Miguel, instinct threw me prone at the sound of a gunshot.

The roof tile afront the Colonel's face exploded in a plume of orange clay.

I looked over my shoulder for the source of the attack. Several houses down, in the direction the Ox headed, stood a woman holding a smoking Derringer pistol, a wilted saffron crocus just visible in her hair.

Several things became immediately clear.

First, the woman had successfully made it back to Jaca after her time on the Ox. Second, she harboured no small amount of dissatisfaction at her abrupt separation from the man at whom she now aimed. Third and most importantly, accuracy with a Derringer was damn near impossible several roof-lengths away. This last point was confirmed as she fired the tiny pistol again.

San Miguel, sword overhead ready to chop the Colonel in half, let out a surprised whimper as the woman's errant bullet found his left leg. He fell to the tile, grasping a nearby chimney to prevent a fall, and dropped his sword in the process.

"Ha! What outstanding fortune!" the Colonel cried.

I scrambled across the tile and helped my dangling comrade back onto the roof with some effort. Although he was thin, his height resulted in considerable weight.

"There we have it. Thank you, Bee. Back to the Ox now. I'll tidy up."

"Mind the line, you blockheads!" Thelma yelled.

I chased after the tow line as it danced towards the last roofs of Jaca. My strong hands gripped the line easily, and I shimmied up to the basket in time to see the Colonel pick up the governor's sword.

"They shall soon come home to roost, Señor Miguel. I wish you all the luck you deserve."

The Colonel tipped his John Bull then was forced to vault the narrow gaps between houses in the direction of the crocus woman. At short length, they were face-to-face.

The crocus woman positioned the Derringer barrel between the Colonel's eyes and pulled the trigger. But there came no discharge.

"You've had your two, love. Lucky for me, you don't shoot as well as you—"

"Colonel!" I shouted. "Mind the bloomin' line!" The tow line had reached the last bit of roof.

The Colonel popped the amber out of the sword's hilt with his handy penknife and flipped it to the crocus woman.

"Pocket it before he sees. I hope your anger falls away, and that if a positive outcome is possible in our union, even if only a pleasant memory, you can value it. I know I will."

"Colonel!" Thelma and I cried.

"Cheers!" He delivered an abbreviated bow and, carried by mercifully long legs, reached the line just as it fell over the edge of the roof. With a trusting leap, he grasped the rope and we flew skyward, flush with the warmth of a just deed well done.

The citizens of Jaca gathered below, books of every size and color in their arms, standing witness to an archangel shot through the leg, perhaps not as divine as he had once claimed.

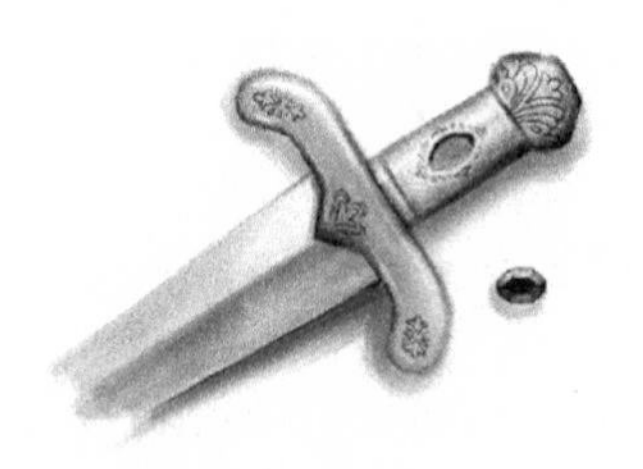

Chapter Twenty

The sword of San Miguel found its new home in the Ox's kitchen.

"Any stubborn roasts will now have me to deal with," Thelma boasted, twirling the weapon of civic intimidation now relegated to dinner preparation.

Sharif was uninterested in hearing about the events of Jaca and wanted to know only when we would be in Britain and back on the trail of the criminal. Initially he had said "the Sphinx" but corrected himself. Only a thick-brained juggler would be foolish enough to still believe him a man of the law, and I looked forward to the day we were rid of him and whatever motives he possessed.

Late the next night, curled up in bed with my magic lantern, I inserted the slide of rose glass painted with an arched-back cat, mouth frozen in a sharp-toothed scream.

A cloud of sweet-smelling smoke settled past my window, and unless a botched pastry was aflame in the kitchen, Sharif was smoking his hookah.

Blast his subterfuge. I'd discover him yet.

I made the Cloud Deck and found the portly man on his back, bathed in smoke, like a sleeping dragon.

"Staring at that magic lantern of yours?" he said.

"How did you know that?"

"You and I are night owls, Beatrix. I observe the behaviour of my fellow nocturnal creatures. You admire those ghastly spirits."

"I do no such thing."

"You're a strange girl."

"I'll accept that as a compliment." I'd never before had a conversation with Sharif alone and couldn't guess what he was getting at.

"It was intended as such. The visible world leaves much to be desired. A fellow *seer* is always valued."

"The spirits I see are born from the lantern's glass and nothing else. A prismatic fantasy."

"Ah, but they are born. Whisked from nothingness into something you can see at the lick of a flame. Is it really so difficult to go one step further?"

"You may have your beliefs, but I do not share them." I attempted to choose my next words carefully. The last time I'd spoken out of turn, I'd queered my standing with the Colonel, and that was still unresolved despite our harmonies over Jaca. I worried far less about my relationship with Sharif, but I had begun to see the advantages that followed tact. "Do you know the meaning behind Antwerp's name?" I asked.

He let out a large plume of smoke.

"Why do you ask?"

"I've heard several different stories about it. I assumed a local such as yourself would—"

"I am an Arab, Beatrix. What of that suggests to you I am exclusively from Antwerp?"

"Let us assume you emigrated. You would still have been required to rise through the ranks, therefore spending a great amount of time in the city."

"And so I am required to know the etymology of its name?"

"I heard tell that there was once a giant who sat by the city's river and demanded a toll of those who passed by. If they did not pay, he would cut off their hand and throw it into the river. This continued until someone did the same to the giant. Antwerp means 'to throw a hand.'"

"How magnificently charming."

"Someone in my circus company spoke of it, and they'd lived there only a few months. I find it just a bit strange you are unfamiliar."

Sharif only shrugged. Perhaps he felt his honor unassailed when it was questioned only by a lowly acrobat. Another substantial plume of smoke rose from his mouth.

"Do you believe we are to find the Sphinx?" he said at length.

I hesitated, not wanting to crack the bell and betray something I shouldn't. Both of us disguised the conversation as casual when both of us knew it to be anything but.

"If it can be found, I have confidence in our ship and her captain."

"A safe and unprosecutable answer. You'd do well in politics. Yes, the Colonel is wise and savvy, but can he direct where the compass cannot find?" He thunked the magnet with his boot and again the compass gave off a hard rattle. It was getting misused a great deal lately. "Can he navigate where none have travelled before?"

"But this is nonsense," I said. "You believe the Sphinx lies in such a place?"

"I do indeed, little one."

"By what judgment?" I asked, nearly adding *fat one.*

"I have been to places half as ætheral for pieces half as valuable. By your comforting laws of reason, some strangeness awaits those who seek the Sphinx." Sharif inhaled from the hookah and smiled. The smoke curled in gnarled tendrils from between teeth the yellow of opium den dominoes. It was an appearance so ghastly, so malicious, I could hardly believe this was the same individual I'd considered benign in the daytime hours.

"Goodnight, Beatrix." He slowly stood and left for bed, leaving a milky pool of ash to float in his wake.

The fraud had evaded the more pointed questions but seemed no longer compelled to claim his initial identity as being true. If adversaries were coalescing, it would be wise to get my own cabal well in order. That meant reconciling with the Colonel.

The night was warm and clear, and I curled up in one of the Cloud Deck's deep leather chairs to enjoy the night sky. My thoughts regarding reconciliation with the Colonel were at length invaded by threads of recto and verso. The riddle's jumble of nonsense words came soon after, and a family of swans ferried me into a dreamless sleep that lasted straight through till morning.

I roused to witness the Colonel bent over the railing, fussing with the nests of the Manx. The adult birds fluttered about with interest but not agitation.

Presumed to be sleeping, I took the opportunity to study the man as he worked.

The Colonel had worn a wristwatch since I'd met him, but only now did I notice that the time and date upon its face had not changed. It could have fallen into non-operation some time ago, but the date was a month away. Had it been broken nearly a year? I did not think the Colonel one bested by failed gears, and certainly not for eleven months. Intentional stasis to mark some future date then? What was to occur in a month? *What was in his heart?*

"Good morning, Bee," he said without looking up from his avian work. "Today promises to be a fine day!"

I should've known my perceived advantage had never actually existed. I sat up from my accidental bed.

"What are you doing there?" I asked.

He was clad in a Chesterfield coat of red and white stripes, an Osiria rose of identical colours tucked in the John Bull.

"One of my favourite obligations: showing these creatures the way home." He straightened from his place at the railing, a baby Manx in each hand. A few adults followed him. "See now how they come to know the Ox." He knelt beside the magnetic rock and gently rubbed the chicks against its smooth surface. His movements were almost ritualistic, and I found myself hypnotized by the rhythm. "There. That should do for now. Takes a bit at a time, but I haven't lost one yet. Incredible animals. Some live as old as sixty if you can believe it."

He returned the birds to their nest and we sat for coffee and tea.

"Is the bed in the Nimble Hare insufficient? I harvested the feathers for the pillows myself."

"No... It's nothing."

"Come now, don't clam up."

In Ziro's circus, my emotions went unnoticed, always. I was now in a culture much more observant and aware.

"I don't understand what's happened between us, Colonel."

"Our row at the lighthouse." He nodded grimly. "You're owed a delayed apology. I stand by my right of privacy, but I also admire the bold. In any case, my mode of condemnation that night was incorrect. I am sorry, truly and without reservation."

I twisted a ballast rope absently in my hands, keeping silent as I watched the impossible heights and depths of the Alpine Mountains slide underneath the Ox.

He took the chair opposite mine.

"You've more to say."

"I'm angry with you!" I said, not realizing the words to be true until I spoke them.

The Colonel gave me his attention and silence, laying way for an explanation.

"You jump to and fro in this basket, absconding from responsibility and blame. You kidnap women and abandon them in the countryside freshly ravaged! You get drunk and cause a catastrophe at sea then turn spendthrift and buy your way out of it. What are you to do when a situation is not for sale or the bank runs dry?" I had worked myself up into such a state that I kicked the brass compass with my shoe, drawing the sad, dull rattle.

"You take issue with my employment of money?" he laughed. "No need to dynamite, fair acrobat. The bank has run dry."

"What?"

"Our new Sicilian companion Augostino now holds all of my fortune. I have money enough for our next few resupplies and not much beyond."

"But... I thought—"

"Currency comes and goes like the snows of winter, Bee. How foolish the man who tries to hold snow after its season has passed. I am usually savvy enough to earn money back, and I rather enjoy putting it to use. Wealth, as you correctly observed, does not always fix what is broken. But when it can pivot my fate or the fate of those I'm engaged with, I allow it to pivot at its highest ability. I try to not just get by in the world, but to live in it with aggressively applied compassion, the greatest quantity of cunning I can muster, and the occasional tactical insertion of currency. What if we were to foster an empire of good will and solution? What if—well, I'd be a bear to test your patience in this state. You appear yet unsatisfied."

I looked at the rattan weave under my feet. Might as well get it all out.

"What is the *Manifest Philopatry*?" I kept my gaze on the deck as long as possible then raised my eyes to meet the Colonel's. "I shouldn't have looked, but I did. Now I have... concerns."

The Colonel reclined deeper into his chair.

"I suppose the nature of a hidden document containing a list of expunged names might be difficult to decipher..."

"Are you a murderer?"

He surrendered to fits of laughter.

"Do you think me one? No, that title I cannot claim. You must understand that I am almost always operating at something, even if the goal is yet unclear to you. Peculiar reasoning I am often accused of, but I am a man of reasoning all the same. I'm afraid I must boldly request trust and patience when it comes to the manifest." He checked a pocket watch, one that actually ticked, then produced a container of tan jelly. The remainder of the jelly was smeared across moustache and lips alike, which he smacked loudly in conclusion.

Before I could remark, a landmark on the ground below diverted my attention.

The lake where I'd first seen the Ox anchored.

"You mean to return me to Ziro?" I cried in sudden terror. "You *are* a murderer!"

"Calm yourself, my dear. No doubt your circus has long quit this town, and I have an appointment to keep."

He flew the Ox low, touching down behind a hill adjacent to Lord Chartish's property. George was asked to the deck and equipped with a cup of coffee.

"If you would be so kind as to keep us inflated for immediate departure, there's a swish of this morning's brew in it for you. Bee, I believe this excursion will be of interest to you, should you like to witness it."

He disappeared down the exterior staircase. I looked at George, who simply shrugged.

"He's told me nothing about this."

I stood in indecision just a moment longer, then disembarked.

A few steps from the Ox, the Colonel turned to address me.

"Ah, wonderful. I see you've come with an escort." Sharif was not far behind me. The Colonel walked back to us. "Sharif, this business is unconcerned with the investigation. Bee alone is meant to bear witness."

"I should like to ensure that for myself," Sharif returned.

"My dear constable, we are many leagues from Antwerp. Even a reach as expansive as yours no doubt has a jurisdiction. You have no license to walk with us now, as neither of us wish your company. I'll thank you to stay comfortably on the Ox." The Colonel's tone was polite but dangerous. Sharif stood his ground a period of time I guess he thought necessary to make a point. Then he shrunk back into the Ox.

We continued on and I sprinted to keep pace with the Colonel's exceedingly long gait, perhaps hustling to my own demise.

"What is our aim?" I asked.

"Your order of business is to observe. I will be the active agent." The Colonel's breath was quite noxious as it passed his beloved yak balm. The pungent paste had a sweet musk that made my stomach turn. But his lips were no longer chapped. Why continue to self-medicate with the room-clearing balm? This was perhaps the most unsettling question of all.

We reached the edge of Chartish Manor's manicured lawn to find a great number of bourgeois on the property drinking and chatting at a large party. Lacy gowns for the women, cummerbunds for the men, and a six-piece ensemble playing Johann Pachelbel for all.

The Colonel flexed his fingers and smacked his lips.

"How fertile the situation! Wait here unseen, won't you?"

He dropped a collapsible telescope into my hands and sprang from our place in the underbrush.

Striding across the lawn with purpose, his always-sharp appearance saw him blend in amongst the smartly dressed guests. For further authentication, he bent an ear or two but never stayed in one place long enough to be pinned down, decoupling from conversations by delivering a limerick and exiting under the laughter. Pivoting from group to group, the easily manufactured social grace camouflaged his dance across the lawn to the tune of "Canon in D." The silky performance delivered him to a side door of the mansion, which he quickly disappeared into.

My gaze wandered to a room on the top floor where a beautiful woman combed her hair. She wore a splendid dress of white lace and I recognised her face in the glass of the telescope.

Lord Chartish's fiancée. But this must be their wedding!

Something pulled the attention of the soon-to-be Lady Chartish. She looked cross, her speech harsh and direct, the hairbrush raised like a weapon. An unheard response came. Her mouth curled into a curious smile. She inquired something. The threatening hairbrush was lowered. The unseen party made her outright laugh. Courtship paced to the wingbeat of a hummingbird! I knew only one man with such supernatural proficiency.

Was the Colonel mad! He couldn't possibly-

The curtains were promptly drawn.

Chapter Twenty-One

"It isn't enough that I suffer your debauched jaunts on the Ox? Now you extradite me to bear witness firsthand?" I shouted angrily at my fire-box captain as we ran through the forest, back to the Ox. "Dabbing it up with every bob tail and tart on the bloomin' continent."

He was positively giddy.

"Believe me, this was not for my enjoyment. The woman makes love like a scarecrow! Perhaps that's justice enough for Chartish."

"Justice enough?"

He wagged a finger at me demanding patience. "Peculiar reasoning, dear Bee. Peculiar reasoning!"

We scrambled onto the Ox and George took flight, the Colonel checking his pocket watch all the while.

"That's it," he coached the Scotsman. "Find the wind just so and here we go."

We passed over the forest line. The cabal of guests had organized into formal seating, all pointed at a grandiose arched trellis, under which stood Chartish and his fiancé, but no, now she had just been pronounced his wife. Her head twisted under an aggressive kiss from Chartish, revealing an Osiria rose tucked into hair a bit more tousled than was expected for a bride.

The Ox's titanic shadow swallowed up the proceedings, and the guests looked to the sky in astonishment. A few ducked in fear as we passed so close overhead I was able to easily see a look of repugnance and confusion on Chartish's freshly kissed face—repugnance and confusion at having just experienced the unmistakable taste of yak urine.

I would guess Chartish realized what the Colonel had done at the same instant I did. We both understood that this was a man of powerful and patient vengeance.

The Colonel claimed his rescue of Jaca was for the sake of his indulgences. But I wondered if he did it for the common people. For today, even in our most demanding schedule, he had taken the time and forethought to conclude a defence of my honour that had begun at a dinner party that seemed so long ago.

George, perhaps sensing our need for reconciliation, nodded his head and went below.

"Bee, I am in many ways a petty man. Vengeful, proud, and stubborn. But I am loyal to my friends. I consider you a great ally, and there is little you could do to disrupt that status. I predict complications of increasing magnitude await us. You implicitly hold my trust. I hope you feel me worthy of yours."

I nodded, unable to bring forth words at that moment. The catharsis I'd pined for so badly brought tears to my eyes, but I would not cry.

"Your hat please, sir," I said in an only slightly quavering voice.

The Colonel bowed low and placed his John Bull in my hands.

"London, please," he said, and left me at the controls.

If there was one thing to know about the Colonel, it was that his brand of reasoning was peculiar and entirely his own. If there was a second thing to be known, it was that his methods often showed results. What appeared as random stumblings to the uninitiated was really an intricate dance the Colonel alone knew the steps to. While I still had a great deal to learn about the flora-crowned hellion, I never again suspected my safety at odds with his interests.

-PART FIVE-
BRITAIN

Chapter Twenty-Two

Learning where I stood, specifically that I was not in the company of a spatially-unencumbered, log-keeping killer, had dosed me with a hearty bit of confidence. Though the Newlyweds assisted a great deal, and our path was much less direct than if the Colonel had been at the helm, I got us to Britain intact. Our destination: Maulgate Prison, tucked in the vast forests outside London.

"What's our play here?" I asked as I eased the Ox into a long descent.

The Colonel's gaze concentrated tightly on the distant prison.

"Christopher was an inmate here. Cellmates are often privy to details others are not. If his cellmate still resides here, we may gain some insight."

"It's an easy pass for me, love," Thelma said. "I fancy a decent picnic after the long legs of trips. Some Scotch eggs'll do nicely for that."

The Colonel nodded.

"Indeed, and a penitentiary is no place for a lady. I suppose it's foolish to—"

"I'll not stay on the Ox," I provided the answer he should've well expected.

"As long as you're aware of the danger, I should value your sharp eyes and tactically caustic disposition."

"Someone's got to gain our next foothold," I lobbed back.

"I'll keep Thelma company," George said. "Should any other prisoners have escaped and taken to roaming the countryside, she can protect me. Picnic'll give my hide some rosy colour."

I set the Ox down in a clearing with only the mildest of jolts.

"I'll join the prison gang," Sharif surprised everyone. Despite the attempt to tag along in Switzerland, his lack of participation had become something of an expectance.

"Very well," the Colonel said neutrally. "Those departing, step to it." He tucked a sprig of purple-flowered vine into his hat. And so, of course, the waistcoat about his torso was the precise green of the vine's leaves, the handkerchief in his breast pocket the precise purple of the flowers.

The Colonel and I... and Sharif, passed through the shady and lush greenery buzzing with animal life.

"This is all an old royal hunting forest, used by many kings of old before it was gifted to a noble family." The Colonel plucked a leaf and examined it with the intricacy of an expert.

Sharif huffed at the Colonel's words for some reason, but added no formative contribution.

"Alright, Colonel, give us just a piece of your mind. What's the play?" I asked, opting for something constructive.

"He won't tell us a damn thing!" Sharif answered for the Colonel. He seemed much more agitated than usual.

"Firstly, Christopher was with me on my Gobi excursion."

"In what capacity?" I asked, mildly shocked. At times, I'd been tempted to think of Christoper as something phantasmic, perhaps even allegorical.

"I had presumed him a traveling partner. Right up until the moment he dislodged me from the Ox, and attempted to steal her. I suppose at that point he became a marooner."

"An attempt at murder?" Sharif asked. He almost sounded impressed.

"He sought the Sphinx as well and grew impatient of my fulfilment of other tasks," the Colonel said.

"Sound familiar, Sharif?" I asked.

Sharif glared at me, but the Colonel continued.

"Mercifully for me, the Ox proved too much for Christopher to handle, and I found it crashed only a few dunes away. By the time I reached it, he'd already fled, likely fearing reprisal from me. Naturally, I feared him dead, as he is of a fiercely Irish complexion and the desert sun is his natural enemy. Though I searched for several days, no freckled corpse did I find. He had spoken of Batavia, and when I failed to locate him there, I travelled to Switzerland on other business, whereupon I made the pleasure of your company, Bee." He spoke casually, as if a journey to the reaches of Southern Asia was no more remarkable than one to the corner store. "Christopher was interned here for his activities in Batavia. His escape came only days before the rather secretive meeting in Antwerp with Ebbing."

The calliope's newspaper flashed in my mind. It had told of a massacre of a family of treasure hunters! Surely Christopher hadn't massacred an entire family singlehandedly? When the Colonel selected rivals, he certainly aspired to great heights.

"I've read of this!" I said eagerly. "He was to be executed!"

The Colonel nodded.

"The caterpillar pace of bureaucracy saved his life. Can't just string a man up the day of his conviction, even if a massacre's concerned. This is London after all. Seems he was provided just enough time to mount an escape."

We reached a fork in the road, where two soot-stained boys, who looked no older than six, played catch with two flat wooden arrows. Between them was a sign that read "Maulgate Prison" at the top, "London" at the bottom.

"A day off from the factory, ay lads?" The Colonel said.

"Tha's right," one of the boys said.

"We're in a hurry," Sharif said to them. "Which way's the prison?"

"Time for a riddle, I think!" The other boy said, not put off by the anger in Sharif's voice.

I made to grab one of the boys, but the Colonel caught my shoulder.

"There are no straight paths, Bee. Only those that fork. Trick's in not minding the fork. Life pushes one along the path without choice, this is unavoidable, however it is at forks that we are granted the chance to fashion something much greater than destiny. What we have here is the playful spirit of Noel Ebbing. Why not indulge it?"

I brushed my blouse, stung with embarrassment.

"The riddle then," I said firmly.

The boys skipped and cartwheeled to trees aside the split road.

"One of us'll always tell the truth," Left Boy said.

"One of us'll always lie," Right Boy echoed.

"You've one question each," they said together.

"Which way's the bloody prison!" Sharif spat, his anger unspoiled by the Colonel's views on the benevolence of choice.

"This way," both boys gestured to their path.

Sharif bounded forward and swatted fruitlessly at Left Boy who gaggled with laughter on his tree branch.

"How 'bout a ladder, mister?" Left Boy asked.

"Or a trampoline?" Right Boy added.

"How 'bout you mister?" Left Boy shouted to the Colonel. "What'll it be?"

"I forfeit my guess."

"You what?"

"I suspect the young lady's query will suffice."

I admit my mind was still on wringing their scrawny little necks. The Colonel may have suspected as much.

"Summon your blood here," he brought his hand level with his head. "A sound mind is rarer than a bundle of knuckles. Show us your prowess, Bee."

I felt the warmth of his confidence but its pressure as well. Ignoring Sharif's grunts of exertion as his frustrated attack continued, I summoned and disposed of several stupid answers. I breathed out and stayed calm. Then I thought of one question, whose answer was telling both in truth and falsehood.

"Which way would the other say the prison is?" I shouted.

"That way!" the boys cried out, directing to the left path. The liar had indicated the opposite path the truth teller would say. The truth teller had indicated the incorrect path the liar would choose.

"Then we go right," I announced plainly, and made for the path.

"Exceptional!" the Colonel boomed with a hearty swing of the arm. "Beyond my own wits, for certain."

"I've no patience for these foolish antics," Sharif took the left path.

"That way lies London," I told him.

"I know it does!" he thundered. "Prison visits are ill-advised for a man of law anyway."

"Come off it. You are no policeman, Sharif!" I charged at last.

The Colonel raised an eyebrow and waited to see Sharif's reaction.

"Keep whatever opinion you must, but I'll not accompany you any further," the squat man spat and waddled down the left path.

"Odd. Men of his size rarely opt for extended leisure walks. Thanks for the lark, lads." The Colonel flipped each boy a coin, and we were on our way.

I waved goodbye to the boys. Sharif's approach, and I must admit my initial one, had been to leave the scene hotly, leaving the youths red-necked and black-eyed. The Colonel's method had seen me with a sense of accomplishment and the orphans bounding away with coins the size of their fists. The Colonel's school of good-will alchemy was certainly the one I wished to be enrolled in.

"Was I wrong to prosecute Sharif?"

"Not in the least. It was a fruit long ready to be plucked. But let us leave the much less interesting mystery of Sharif to idle for now as we enter a potential catalyst for the much more interesting one at hand. Why are we here, Bee?"

I thought hard, not wanting to spoil my successful play at the riddle.

"Christopher was present at an appointment of the utmost secrecy an extremely short time after his escape."

The Colonel nodded.

"You think he learned Ebbing was to be at The Cross Eyed-Cricket while still confined here? Meaning one of the prisoners or guards may aid in our exploits."

"Top marks. We're going to start with his cellmate. With any luck, we'll meet the man forthwith."

He nodded up the path. The perimeter walls of Maulgate, which I thought rather low for a prison, edged a large clearing surrounded by thick forest. A guard tower jutted out of the main building like a great concrete tent pole yet to be adorned with a tent. The front gate hung at an angle on rusted hinges. The facility appeared to be in tremendous disrepair, same for a man standing abreast of the front gate, loudly lamenting his station in life.

"Observe immediately this man's condition," the Colonel said. "Managerial by the way he speaks, under-appreciated in his work if he is appreciated at all. Let us see if words of recognition can have an effect."

The man reached a pinnacle in his lament to no one.

"Not enough money to repair even the walls. I ask you, are the walls of a prison not of the utmost importance? Unless they want inmates running—" He stopped, noticing the Colonel and me. "What is it now?" he moaned.

The Colonel spoke cheerfully.

"Come now, is that any way to greet the providence of change? Your superior manner and spruce appearance suggest you are the administrator of this facility. Am I correct?"

The worn man puffed up a bit at the Colonel's courtesy.

"I am indeed."

"My name is Colonel James Bacchus. This is my coadjutor, Bee."

I had no idea what a coadjutor was but did my best to look the part, delivering a slight bow as the Colonel continued.

"We desire to speak with one of your prisoners."

"Which one?"

"The cellmate of a man named Christopher, the prisoner who esc—"

The warden held up a finger.

"Do not say the word. Do not speak of what Christopher did. Why do you wish to speak with his cellmate?"

"We are something of independent investigators," I said.

The warden seemed surprised I'd joined in the conversation, but he turned to me, voice crackling with hope.

"You're tracking Christopher?"

"Yes."

"For what agency?"

"None but our own."

The warden thought about this. He pulled us both close despite the fact we were quite obviously alone, save for the squirrels and hares.

"You operate out of the public eye?"

"Yes," the Colonel reassured. "Your assistance would undoubtedly be invaluable in the apprehension of Christopher." I noticed he left out any pledge to return the escaped convict. Although the Colonel hadn't spoken of what he planned to do if and when he acquired Christopher, I assumed it would be justice of his own creation, which likely didn't include re-incarceration in a prison that looked as if it could scarcely hold an invalid.

"Oh, how wonderful!" The warden shed any resistance and became chummy as a childhood friend. "Merciful fortune has found me at last. The pair of you look most capable indeed! Do please come inside. Welcome to Maulgate. I am Warden Cain."

He shook our hands and we traversed the prison yard, following what once must've been a square man, edges worn soft from high expectations and a low-walled prison.

"Please disregard my temperament at the gate, but with Christopher's... unscheduled departure... I've been under a great deal of pressure. Cricket statistics and prison escapes are both a matter of public record and public interest. Stumps and breakouts are the most egregious smears possible. I'll do anything to bring Christopher back within these walls."

"Naturally," the Colonel reassured the distraught man.

"We've got loads of degeneracy in here, serving their time for one shadowy thing or another. Swindlers, sleep talkers, sleep walkers, ventriloquists, jugglers—"

I uttered a grunt of agreement at the mention of jugglers and their degeneracy.

"—Even a fellow who can pluck his glass eye out and roll it around his hand."

"Such a collection of trickery and guile no doubt demands a keen eye," the Colonel said.

"And I have as much! Two even! But I can only do so much with what I am given."

"Forgive my broaching of a sensitive matter, but may I conclude that this is the place of Christopher's departure?" The Colonel gestured to an indented portion of the wall where a guard had been posted.

Warden Cain's eyes watered a touch.

"Yes, the building material is far from the highest quality. Tree branch came down in a storm—" Warden Cain clapped his hands. "Wall took a hit. I've sent in numerous requests for repair funds but, as it stands, the crack grows larger every day."

"There, there."

The Colonel handed Warden Cain his purple handkerchief and the weeping administrator cleared his nose. The Colonel strolled over to the escape point and poked about, taking a particular interest in the sun above the treetops.

"Interesting, interesting," he mumbled, rejoining us near the jailhouse. "I must admit, I've found myself in similar locales on the odd regrettable occasion, but never have I witnessed one as well kept as this, considering."

"Thank you." Warden Cain wept lightly with gratitude.

The Colonel was certainly right about simple words of recognition and encouragement, although his admission of previous incarceration was, if true, a touch unnerving. Warden Cain offered the used handkerchief back.

"Quite alright, old boy. Consider it a tax for your hospitality. If we may impose upon it further," the Colonel said, "I would cherish a meeting with the cellmate."

"This way," Warden Cain said, still bristling with pride at the Colonel's compliments. He likely would've trusted the Colonel to entertain an unwed sister, unchaperoned.

"Christopher was in our best cell. Still got all its bars!" Warden Cain announced proudly as we entered the creaking facility.

"Done a quarter stretch or two, have you?" I whispered to the Colonel.

"Who of any interest passes through this life without a misunderstanding?" was his teasing response as we ascended a set of rickety stairs. Passing through ancient doors of rusted metal, we arrived finally at a cell block, anchored at the far end by two gorillic guards standing watch at a fully-barred door.

A soaking wet guard called up from the bottom of the stairs we'd just climbed.

"Warden," he huffed, "we've suffered another burst joint. Whole armoury's flooding!"

"Mercy in heaven," Warden Cain dragged hands down his worn face. "I should never have proved my skill with plumbing. If more than a thimble-full's spilled, they call me. Start with the mops, I'm on my way," he called to the dripping guard. "That is Christopher's cell there at the end. Those men will see to your safety, but be wary at all times regardless. Despite the relentless chorus of the prisoners, none here are innocent. I wish you luck, detectives. I'll thank you to bring Christopher back to me."

He shook our hands and raced off to plug the leak.

"Poor bloke's been given command of a sinking ship," the Colonel said and shook his head as we walked down the cell block.

He seemed unconcerned with our surroundings, but I kept closer to his side than normal, peeking about his belt to ensure the rapier was at hand. The prisoners shouted at us, some with pleas for salvation, some with threats of disquieting detail.

The man with the glass eye made his identity known by throwing the false organ at us.

"A souvenir for Jasper?" I said nervously, picking it up.

The Colonel walked over to the inmate.

"I say, is that you, Porter? I wondered how many one-eyed miscreants could be in London."

"Colonel Bacchus. How're you?" The one-eyed man recognised the Colonel once they were close.

"Avoiding the bobbies thus far."

"I'm not one to call in a favour seconds after reunion, but have you any comforts? Cigarettes or chocolate perhaps? I did hide you from the Derringer Sisters once, did I not? They must've had a hundred fliers about town, warning of an immoral pleasure seeker."

"You did indeed grant me shelter, and allow this to be my first repayment."

Out of sight of the prison guards, the Colonel passed the sprig of flower from his hat into Porter's cell.

"Chinese wisteria. A rather voracious bit of vine that can bear a man's weight. Just be careful not to eat any, if you could even manage."

The Colonel winked and walked off. Porter gave me a toothless grin. I stuck out my tongue and tossed him back his eye.

"Cheers, half-pint," he said, examining the wisteria with his good eye.

"Deserving of an early release, is he?" I whispered to the Colonel as we approached Christopher's cell.

"A relatively harmless man. Even the rabbit justly caught in a snare merits a fighting chance."

We reached Christopher's cell and the standing guards stepped aside. What sort of ruffian awaited us, and at what moment would he strike?

We entered to find a young man, not much older than myself, craning his neck to see out a high window in the direction of the Ox. His movements were limited to the meager allowance of a second prison: a crush cage roughly the dimensions of his body, normally used on bears in the Orient.

He wore only tattered pants, leaving unconcealed a wavy serpent tattoo that ran around his chest and back like some loose necklace. Waves of blond, almost-white hair had begun to reappear on an otherwise smooth scalp, likely shaved for lice when he entered the prison. His figure was rail-thin, rich brown eyes shining above pronounced lines of fatigue that defined the top of his angled cheeks. His face appeared angry and distrusting, but also... handsome.

"What flag do you carry then?" The prisoner addressed the Colonel. "Too tall and fair skinned to be Nodd. Valirov is it then? Distant cousins come for revenge?"

"We are none of these things, sir. But you are undoubtedly a Hackett," the Colonel said, obvious interest in his voice as if a connection in the case had just bloomed.

"That's right," the young man answered with pride.

"Young Master Hackett, I assure you we have no position in your deadly trifecta of treasure hunters. We call on you today in the hopes of learning something about your cellmate."

"Christopher?" The young man's demeanour softened a touch with curiosity. "If you're neither Nodd nor Valirov, just who are you?"

"Clearly one with atrocious manners. My name is Colonel James Bacchus and this is my coadjutor, Bee."

I nodded to the prisoner, praying I hadn't blushed.

He studied us a moment longer then relaxed, suggesting he thought we presented no immediate threat. "I am Elmhurst Hackett. I recognise your balloon from the skies above Batavia."

"Indeed you do. I knew not whether Christopher was hunting Valirovs in the company of Nodds or Hacketts, but this pretty well settles it."

"I had no part in the hunting party. I disagree with how my family—" He stopped himself before continuing. "I've no wish to be rude, but I have even less interest in speaking ill of my family to strangers."

"Nor is it my intention to have you do so," the Colonel said.

"How did Christopher escape?" I asked, partially just so Elmhurst would know my voice.

Elmhurst studied our faces again without apology. I hoped he saw we were good people, worthy of his disclosures.

"It was a plan of my own devising. I had thought Christopher and I friends. We intended to escape together. You may have noticed a weakness in the perimeter wall."

I nodded, again hoping reddening cheeks hadn't betrayed the flush I felt.

"The top had crumbled just enough that one could, provided enough fitness and aim, vault through the point. There are three days in the year this action was most advisable."

Aided by the Colonel's behaviour outside, I guessed the reason.

"The sun. It would be directly in the guard's eye for a time."

"Yes." Elmhurst smiled at me, his attitude now much more receptive. "Perhaps obviously, the second day would have been the most optimal. I was going to wait. Christopher made the jump on the first day. Now a guard is stationed there and I am not permitted movement enough to scratch my nose. The loophole has been closed several times over."

The Colonel scratched Elmhurst's nose.

"Mercy! Thank you, sir."

"Have you any idea as to his whereabouts now?"

Elmhurst smiled.

"Colonel, do not play ignorant. You know as well as I do he still seeks the Blue Star Sphinx. As does my family, as do the Nodds, as did the Valirovs. What is your business with Christopher?"

"Private, I'm afraid."

"Do you wish him harm? Even though he left me in this place, I have no wish to see him harmed."

"I do not wish him any particular harm."

The Colonel said this evenly, though I couldn't decide if I believed him. Elmhurst may have been too earnest for his own good. What did he think the Colonel would say when additional information was at stake?

"The pair of you do not seem without virtue, so I hesitate to make this offer. I can send you away with directions to my family's estate, as well as a letter of introduction. There, you may gleam more information about the Sphinx. They will be glad to take your information as well, of course, so do not accept this offer without deliberation. My family is—" Elmhurst hesitated, "They are rather... dedicated. Should you prove nothing of value to trade, it could be quite dangerous. They, like I, will no doubt recognise your balloon from Batavia."

"And that is why you are here?" the Colonel asked.

"Indeed. The beach the Valirovs died upon was British territory. The Nodds were rather helpful in implicating my family, and the authorities were rather eager to make an arrest once we returned here to Britain."

"I wouldn't guess you cold-blooded enough to murder," I said.

Elmhurst seemed pleased by this.

"You're right. But it doesn't matter. Someone in my family had to answer for what happened. They made the offer to take a dozen of us, or my father, or me. Looks impressive in the papers to break up a dynasty like ours, you see."

"And your father remains free?" I asked.

"He has work still to do. It was my mother's decision. She—" He said the words with hard conviction, but the belief behind them seemed less certain. "Again I must stop my errant tongue."

"And Christopher?" the Colonel asked.

"Arrested with me. He was simply caught up in the whole affair. With no family to bargain with, he had no choice in the matter."

"So be it," the Colonel said. "We accept your offer of introduction."

"As you wish."

"May I make a request?" the Colonel added.

Elmhurst nodded.

"I should ask you say nothing of seeing the balloon. I feel it would complicate matters and—"

"I was to suggest the same thing myself," Elmhurst interrupted.

"Really?" The Colonel looked intrigued.

"You appear to be well-meaning. If my family were to lay eyes upon your fantastic balloon, I should think your deaths would be a certainty, as opposed to a mere likelihood."

"Right decent of you."

The Colonel held a bit of parchment near Elmhurst's hand and the prisoner wrote a note to his mother.

"I wish you luck, truly, and hope we meet again," he said on our departure.

Despite my best efforts, I looked over my shoulder. My heart was wrenched by the melancholy smile upon the prisoner's face. He said he was no murderer, and I believed him, but he had admitted association with the crime. If I couldn't accurately gauge the Colonel, how could I gauge this man I'd just met? My powers of character judgment were being strained at every turn and not always succeeding.

We left the prison, wading through ankle-high water before passing through the front gate that had now fallen off its hinges.

"Colonel, what exactly happened in Batavia?"

"The Russian family of treasure hunters, the Valirovs, purchased the first issue of Ebbing's riddle. They were in the vicinity of Batavia, perhaps having found the Sphinx, perhaps not, when they were set upon by the Hacketts and Nodds, rival fortune-seeking families. I followed Christopher there, and witnessed the aftermath."

"What was it?"

"Bodies. All along the coast. Bullet-ridden, but not water-logged. They were ambushed on the beach, where most died. A few made it to their ship, but it was wrecked in the haste of an escape. It's from that very floatsam I discovered the compass now set within the magnet on the Cloud Deck."

"You preyed upon the debris for profit?"

"Don't be simple. I was searching for survivors, intending to provide aid. But there were none. The handsome compass glinted amongst the wreckage, somehow missed by the scavenging murderers. The Valirovs were ruthless treasure hunters just like the other two families, but they were also explorers. Were I to wreck the Ox, I should like some piece of her to continue on so that the journey is never finished. I assure you the piece is of little monetary value. Common brass."

I chose to believe him.

"Let's open the letter then," I said to the Colonel.

"Lady Beatrix, it is not addressed to you."

"But surely you don't trust these Hacketts."

"You know I don't. The reasons the note will remain private are twofold. First, the Hacketts are very accomplished, world-class thieves. I infinitely doubt their prince would spell out essential information on a note handed to someone outside the bloodline he's known for less time than is required for bread to rise. No doubt any vital details are encrypted within a code requiring some familial cypher. Second, and of greater import, opening the letter would be behaviour unbecoming of a gentleman."

"Unbecoming of a gentleman? You bring infidelity down from on high and employ animal excrement as a tool of revenge, and you speak of *gentlemanly behavior?* You can't be serious!" I laughed.

"I am indeed. And before you give voice to my carousel of vices, remember that no white smoke signalled my appointment. I am not infallible and am horizons away from saintliness. Just the same, I *will* claim a certain air of sophistication. We've all a few odd apples in our bushel, but that serves as no justification for a rotten crop."

"Fine, but delivering the letter and absorbing into the bosom of the Hacketts feels foolish."

"The best information is often clutched tightly by the most dangerous agents. I'm afraid close proximity may be essential at this juncture. We've learned all we can from a safe vantage. Fortune cannot find those hiding in the hedgerow with their digits crossed. But don't lament our demise just yet. The Hacketts will be most curious as to what we know as well. There exists leverage on both ends. If Billingsly is successful in his decoding, we'll depart that very moment. Is that satisfactory?"

"It is. What is the trifecta you spoke of?"

"Ah, my cursory interest with treasure hunters is proving quite valuable. The Hacketts, the Nodds, the Valirovs. Ruthless treasure hunting families whose hatred of one another is downright biblical. The Hacketts and Nodds fight most fiercely. The Valirovs were regarded as the most ruthless of the three, perhaps why they were targeted for elimination, I know not."

I twisted a small knot in my dress, debating whether or not to ask about Christopher.

"Do you think Christopher helped kill the Valirovs?"

"I cannot honestly say. But I do believe I've identified our beloved detective at last."

"Sharif?"

"The Hacketts are known for their rapacious eyes and wasting frames. Elmhurst fits the bill quite well."

"I found his eyes rather fine," I said before any thought of censorship.

The Colonel raised an eyebrow to me.

"Really?"

"Finish your explanation," I commanded.

"The Valirovs are expressly Russian, often misinterpreted as unfriendly. And the Nodds? Dark-skinned, vertically-restricted, heavyset, and London-based. Sharif regularly displayed a predilection for treasure hunting and made his exit only when we were to meet a Hackett. I suspect he stayed until the very last moment to extract every bit of information he could."

We arrived at the Ox to find the Newlyweds packing their picnic wares back into the Bulkhead. I filled them in on Sharif's departure, our visit to Maulgate, and the newest revelation.

"Sharif. A treasure hunter," George tried it out. "Aye, fits."

"He's made for his home in London," the Colonel said. "If we're lucky, we'll be rid of him for a time. Always wise to juggle as few knives as possible. Nodd conjecture will have to wait as we must fly for the Hackett Estate. I believe finding it will be volumes less difficult in the light of day. Any Scotch eggs left?"

"Sorry, dear. We had one left, but Jasper up and made off with it," Thelma said.

The Colonel grumbled something about revenge against the blasted packrat and stomped up the exterior staircase to start the burner.

Chapter Twenty-Three

Lord Chartish's Swiss estate was the finest property I'd ever seen.

Until I saw the Hacketts'.

Having landed the Ox some distance away in an emptyish patch of forest (and taking a moment to set some concealing brush upon the Ox, which amounted to a green tea cozy upon the hide of an elephant), we found ourselves walking lengthwise up the Hacketts' front lawn for several minutes towards the colossally pillared mansion at the lawn's conclusion.

"A bit of butter upon bacon, innit?" Thelma said.

"Conspicuous a place as I've ever seen," George agreed with a wrinkled nose.

"Remember all," the Colonel said, "whatever you do, make no mention of Sharif. If this lot even *suspect* we are affiliated with the Nodds, I'm sure it will be to our tremendous discomfort."

A battalion of slender men hustled from around either side of the mansion (taking some time to meet in the middle) and we were greeted by the hollow eyes of a dozen gun barrels.

One man stood shoulders above the tall group, his height even greater than that of the vertically-substantial Colonel. As brutish looking as Ziro, his face was slightly battered, covered in still-healing wounds like a poorly-trained prize fighter weeks after a tough bout. His mad eyes were set into dark circles of skin that looked not to be injuries, but normal characteristics of the unfortunate face. I could only pity the other party that had been foolish or unlucky enough to tussle with this statue of dark brawn.

"What's your business?" he snarled.

The Colonel said nothing, but with deliberate transparency, extracted Elmhurst's note from his waistcoat and handed it over. We remained at gunpoint while the monstrous man took his time reading. After a time, he regarded us again.

"You're too fair skinned to be Arabs, too jolly to be Russians, yet you could be hired spies for either."

"I know not how to disprove that which I am not," the Colonel said.

"Just one last opportunity to rattle you loose should anything be awry. My son speaks well of you. I am Lindenhurst Hackett." The mad eyes softened, rifles were lowered, introductions made, hands shook. "You wish to stay with us then, Colonel Bacchus?"

"Your son proposed as much. It is no secret we both desire the location of the Sphinx for reasons that are our own. A brief stay may prove mutually beneficial."

"In that case..." Lindenhurst bared his huge teeth in an ill-fitting grin. "Welcome to Hackett Manor. You must be weary from your walk from the prison." He nodded at the traveling packs we'd equipped ourselves with to suggest travel on foot.

"We will admit some fatigue, as we haven't all the metres of your common stride." The Colonel slapped playfully at Lindenhurst's tree trunk legs, making the giant jump. The brute turned around in the same movement in an attempt to conceal his alarm and gave a thunderous clap of his hands that echoed even in the vast openness of the lawn.

A butler in a top hat stood at attention before the front doors of the manor.

Unable to help myself, I cried out in excitement.

"Beatrix, what's the matter?" George asked with concern.

"It's nothing really." I blushed feeling a bit foolish. "I've just never seen a butler in a top hat before."

"Somethin', isn't it?" George agreed with a wink.

Above the manor's entrance gleamed a colossal golden seal of the Hackett family crest: a serpent twisted around a shield that bore the cross of St. George and a banner that delivered the message: *that which is precious, shines*. Perhaps to prove this point, the serpent's eyes were glittering sapphires.

The top-hatted butler opened the main doors and Lindenhurst introduced our names to a woman wrapped in a dress of stiff grey cloth, a broach of the family crest clasped about her collar. Beneath tightly bound hair the colour of bone and a face thin even for her family, the woman looked with disdain at our shadows that dirtied the pristine white marble of her estate. As was Hackett tradition, murderous stares gave way to open accommodation after our value had been explained. All Lindenhurst had to say was we *may* have an *idea* where the Sphinx *might* be, and we were as welcome as a forgotten coin discovered in a pocket. Here was the matriarch of the matriarchy. As frightening as Lindenhurst the rooster was, I had a feeling the hen was the one to watch out for.

"I am Madame Hackett. Welcome to my estate."

Chapter Twenty-Four

The magic words for the Hacketts: *Blue Star Sphinx.*

For the Colonel: *dinner is served.*

We were shown into a dining room that put Chartish's to shame, our captain's mood greatly buoyed by his dinner spirits: elation brought about by the prospect of the day's final meal. In his dinner spirits, the Colonel seemed more at ease and more recognizable as a person with his thoughts and words much less calculated.

Seated around an impossibly long table were myself, Thelma, George, the Colonel, Lindenhurst, Madame Hackett, and forty or so Hacketts we were not given the names of. There appeared no outlier amongst the pale and skinny figures, no new spouse of distinct appearance that had yet to assimilate. As if reading my thoughts, George mumbled something about kissing cousins to Thelma, at which point I felt her leg move to shin-kick him into silence. The Hacketts had the air of European royalty of old: physically frail and vaguely incestuous. Both the men and women were dressed in low-necked tops that proudly showed off the same serpent tattoo we'd seen on Lindenhurst. Madame Hackett alone wore a collar, her allegiance beyond question.

A gasp of horror escaped me as I noticed the same ghoulish tattoo ringed on the still-chubby neck of a newborn.

I brought my gaze down to my bowl as it was filled with a thin broth, but I could already feel Madame's sharp eyes upon me.

"The relative size of the serpent will diminish as the canvas grows," she said, as if this explanation would remedy my shock.

"Why not wait?" the Colonel asked in between spoonfuls of broth.

"You'll notice," Madame Hackett said, angling her spoon the slightest bit to permit a few drops of broth I doubt would have satiated even a Manx, "some in this room bear serpents with a certain texture. While we must permit the inclusion of outsiders by marriage, it is useful to show who has been a Hackett from birth. The natural expansion of skin during aging produces scales on the snake. Those with many sharply defined scales are closest to our heart." Madame touched Lindenhurst's hand and he nodded in agreement. "Those without—" she cast a glare at a young woman with a smooth snake tattoo," —are to be trusted only so far as absolutely necessary."

"Just a laugh a minute in this place, innit?" George said under his breath and a muted flourish of kicking resumed.

Madame snapped her fingers and the servants stepped forward, relieving us of our soup bowls. The Colonel managed to scoop several more spoonfuls before his was whisked away.

"Now," Madame announced, "let us retire to leisure and champagne."

The Colonel choked on his last bit of broth.

"Retire? But we've only had the soup. What of the rest of the meal?"

"The soup was the meal," Madame said, unaffected.

She snapped her fingers and the rest of the Hacketts returned dutifully to whatever hidden enclaves of the mansion they'd come from. Lindenhurst, whose muscular frame looked as if it could use another few litres of broth, made no complaint as he stood aside his wife's chair and waited for her to rise.

We followed Madame and Lindenhurst through marble halls and fountained courtyards.

"Look there!" I tugged on George's sleeve and pointed at a passing butler. "Another one in a top hat!"

"Aye, looks as if they're full up with 'em."

We were led to a disconnected wing of the mansion that must have rivalled the finest museums of Europe. I had never been to an actual museum, but surely none held such a wealth of treasures. Some of the pieces were so famous, I knew them by name.

Thelma attempted to touch one of the many tiaras, but George slapped her hand away.

"More riches than the Queen of Sheba, wouldn't you say?" Madame noted proudly. "These bracelets and amulets here are Incan gold. This copper scroll is Hebrew and tells of even more treasures to be found. That, a jade sword from the Orient."

"Quite the haul," I noted.

"Any of it edible?" the Colonel murmured under his breath.

While the collection of valuables was quite eclectic and international, I noticed a commonality: sapphires. The room was positively infested with hundreds of the blue gems that glittered in the lamplight, making the room appear as if it were underwater.

The Colonel bent far forward to study a bronze sculpture of an angel.

"This is from a riddle of Noel Ebbing, is it not?"

Madame answered carefully.

"You are familiar with Ebbing?"

"Come now, all in this room are well aware of the man. No need to withhold that admission."

"Yes, our family has purchased many of his puzzles and enigmas over the years," Madame said.

"Including his ultimate one?"

"We sought to, but he was killed before we'd a chance to do so. Somewhere in Brussels, wasn't it?"

"Something like that. The Valirovs managed a copy, didn't they? Before they were all killed."

"Yes, we read of that," Madame said.

"Ambushed I believe," the Colonel continued innocently. "Killed like corralled livestock…"

Lindenhurst stormed over with such speed he nearly knocked over a dusty Roman vase.

"Yes, yes! We were in Batavia. Don't think we haven't recognized you."

The Colonel remained entirely calm.

"I merely wondered if they had—"

"Why else would we all've been in the South bloody Seas? And where is your charming little balloon, *Colonel*?"

"Wrecked not far from Batavia, I'm afraid. I was rather unaccustomed to the winds in that part of the globe."

"How unfortunate for us you didn't perish as w—" Lindenhurst began, but Madame's hand streaked across his face.

"My dear husband, I think you could do with a brandy to douse your rage and numb your tongue. That will do for the evening."

Lindenhurst glared hotly at us, then slinked off like a kicked dog. The welcome tour abruptly ended.

Two rather burly top-hatted butlers made their presence known and courteously escorted us from the museum. I flicked George and excitedly pointed at their hats. He nodded and pointed to the back wall of the museum where a short pillar stood draped in flowing velvet cloth, folded into a nest, awaiting a yet acquired prize I had not to guess the name of.

"The museum is viewable at any time, provided you have an escort. The rest of the property is likewise at your disposal, all except for the garden house. Servant's quarters are no place for a guest."

"Think I'll have a walk around now," I announced and departed the stuffy gathering. I'd had about all I could take of our hosts for the moment and wandered the absurdly expansive grounds, occasionally passing one of the many serpent-branded residents in my exploration. I had to squint to confirm it was the Newlyweds extinguishing their light in some top floor of the mansion.

Passing through one fountained garden after another, I walked along a lake still humming with the aquatic activity of fish in the warm evening.

These Hacketts were unlikable to be sure, but vile? It was hard to say just yet.

Through another of the yellow windows of the manor, I witnessed Lindenhurst alone in a study, emptying glassfuls of brown liquor down his throat with frightening speed. Unable to keep his balance, he collapsed into a nursing chair. Not only was the man of scant temper, he was a fiend for drink. If I'd ever been granted power without limit to disallow a relationship, it would've been that of man and drink. It transformed good men into bad, and bad men into monsters. I was no Puritan, but to be rid of the stuff altogether would've suited me just fine.

My heart was then seized by a horrible realization. All were accounted for in my wanderings except for Madame and the Colonel. I quickened my pace, sticking my head round corners and throwing open pantry doors. The Colonel's *activities* were his prerogative, but in this instance, we could do without the complication.

"Toast the bloomin' fool," I muttered. "He'll go and bring the roof down on our heads."

My wordage increased in salinity as I continued to ambush one empty hiding place after another. A young maid overheard my language and was so scandalized, she dropped the tray of liqueur she carried.

The Colonel dashed out of a study down the hall.

"Bee? What's happened?"

"Look what you've done," Madame hissed at the maid after emerging from the same room. "Clean it up. I'll fetch the drinks."

I bent to help clean the glass, but the maid insisted.

"Please, miss, let me."

I followed the Colonel into the study.

"You... you... incorrigible rake!" I charged.

"You think I've an interest in Madame Hackett? There shall be no pelvic exploits this evening. That is unless..." The Colonel leaned back into the hall where the rather pretty maid tidied up the glass.

I pulled him back into the study.

"Don't be a scoundrel! Colonel, please. I don't like this place. I have a terrible feeling about it all."

He composed himself and cleared his throat.

"You're quite right. I've no wish to make our stay last a moment longer than necessary either. I shall assume tremendous focus and dedicate myself to the task. Now, find yourself occupied elsewhere. Madame doesn't care for you."

"I beg your pardon?"

"Don't act wounded. Why should an opinion such as hers weigh on your dispos—Ah, salvation from on high, and lo, it comes in liquid form." Madame had returned with the drinks. The Colonel kicked at my feet to shoo me away.

I did not disappoint.

Quitting the company of a woman as cheery as Madame Hackett and the blasted Colonel was my distinct pleasure. They began to discuss snakes, of which the Colonel of course had an opinion. His voice echoed in the hallways as I quit the mansion.

"The admirable amongst us do the best they can with what they have. For creatures with no arms, no legs, and a perpetual bounty on their entire species, snakes have done quite well in fact."

I rolled my eyes, mercifully passing the point of earshot, and crossed onto the front lawn.

The black of the surrounding forest was top-edged with a smoky orange glow from the furnaces of London's many factories. A shiver upon my spine improved my posture. Someone or something watched me from the darkness of the trees, I was sure of it. I had felt this gaze before, and yet I could not specify where or when.

"Hello?" I said foolishly into the wooded void.

Unsurprisingly, no answer came from the forest.

"Beatrix, isn't it?" A voice came from behind me. Lindenhurst Hackett, out for an evening stroll, or stumble as it were. "'Lo, Beatrix," he mumbled.

"Master Hackett."

"Lindenhurst. You call me Lindenhurst." His words were weighted unevenly in his drunkenness, and something in the man's tone suggested he thought himself a predator stumbled onto easy prey. "There used to be a prize buck that grazed about the property." He loosely gestured to the forest.

"I'm sorry?"

"It was killed by the Nodds! Do you know of the Nodds?"

"Fellow fortune seekers, are they not?" I didn't like the direction of the conversation.

"Fellow nothing." He spat on the lawn. "They play at the game but do so with no discernible skill. They are given to wanton tricks and vandalism, such as killing the buck. But they didn't finish on top there." Lindenhurst Hackett's thin, purple lips curled into a wicked smile. "They adorned that hole they call a home in London with the buck, stuffed as a prize. Well, we had at it, my boy and I! Set it aflame so their only trophy is a pile of charred bones! Took a bit of their home with it!" He cackled at the memory. "Ah, well. Where is your mother in all this?"

Now it was my turn to laugh, understanding what he meant.

"The Colonel is not my father. We are of no relation."

"What is... what is the nature of your connection?"

I opened my mouth to respond, but no answer came. I did not quite know what to say. Chance had crossed my path with the Colonel's in Switzerland and it had been to our mutual benefit to escape those who wished us harm. I still hadn't even discovered what a coadjutor was.

Lindenhurst read my indecision.

"In that case, permit me to provide a friendly warning. The Colonel is famous, as you must know. An elusive man of mysterious ways and means. He seeks my son's cellmate, of that we are certain. But for what purpose? Revenge? What shall he do once he has his hands firmly around the man's neck?"

"You know his intentions?" I grew impatient of the drunk man's whims.

"Ah. Neither of us know. And that is the point. Some may call the Hacketts pilferers and opportunists. Raiders and looters. I do not accept those labels, but I understand why they are placed upon us. Because we are clear about that which we desire. You have seen the very pedestal for our goal."

"Proud of your greed then? You seek to convince me it signifies some sort of nobility?"

"Only certainty. Our intentions are defined. As are the Colonel's. But then of course we are left with the obscure. You, young Beatrix. What is it you seek?"

"It is of no concern to you," I said.

"Perhaps it is that you yourself do not know." He poked me hard in the chest, then stumbled backwards, holding his hands open in supplication. "I offer only an open hand. If your feet cannot find purchase, and there are none to throw you a rope, you need think only of my offer, and there you will find peace."

"What offer?"

"Forget this illusion of cooperation, of sharing information. Tell me what you know truly, and join us. Our goal will become yours and we shall see it accomplished together."

I laughed. He demanded defection from those I cared for most, and the trade offered was the company of Hacketts.

Lindenhurst delivered a triple distilled bit of spittle at my feet.

"You and yours take this rather lightly. Consider the Valirovs took it rather seriously and still ended up in early graves. Enjoy your fate." He walked an inefficient path back up to the mansion.

A moment later, a figure briskly approached down the same walkway.

"Found the courage to try and sort me out, have you?" I raised my fists.

"Ah, ready for a sporting bout?" The Colonel raised his own fists and began to hop about.

"Oh, it's you."

Disappointed I wasn't game for a quick boxing match, the Colonel dropped his arms.

"You weren't... caught with Madame were you?" I asked.

"Don't be perverse. I left her company of my own volition. All is as I expected, and nothing is more disappointing than things turning out as expected. I'm beginning to suspect these lauded treasure hunters are quite innocent of any original thought."

"Lindenhurst was just going on about the Nodds and some yarn about an immolated stag."

"Dull, dull, dull. The Nodds are the anti-Hacketts and vice versa. Both families known chiefly by their disdain for the other. Suffice to say they are not on borrowing terms, hmm? I too waited for the Nodds to be brought up, and sure as sugar, Madame couldn't get there quick enough. I despise quarrels between families. Spoiled babies and withered elders who feel entitled to a grudge over a transgression neither side can accurately recall. I've come across these types before. They both clutch to the rivalry, so much so that should one loose the other, both would fall away into nothingness. The rivalry defines their mere existence!"

"If you've had your fill of Nodd talk, there's always the Sphinx," I teased.

"Can you believe it? Such a tremendous enthuzimuzzy over a hand-scored rock! My word, what has happened to man's imagination?"

"And threats of death for good measure. What is our plan then? Are we to depart?"

"No, nothing has changed. Here lies our best chance of disclosure. There is an energy in this place, even if it is a dark one. Come now, our only method of escape lies in dreaming, let's not put it off."

We made for the manor and I kept pace with the Colonel's long stride, still feeling the surveillance of some unseen ghost from the forest behind.

Chapter Twenty-Five

A week of sparse meals and tense interactions passed. The Hacketts were content to speak only on two subjects: the Blue Star Sphinx and the Nodd family. The Valirovs were far from praised, but as the Colonel had said, the true rivalry lay with the Nodds.

The initial excitement of Lindenhurst's museum outburst settled into a stalemate that began to drag for all involved. I trusted our stay was not proving the informational gold mine the Colonel had hoped for. Either the Hacketts knew little regarding Ebbing and the Sphinx, or they were quite astute at pretending as much. Lindenhurst was perfectly right about the illusion of cooperation.

While the top hats never failed to give me a thrill, the rest of the mansion's finery had become humdrum in short order. The only things of interest were the garden shed, proclaimed off limits from the start, and the massive barn at the rear of the property, prohibited later in our stay. While the forbidden labels made both quite tempting, they were kept under heavy guard.

My thoughts had returned with regularity to the young man twice locked in Maulgate Prison. True, Elmhurst was unlikely to be an ally, but I found him alluring just the same. He wasn't unpleasant to look at, and there was something sad in his eyes. It was said women were drawn to sad eyes like fish to a lure, and it seemed I was no exception. Elmhurst met the cosmetic requirements of being a Hackett: tall, thin, and snake-marked, but that's where it ended. He spoke with none of the vitriol that came from all other family members. Could he help the family he was born into any more than I?

Unlike the barn and the garden shed, the Hacketts' stables were not off-limits, and I encountered no one as I took a small steed off into the generously moonlit night. Slung about me was an extra bit of rope from the barn and two wineskins from the kitchen. The horse was strong and obedient and we raced in the direction of Maulgate Prison at a good clip. I thought of the circus horse, Charles, and hoped he had found happiness in the Swiss mountainside as the Colonel said he would.

At length, I spied a yellow flame atop Maulgate's guard tower. The sight reminded me of Billingsly's lighthouse, excepting that this flame seemed well-attended.

A guard on night watch sat in the tower. Near the crack in the perimeter wall came grumbling and lamenting I easily identified as coming from Warden Cain. In addition to being the most-skilled plumber, it seemed the beleaguered man's masonry skills were equally superlative, as he was personally laying brick and mortar at the place of Christopher's escape. His soliloquy of woe carried softly through the tree trunks of the forest like the tune of some dismal fairy. I tied a clovehitch for my horse and crept closer. The guard in the tower above was either whistling or snoring, hat over his eyes in either case.

A spiderlike tingle ran hollow down my back. The watcher in the forest was upon me again. But no, this was not the same familiar gaze. I cannot say exactly how it felt different, just to say that it did. I scanned the dark forest protected from moonlight by the canopy above.

Then I saw it.

A figure, not much larger than myself, clad in what I could swear were the burgundy keffiyeh and scarf of Sharif. I stared into the shadowed face in between, where the glint of two eyes were barely visible. The figure blinked then leapt nimbly into a tree above and was gone.

This couldn't have been our departed crewmate. The figure was nearly as graceful as I.

Another mystery member had joined the League of Beatrix Voyeurs, but now was not the time to chase ghosts through the forest. They could enjoy a view of my backside and the soles of my feet.

Slinging a bit of rope I'd brought over my shoulder, I sprinted nimbly along the edge of the forest, past Warden Cain who had run out of bricks for his repair and now used rocks from the prison yard. Most were no larger than a skipping stone, and I thought the maddening task fitting for the poor man with all the luck of Sisyphus.

A wheelbarrow lay forgotten amongst the trees, and I rolled it to the perimeter wall, wincing with every squeak of its rusted joints. I tied my rope to the base of a tree and tossed the bundle over the wall to allow a point of future departure. Then, with a running start, I vaulted from the wheelbarrow to the top of the wall with ease.

Climbing the side of the prison building proved more difficult. I leapt from crevices of chipped rock to rusted bars quite sharp in places. I was determined though, and in a short amount of time, my hands closed around the bars of Elmhurst's cell.

And there he was. Sleeping upright in the crush cage, a sheet of blue moonlight dividing his resting face and snake-ringed torso.

"Elmhurst," I whispered.

He gave a start but mercifully did not cry out. A moment later he found me.

"Beatrix?"

He'd remembered my name!

Part of my mind said of course he recalls your name, prisoners aren't meeting loads of new faces on a regular basis. Another part of my mind, or perhaps my heart, told the first part of my mind to stuff it.

"What are you doing here?" he said.

"I've come to see how things are here, with you," I finished stupidly.

"Not much new to report here." He grinned wryly. "How are things at the estate? Does my family treat you well?"

I'd no desire to slander the imprisoned man's family, but he read the look on my face.

"I know they can be quite... Well, you must know how they are by now. But we're not to choose our families, are we?"

"No, I suppose not." I smiled. "Are you locked in there all hours of the day?"

"The warden's been very careful with me ever since Christopher escaped. Our incarceration was of great public interest, and he's determined not to have us both slip the noose." His face fell then. "As such, my execution's been moved up. If the law has their way, I'll be dancing upon nothing in a week's time."

"We must spring you," I nearly shouted, wincing at my outburst. "How on Earth can you be so calm about it all?"

"It's unwise to rely on things yet to come, but I'm certain I'll be rescued."

"By your family?"

"Perhaps," he said. But it was obvious he believed rescue would come by some other benefactor. "If I can be of further value to my family, they may collect me. But I do serve a purpose in here."

"Don't speak that way."

"I don't mean it unkindly. That is how we Hacketts are." He was right. If any family were to see their son on death row as a useful play, it was the tattooed skeletons we were currently guests of. "This prison can be dangerous. I must ask you not to visit again, and you must promise not to try and rescue me." He had read my face well.

"But—"

"Please, Beatrix. I have faith I'll be extradited. You must trust me."

"I nearly forgot," I said, unslinging the wineskins. "I've water or wine if you'd like any."

"A bit of wine would be the most tender of mercies. The prison's own cellar is quite wanting."

I stretched my arms through the bars and was just able to send a stream of purple liquid through Elmhurst's formed cage.

"A million thanks," he gasped when the skin was emptied.

"May I ask you something?"

He gave a restricted nod.

"Did you set fire to the Nodds' home?"

His eyes dropped in shame.

"My father told you of that, did he? Yes, I must admit the deed. I've no excuse other than the foolishness of youth. It was merely to burn the prize buck, and the blaze was quickly extinguished." His face was red. "I do try these days to live with greater honour. Have you had any luck with the Sphinx?"

"No," I said. "It seems as if our two parties are at an impasse."

I heard the guard shifting around in the tower above, his nap drawing to a close.

"I should be on my way," I whispered.

"Keep good faith. Something will give and this stalemate will dissolve. And worry not about my neck. There are others that care for me beyond my immediate family. I thank you for the wine and for your concern as well, Beatrix." He smiled his gratitude and my heart warmed.

"Good luck, then."

I made my exit.

My horse navigated the underbrush on the way back with ease, allowing me freedom to think. Were the Hacketts really unconcerned that one of their own was to be fruit of the gallows? Who was this person or persons who meant to rescue Elmhurst? Was he really so confident in their ability to save him? Had I a fondness for this prisoner I'd felt for none other before?

The excited yells of many men ahead took my attention. I halted the horse and continued on my own two feet. Firelight in a small clearing was divided by the edging trees, leaving long dancing spikes of shadow and light. A ring of torch-wielding Hacketts had surrounded something on the ground. Wondering if this was some bizarre Pagan ritual, I climbed a tree for a better look. Within the circle of Hacketts, Lindenhurst raised a sword, intending to decapitate two men in cloaks of powder blue.

The Mirrors! Ziro's bloodhounds had found me!

With an instinct I would nary understand later, I jumped from my perch into the execution circle.

"Wait!" I cried.

Several of the perimeter Hacketts nearly ran me through before I was recognised as no threat.

Lindenhurst stayed his blade and those of his men.

"Beatrix? Return to the house. You've no business here."

"But these men are known to me."

"These men are Nodd spies!"

"They are nothing of the sort. They are known to me and have been so for a long time."

The Mirrors looked calmly up at me with four feral eyes of grey and yellow. *These* were the familiar eyes that had kept watch of me from the shadow of the forest that first night.

"What is their business here?" Lindenhurst asked.

"To locate me," I said. "They were likely awaiting the correct moment to snatch me up and return me to bondage. I fled my previous employ with less than proper notification."

The Mirrors looked back at the ground, their hands secured with cord behind their backs. Whatever the reason, they had long ago decided to live their lives in mute and had not deviated since. I knew they would reveal nothing, not even to save their own lives. For some reason, I had taken up the flag for them.

Lindenhurst smiled. I had demonstrated that I knew these men and didn't want them killed before my own eyes. He had, at last, an advantage on our party.

"They are trespassing in a royal hunting forest. I am well within my rights to carry out justice as I see fit." Lindenhurst rested his blade on the nape of Ammoniac's neck and waited for me to take the bait. I had no choice and took it.

"I will help you. I will help you in exchange for their release." I heard these words, in awe that I had said them. These two mercenaries were the jailers of my youth. Lindenhurst was doing me a rather large favor by offering to remove them from my life forever, and I was intervening? Trading valuable information to keep one eye open at night?

"You have one sentence with which to barter, so choose it carefully." Lindenhurst strode over to me, using his sword as if it were a cane. His enjoyment was evident. "If you lie, or if I judge your information to be inconsequential, their heads shall be promptly removed."

I tried desperately to cope with the situation I had put myself in. I had only the riddle or the location of the Ox to trade.

The Ox was my *home*. I would never give her up. The riddle then? Was I really to assist this deplorable family in their acquisition of the Sphinx? I would love nothing more than to rid myself of the Hacketts' presence altogether, and providing the riddle would put them on the very path we meant to follow. But enemies or no, I could not allow bound men to be slaughtered.

"At the Treble of the fare see. Caught the point where the rite and vial joyless, and the ships find less. Where the lord comes to instill on lakes of white columns at hand. Deaf dyes a male, knew and drink. Predator to hymn and be silent to remain of the daughter. Single within your buried and meat the part. The active you will have divided at the pro of future pulling many."

The Hacketts in the circle looked completely bewildered. As did Lindenhurst. Proper responses to the nonsense I'd spewed, but this was valuable nonsense.

"That is the extent of our knowledge. I swear it. The ultimate riddle of Noel Ebbing, found in a false pocket upon his own corpse." Lindenhurst looked dissatisfied, but before he could proclaim as much, I continued. "It has confounded our party, but surely explorers as seasoned as the Hacketts will be able to tread where we could not."

It was flattery. Everyone in that clearing knew it, including Lindenhurst. But it worked nonetheless.

"The sale is made. Loose the spooky twicers."

A Hackett cut the cords that bound the Mirrors. They stood, and when it was clear none in the circle would prevent it, they fled weightlessly into the forest beyond.

"You lack the stomach required of a treasure hunter," Lindenhurst whispered to me. "If this information yields no results, your friends' fates will be visited upon you."

I thought about making a smart remark but held my tongue.

Lindenhurst pinched the back of my neck and set off with his hunting party. No doubt they would begin to work the clue right away. On one hand, I wished them nothing but frustrating failure. On my neck however, I wished them nothing but success.

Chapter Twenty-Six

How was I to share with the group what I'd done? I could conceal it, but for what purpose? The Hacketts wouldn't concern themselves with my integrity. Even if keeping the disclosure a secret would be to their advantage, the family was so stupidly proud they were almost certain to make their gain known.

Departing the stables, I found Madame Hackett smoking a long, expensive looking cigarette at the property edge, neatly tapping her ash into a cluster of ivy.

"Ash helps them grow," she offered with easy confidence.

"I'll double-check with the Colonel," I volleyed back.

I made to walk straight past her.

"My husband made a failed ploy for your allegiance the other night. I must apologize for his uncouthness. I didn't ask him to do that." She spoke to the forest, as if she couldn't be bothered to give me her attention. "I must inquire once again. Not because I am foolish, but because you are smart. Which of the Sphinx's suitors possesses the most experience? Which has been after it the longest? Which has the most resources available? Which has a new trove of information to work from?"

"They've told you then?"

She continued, as if I hadn't spoken.

"It is with the House of Hackett you seek to ally, Beatrix. You have given us valuable information, thereby nesting your transition. You would not only be welcomed with open arms, but rewarded with a share of the treasure."

"Lop off one of the Sphinx's ears, will you?"

Madame frowned and gave me her attention at last.

"Stupid, silly girls don't last long in this trade. Make no mistake, this is no offer given with frequency."

"And what of your son?"

The confidence was gone, replaced by genuine confusion, as if I'd spoken in another language.

"My son?"

I pointed in the direction of Maulgate.

"Elmhurst awaits the noose! Have you no concern?"

She gave a knowing smile.

"Handsome boy, isn't he?"

"What he *is*," I corrected, "is in tremendous danger. While you grab at Sphinx-scented straws, he awaits certain death."

"Given the random band you travel with, I might assume you do not understand family, and you certainly do not understand mine. My son is doing a Hackett's duty. He may be asked to give up a great deal, but not without purpose. He has quelled the law's—"

"He is your son!"

"And he is of no relation to you whatsoever. Mind your doting eyes, and be certain not to overstate the value of a captive man's attention. Am I to assume your answer is no?"

I kept her gaze, incredulous, then stormed in the direction of the manor. I had given her an answer, and she had given me one as well.

I would confess my gaffe in the morning. For down a certain path, even if at a great distance, lay the life of Madame Hackett snarled with lies and manipulation. One of many possible ends to my story I would not succumb to. Here was a fork, and I would relish the choice provided.

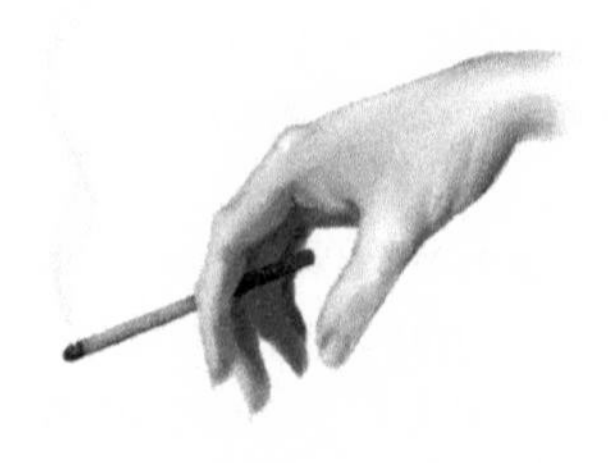

Chapter Twenty-Seven

"So that's it. They've gained the riddle and we've gained nothing. I'm sorry. I've let you all down."

The Colonel and the Newlyweds sat in silence following my confession of disclosure. The four of us sat on one of the manor's many balconies, taking a late morning tea.

"Lindenhurst, that sorry bully. I'll bloody his upturned nose," Thelma said suddenly.

"Beatrix, you really shouldn't be out on your own like that." George eased the riled Thelma back onto her chair. "I'll be your escort anytime you'd like a stroll."

"Quite right," the Colonel said. "The Hacketts are not to be underestimated in their willingness to employ violence, and the Flemish twins may yet be lying in wait for another attack."

Where was the outrage? The condemnation? The whipping? I'd suffered us a tremendous loss and they were concerned with… my safety. I began to weep.

"He's injured you!" Thelma erupted. "I'll knock his block off!"

Now it was my turn to bring her back to her chair.

"No, no. It's alright." I reined in my emotions. "I'm just… I'm glad to be amongst you."

George and the Colonel, if I may say, acted as some men do when confronted with excessive emotion. They radiated discomfort and busied themselves elsewhere.

"Give no thought to the fortitude of boys," Thelma told me, delivering a welcome hug. "Let's have another cuppa. Then you can join me in sewing if ya like. George's gone and snagged his cap on a branch, torn it somethin' fierce."

"I don't know how to sew," I admitted, wiping my face dry.

This revelation scandalized Thelma more than my surrender of the riddle, and we were soon with our cups of tea and balls of yarn in the warm midday sun.

In between Thelma's expert lessons in sewing, knitting, and needlepoint, my thoughts took to the Mirrors. I could still feel them lurking in the forest, for what purpose I was now unsure. Did they still mean to capture me? To kill me outright? They were singular creatures, motivated by only one thing at a time. When I had known them, they were ruled by loyalty to Ziro. I never knew why, and this was the most unsettling thing about them to me. To not understand why another does something, especially something as engrossing as dedicating their life to a cause, can inspire great fear. How was one to negotiate? To empathize?

Thelma marked my wandering attentions, and I confided in her my concerns.

"Show a beaten mongrel kindness and they'll sometimes surprise you," she said. "It is clear to me these two men owe their very lives to you. Why shouldn't they recognise it as well?"

"They are strange men. Peculiar."

"Dearie, don't forget I keep the company of the Colonel," she said, and we chuckled. Her hands were a blur atop George's wounded cap, and I marveled at the talent.

"You're so practiced."

"Oh, it's nothing. Essential knowledge for flying on the Ox. George and the Colonel know it too. Y'can help me with the envelope later, always needs a bit a stitchin' here and there."

"Perhaps I should practice first on something with less fatal consequences should one of my seams pop."

"I think that'd be wise. What do you have in mind?"

I thought for a moment.

"I've an idea, but I'd like it to be a surprise."

"Alright, well, here's yer colours." Thelma slid the basket of yarn to me with her foot. "You've got a bit more rose to your cheeks these days," she observed over the effortless dance of her needle.

"I... there's a... the young man we met in the prison."

I expected her to ooh and aah, to make a joke of trying to embarrass me. But she was no immature girl of my own age. Thelma just smiled softly.

"Ah, I see. Young Master Elmhurst, isn't it?"

"He's a Hackett, but he's not like the others," I said, defending Elmhurst from an attack that had not come. "I'm worried for him. He's to be hanged."

"And we're sittin' here playin' with yarn?"

"He said he has a way out already. Made me promise not to try and do anything myself. But if he's not out soon, I'll be forced to do... *something*. I'll not stay and see him hanged no matter what I promised."

George stepped onto the patio and cheerily inspected Thelma's work on his beloved cap. As far as I could tell, it was the only possession he valued.

"But you've used the wrong colour," he exclaimed. "The hat is auburn! This stitching is scarlet!"

After her labours of careful stitching, Thelma looked primed to pop her ungrateful husband on the nose. To diffuse the situation, and since my fingers were already getting cramped, I jumped from my seat.

"I think I'd like a stroll," I announced. "Does your offer of accompaniment still stand, George?"

"A'course, love, be happy to," he said, oblivious to the pitfall he'd narrowly avoided. He kissed Thelma on the cheek, the "wrong" thread already forgotten.

I stashed my secret project at the bottom of the yarn basket and we were off.

"My word, she's really done a bang-up job here," George said, inspecting his cap as we traversed the lawn. "And don't you fret, Beatrix, I can still keep up with the best of 'em. We don't even have to talk if you don't like."

"You make it sound as a punishment," I said as we left the Hackett mansion for its lawn.

"That a 'course depends entirely on who ya ask."

"Well, not to worry about the pace. I'm afraid my physique has suffered since leaving the circus. Halved rations and daily performances kept me pretty lean then. Now I laze about on a basket that travels for me, amongst the finest cooks in all of Europe!"

"Now you can empathize with my belly," George slapped his round stomach. "Beatrix?"

"Yes?"

"I can't help but notice we're headed in the direction of the off-limits barn. Shall we change course?"

But of course he knew that was our destination.

"Thelma told me of your days as an infantryman," I said. "How would you feel about re-enlisting under a woman's command?"

"I've been under a woman's command since I met Thelma," he winked. "But delivering you to danger would make me rather a poor escort."

"I've done naught but hurt our cause, and we're quagmired on this horrid property. If seems our departure will come only from direct motivation, I'd like to be the one to provide it. If you feel aged out of the required action…" I teased.

"I'm a stone, or two, or three, heavier than I was then, but reliable as foul weather in the Highlands. You've no debt to us, Beatrix."

"Please," I implored. "Let me contribute."

George's jaw cycled in consternation.

"Fine, but you're to be extra careful."

"Oh, thank you!" I slapped his arm and was genuinely surprised at the brawn concealed beneath. "Right then. Your part does not require stealth. In fact, it's quite the opposite."

"A distraction, is it?"

"That would do nicely, thank you."

George tipped his cap then strolled casually across the back lawn towards the rear patio. He approached the Colonel, who stood drinking a brandy with some of the Hacketts. His plate of the day's pitiful lunch: peppered lettuce, lay untouched nearby. Our captain's once elevated dinner spirits had been deflated by the *cuisine de Hackett*, and this, more than anything, may have inspired his own renewed efforts to free us. The whole group of Hacketts were enraptured by some anecdote the Colonel was concluding.

"'What's a fice amongst friends?' the Prime Minister said."

"I'm not familiar with the word," Madame interrupted.

"A fice, Madame, is a small, windy escape backwards, more obvious to the nose than the ears, that is frequently, by old ladies, charged on their lap-dogs." The group erupted in laughter and polite applause. The Colonel had just begun a bow when George knocked the brandy out of his hand and slapped him across the face.

I held my breath. Surely he didn't think I'd asked him to do that!

The Colonel recovered from the blow and grinned. He gamely assumed a fighting stance that was foreign to me.

"Karate!" George and the Colonel shouted in unison at one another before engaging in a furious bout of sporting combat.

The Hacketts were immediately drawn in by the physical display. I too stared as the men advanced and retreated in a flurry of blurred limbs until I recalled this was meant to be a distraction for the Hacketts, not me. The Hacketts standing watch outside the barn were drawn closer to the commotion on the patio, allowing me to slink up to the vaulted building with ease.

Sounds of tools and machinery emanated from inside, but a sound more curious came from somewhere around the corner, at the rear of the barn. Something was being eaten.

Half-crouched and furiously chewing, Lindenhurst Hackett ate a cut of red meat. I refused to make any kind of guess as to where the flesh had originated, but it was clearly raw. The man stopped chewing and looked over his shoulder, mad eyes popping white above the smear of blood and juices. I did not think. I ran.

The monster followed, and threatened to outpace me. I darted round the garden shed and found a half open door. I slipped into the darkness without deliberation. Lindenhurst stalked past the door's crack a moment later, chin dripping, hands rigid. I held my breath. The giant's footsteps faded as he stalked to some other part of the property. What was this revelation? There was no crime I knew of that forbade the eating of raw meat, but doing so in secret with only one's hands was… distressing. I'd wanted a means to escape, not another reason to do so.

This was too much. I'd sleep alone on the Ox if I had to, but I wouldn't spend another night amongst the slithering Hacketts, waiting for one to strike. My thoughts became so real in the darkness that I could swear I heard the slithering and hiss of snakes.

The heart of the shed was in total darkness. As I turned to leave, one of my feet set down only a hair farther into the black, an unremarkable distance… provided one is not at the edge of a large pit. As I began to fall, my acrobatic mind took the reins and I'd just enough time and reach to push off the ledge and vault into the void before me, high enough to grasp a low rafter of the structure. How many times my former profession had saved my life, I could no longer count.

My movements excited a good many of something in the pit below me. I didn't need the Hacketts' seal as an additional clue, the animal sounds had been real. A thousand ropey bodies curled and flopped, agitated by my intrusion. Putting the ghastly fate I'd thusfar narrowly avoided out of my mind, I swung my body and let go, soaring through the ajar door to the safety of firm grass outside. My exit spilled sunlight onto the horrible pit of snakes that hissed more furiously than ever as their green and black bodies threaded the cavities of several human skeletons.

Mine had nearly been amongst them.

I ran towards the back patio to inform my comrades of the horrors I'd witnessed, paying no attention to the sounds of construction spilling from the barn. My curiosity for that mystery had been extinguished for the time being. I traversed the barn's broadside and was about to break for the patio when a hand that was much too soft to be Lindenhurst's clasped over my mouth. I moved to strike, but a different pair of hands bound my arms. In a moment's time, my hands were tied, a sack had been placed over my head, and I was being lead roughly through the forest, away from the Hacketts' property.

Chapter Twenty-Eight

The wretches. The traitors. The goddamned weasels.

I had freed the Mirrors from certain death and this was how they saw fit to repay me?

Blinded and bound, I'd no choice but to keep my captors' pace as we pushed through the forest for, what? A death more private? For a berth that would see me back into the employ of Ziro? I could not decide which was worse.

The springy carpet of forest floor eventually turned to the manmade surfaces of cobblestones. The musky smells of oak and fern were usurped by smoke and horse manure. We were in London.

Ziro had never seen fit to tour London since it was a crowded market for entertainment and thus less exploitable. I'd often daydreamed about visiting the largest city in the world. In none of these visions did I arrive in a gilded coach, rolling upon palm fronds and rose petals, but hooded and handcuffed wasn't quite what I'd imagined either.

I experienced the horrible sensation of stepping onto nothing and stumbled down a staircase. I insist, yet again, my acrobatic trade kept my neck unbroken as sightless, I danced down the staircase's decline until I ran full speed into something large and soft. The sack upon my head was removed, and I stood face-to-face with a squat, dark-skinned man.

Residing in the Hacketts' propaganda for many days brought the answer to my lips immediately.

"Nodds!"

"I said to be gentle about it," the fat man shouted. "My name is Basir. These are my brothers, Abbas and Hamzah."

Two men, the same size and shape as Basir, descended the staircase behind me, much more slowly than I had.

"I apologise if they were not courteous. Please come inside." Basir turned around and walked through a door barely large enough to admit him. Just like the Hacketts', a family crest crowned the door—a gigantic bat held crossed swords flanked with lettering I guessed to be Arabic.

Basir's head popped back out to check my delay.

"By blood spilled, you will know thine brother," he read for me. "Hopefully unnecessary in your case. Come."

Abbas and Hamzah pushed forward and I was carried by the tide of Nodds into their dwelling, past the blackened antlers of a trophy buck mounted on the wall.

"One of our prizes from those dog Hacketts," Hamzah announced proudly.

"They went and defiled their own forest spirit." Abbas added, and they laughed.

It was the same stag Lindenhurst had bragged about defiling. So both sides counted it as a victory. Of course they did.

Deeper and deeper we walked, past low-burning lamps rendered even dimmer by the thin haze of smoke that filled what looked like a wooden cave, the walls pockmarked with alcoves of curious children and coldly staring adults.

The family's search for the Sphinx was everywhere—mounds of weathered traveling gear, heavily inked maps of dead ends and lists with strikethroughs of black ink. One alcove was crowded with books on chemistry and alchemy, and in its centre, huddled above piles of metal powder and flints, was the burgundy figure I'd caught following me near Maulgate. I could see the eyes more clearly now, a brown so dark they were nearly black, narrowed in loathing for me. Could this be some nefarious prince of the Nodds, sent that night to murder Elmhurst? Had I saved Elmhurst's life? Basir disallowed any revelations as he guided me yet deeper into what felt like an endless den of wood and smoke.

Further recesses contained more shy children, an elderly man playing a zither, and women adorning themselves with colorful shawls as if preparing for a celebration.

The smoke was now so thick that if Basir hadn't held out a hand to stop me, I should have run straight into a doorframe before us, entirely concealed by the puffs of thick smoke that swelled from within.

"She's here," Basir announced into the grey.

"Bring her inside."

Basir nodded at the doorway, and I entered.

With my visibility hindered, I walked the perimeter of what turned out to be a dome, its walls pitted with hundreds of shelved holes. A catacomb of precious metals and gemstones, each nook glowing dimly with the treasure inside. Peering at me from the hollows were hundreds of animals —a dove of black moonstone, a frog of purple zoisite, quartz crocodiles, and too many jade dragons to count. The Hacketts desired the Blue Star Sphinx principally for its sapphire quality, the Nodds for its animal shape. I had to admit both families' collections immensely impressive. Truly, the treasure hunting elite.

In the centre of the room, amongst a throng of pillows, a man smoked from a hookah as he patiently watched me take in the crystalline zoo.

"A bit of ventilation would save many a stubbed toe," I told him.

"Hello, Beatrix."

"Hello, Sharif."

"Were you brought here gently?"

"Yes," I said absently, trying to understand what this all meant.

"You've been at the Hacketts' mansion for some time now. Shall I assume you've allied with their cause?"

"Why would you keep your identity a secret? Why pretend to be a sheriff in Antwerp at all?"

"Would the Colonel have let a treasure hunter aboard his precious Ox? Subterfuge was a meager price for my ticket."

Gone were the keffiyeh and scarf he'd always worn. On his forehead were several bruises and bumps, barely visible as they were nearly healed. Where had I seen this appearance before?

Lindenhurst Hackett. Both men had tussled in the recent past.

"It was you who met Ebbing in the bar. You and Lindenhurst." I realized this as I said it aloud. Sharif expelled a long stream of smoke, letting me piece things together. "Ebbing brought you both out with promise of the riddle. When did the fight break out?"

"When we learned Ebbing meant to sell it to us both. The price he demanded suggested exclusive rights. One of the few things Lindenhurst Hackett and I have ever agreed upon."

"Who killed Ebbing?"

"Does it matter?"

"Of course it matters!" But how could I believe him anyway? Caught between snakes and bats, it was wise to trust neither. Perhaps I'd put that wisdom upon my own crest.

"It's possible you don't realize how dangerous the Hacketts are. I, for instance, was accosted in their cursed forest and robbed after we parted on the road to Maulgate."

"Robbed of what?"

"While I was able to conceal the notes I borrowed from Billingsly on nitroglycerine—"

"The notes you stole!" I said, but he ignored me.

"The snakes were successful in locating my Ox journal."

"Your Ox journal?"

"Why should the Colonel alone possess the power of flight, especially when he does not even use it correctly! I took great pains in transcribing that vehicle to paper with the purpose of recreation. Now that plan's been spoiled, but I've got you."

"Me?"

"You and the Colonel were enraptured with forks when I last left you, so I'll provide another. Down one path is cooperation. Join the Nodds, convince the Colonel to do the same, and together we can outsmart and outhustle the Hacketts to win the Sphinx."

I could hardly believe it. The two families that thought themselves infinitely dissimilar ended up indistinguishable.

"Lindenhurst gave the same offer, and I'll give you the same answer. No. What's down the next path?"

"Perhaps you'd like longer to consider. Down the other path, you become a bargaining chip. If you'll not play salesman to the Colonel for me, you'll play bait. Stay a while and think about it. Take a seat. There's something I'd like you to see."

I didn't move.

"Basir." Basir waddled through the door. "Sit her down. Somewhere with a good view."

Basir's heavy hand persuaded me to sit.

"Serpent tattoos are a paltry commitment. It is time for you to witness true dedication. This is a tradition witnessed only by Nodds, but since you are a special guest... Hamzah! Bring them in."

Hamzah led a line of adult Nodds into the room, all dressed in fine clothes. Most took their place along the wall. One alone, a young man, stood in front of Sharif.

Soft noises came from throats. Grunts that fell into a rhythmic chant. The grunts solidified into words, words I remembered from the crest.

By blood spilled, you will know thine brother.

Over and over again, faster and faster, until the sound was a perfect song of layered voices. The smoke made my stomach turn. The shouting made my head ache. I'd had enough of the ritual already.

The chanting stopped.

Sharif pulled a knife from his waistband and drew it across the young man's neck, releasing a curtain of dark blood.

I stood in shock, but Basir's strong grip pulled me back down.

The injured man wavered only slightly, a mask of forced calm upon his face. Then, very carefully, so as not to disturb his shallow wound, he embraced Sharif. The family perimeter erupted in shouts of congratulations, and for the first time I noticed a thin scar across each of their own necks.

Tobacco and hashish were replenished and smoking resumed. The wounded man gestured for the hookah. He inhaled, then expelled a bit of smoke through the line in his neck. I was sick on the floor amid deafening cheers.

Sharif pushed through the celebration.

"You know where to take her. Hamzah, you go as well." He looked at me without pity. "And be persuasive."

I was taken from the room, one Nodd in front, the other behind. The once bustling den was empty, the adults all gathered in the treasure room, the children hidden in nooks and crannies. Even the mysterious alchemist was gone, though I hadn't seen the burgundy headdress at the ceremony.

We approached a black metal door, not much larger than that of a furnace.

"This must be me," I sighed.

Basir had no banter to trade back. Instead, he struck me in the stomach. I doubled over and heard the hinges of the door squeak.

Hamzah lifted me by the back of my blouse and tossed me, with merciful skill, through the opening. I landed hard against a stone floor, receiving several fresh cuts and bruises. The door closed, delivering me to total darkness. A key turned, a bolt slotted, and footsteps faded away.

There was a strange energy to the room. The air felt humid and rank, filled with a soft… rustling?

I tried to feel for the door but found my bearings had quickly collapsed in the darkness. My hand instead closed over something that scraped across the floor. It felt almost as a rock but did not have the cold it should have. The surface was light and porous, with holes, some smooth, some jagged. A line of smaller rocks along the bottom. Teeth. I held a human skull.

I tossed the skull in terror and unleashed one much greater. A thousand angry wings filled the air, screeching, clawing, biting. I covered my face with my arms, pressing myself as flat against the stone floor as I could while the bats fluttered against every part of my body.

I willed myself to stay still and silent.

After what felt like an eternity, the bats settled above once again.

I was no coward around wild animals—heaven knew I'd dealt with enough of them in the circus. But to experience a thousand bats, in a closed space, entirely through touch, was too much for me. I kept my sobs low and allowed them to pass in their own time without shame.

Did Sharif think this would win my allegiance? It was a bloody farce. He knew before the offer that I'd not join him. This was punishment for fun. Torture without aim. I was a mouse for the cat to paw around at its leisure. Then I would be leveraged against my friends, causing them yet more strife.

Did they know of my abduction? They must by now. Thelma would be worried sick. If she found out George had been a part of my dangerous plan, his life was likely more in danger than mine. Perhaps the Colonel had tracked my kidnappers and would appear at any moment, primed to rescue with a keenly deployed bit of chrysanthemum and a witty—

No.

Ascribing such perfection was a foolish thing to do, and there was no flower I knew of that could pick a lock. I would be forced to await whatever wrath and barter Sharif had in mind. I saw no other means for my liberation outside the intervention of an angel, and though I was no churchgoer, I'd gladly accept the help. In this predicament, I'd welcome the intervention of a demon.

Chapter Twenty-Nine

A tight chill ran the length of my spine. Surely no draught could reach this far underground. What was its source then?

Careful not to rile the bats, I found the cold metal of the door. Tracing my fingers across the flat surface, I located the keyhole and put my eye to it. Two Nodd guards slept in the faint light, snoring loudly.

Then the lamps were snuffed, one after another, until the outside space was as dark as mine. My mind went immediately to the Spectre of my magic lantern. Had my silent prayer summoned the demon to claim me at last? I crawled away from the door, awaiting the impossible.

The bolt withdrew and the door creaked open. None entered that I could tell.

A light, cold hand grasped my wrist as another wrapped around my mouth. The Spectre had come for me, I was certain. I could cry out, but to what reward? Waking the abusive Nodds was less in my interest than following some cold-handed ghost. So I followed where I was led, deeper into the bowels of the Nodd home or towards an exit, I did not know. At long last a door opened. It was nighttime outside, the reflected moonlight just bright enough to illuminate narrow stone stairs that ascended to the streets of London. My liberator was revealed at last, dressed in a cloak of powder blue.

"Ammoniac."

Instinctively I recoiled, bracing for an attack.

"Where is Javellisant?" I asked, looking about for the ambush. The two of them would never have been apart this long.

Ammoniac continued up the stairs and beckoned me to follow. I hesitated. True, he had just now freed me from that horrid bat cave and whatever was to follow, but before this moment I had known him and his brother only as antagonists of the worst order. I chose to believe that a mongrel shown kindness could change. I followed.

Running past a pair of butchers chatting over a late-night cigarette, I heard talk of Noel Ebbing and his final mystery. Ebbing's murder was known from Jaca to London, but did the populous know of the Blue Star Sphinx as well? I considered putting this question to the butchers but kept pace with Ammoniac instead. I did not think he'd wait for me.

I chased Ammoniac through parts of the city where one was encouraged to "keep two upon ten," lest you be burgled by a passer-by. But aside from the butchers, I saw only the remnants of the late-night pub crowd. Two men on the street curb passed a pint glass back and forth, neither noticing it had been long-since emptied. One vowed loudly he would be the one to find the Purple Diamond Sphinx. He'd a few of the details wrong but confirmed enough: the identity of the legendary gem was widespread.

So silent and swift was Ammoniac's progress that I nearly lost him several times despite the bright blue cloak. The wraith was concerned with none of the dwindling festivities or slurred rumours, never breaking stride as he made for the Hacketts' royal hunting forest.

At the edge of town, we passed the charred remains of what must have once been a handsome residence. A wolf of hammered metal stood frozen in a howl amid the skeleton structure. The name of Valirov came to my mind. Could this be the charcoal scraps of a once-great treasure hunting dynasty, raided and burned once news of the Batavian massacre reached London? How many treasures held by Nodd and Hackett had been cleaned of Valriov blood and ash? A derelict old woman shuffled in a loop nearby, her eyes lost and downcast. Was she some woebegone remainder of an eradicated family?

Or perhaps I was witness to a derelict house, a vagrant woman, and nothing more.

I had not the luxury of finding out. Ammoniac pressed ahead, slipping into a bramble of bushes at the edge of the forest.

I vaulted logs, I swung from branches, but at length, I lost my swift savior.

I'd known the Mirrors to break their employment or perhaps servitude to Ziro in only one, brief instance. The Tale of Bartholomeus was well known in the circus.

Bartholomeus was a blind, gentle peacock the brothers had picked up in Prague. More doting identical Flemish twin owners, no blind peacock ever had, subject to all the luxuries they could provide in a traveling circus. One day Bartholomeus disappeared, and rumours were whispered that a hunter in our town of engagement had shot the peacock as he loitered outside the tents. The circus moved on the next day, but the Mirrors were uncommonly distracted in their duties. A juggler who attempted to free some coin from Ziro's lockbox had been caught in the act by the Mirrors and merely sent back to his tent instead of the usual flogging. Then the twins left. Absent for three days' time, during which I imagine they'd located an unsuspecting hunter who then suffered the grieving wrath of Bartholomeus' owners. Upon their return, the brothers both had a peacock feather earring dangling from a bone too thick to be avian. It looked to me like a finger bone. Perhaps a trigger finger. Ziro had been wise enough to let the matter of their disappearance go, and all returned to normal.

"Ammoniac?" I spoke to the empty forest. Another step forward and I nearly tripped on a body in a blue cloak. Had Ammoniac stumbled?

No.

It was the lifeless body of Javellisant.

Who had done the deed before me? What party stood to gain from the death of a ringleader's henchman?

Ammoniac's gentle hand covered my mouth. He nodded to the path behind us where a line of lanterns bobbed low to the ground. The Nodds had discovered my escape.

Ammoniac removed his brother's dagger and placed it upon his own belt, then leapt into a tree above.

Heavy footfalls crunched branches with clumsy weight. Either a party of elephants had migrated north from Africa, or the Nodd hunting party was nearly upon me.

I fled in what I thought was the direction of the Hackett property, but soon came again upon the light of a search party. Had I travelled the wrong way? Had the Nodds flanked me? Surely their portly frames could not accommodate such agility. Then I heard the voice at the head of the group. It was not Sharif, but Lindenhurst. I took cover in the underbrush.

"She's defected to the Nodds. I'm sure of it!"

"Ahoy there, Lindenhurst. Have you found her?"

It was the Colonel.

"No. And I wish no more of your involvement. Your Nodd sympathies are exposed at last. Remove yourself from the property with haste."

"There's blood on his sword!"

George's voice.

"I came upon one of your cloaked agents in the forest and cut him down," Lindenhurst growled. "Our hospitality has been rewarded with betrayal!"

"If the blood is hers, you'll not live to see the sun," the Colonel said.

"I will not be threatened by a gallivanting minstrel in my family's own forest!" Lindenhurst said explosively.

"A minstrel, am I?" the Colonel shouted, accompanied by the unsheathing of his sword.

"Here I am!" I cried, springing forth.

The Colonel, George, Lindenhurst, and his band of men stared at me.

Before any of us were laboured with a response proper to the situation, a lantern was extinguished. Then another. And another. All snuffed by a swift hand stabbing down from the canopy of leaves overhead.

"Encircle me!" Lindenhurst screeched at his men. "The slain has returned for my head!"

The forest lit with the fire of a dozen gun barrels.

In those frames of light, I saw a bejeweled dagger streaking for Lindenhurst's heart deflected to his face. The blade split open the broad cheek. More gunfire showed me a wisp of light blue cloak vanishing into the foliage, heavily stained with spots of blood where several bullets had found their mark.

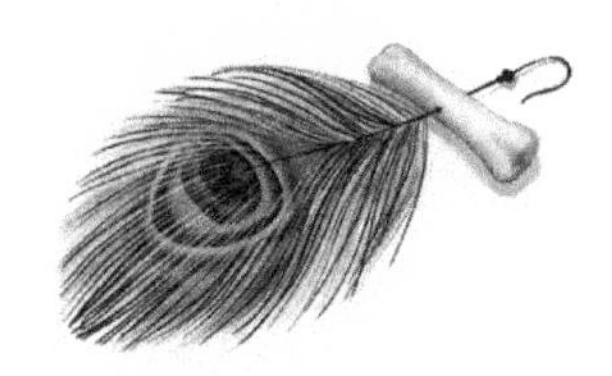

Chapter Thirty

Never in my life was I so glad to quit a forest. The Hacketts' maze of branch and bush held delights only for the sinister: lurking voyeurs, clandestine executions, and warring hunting parties.

When the lanterns had been relit, and the Colonel and I had made sure the other wasn't injured, I'd begun to ask where George was. The Colonel shook his head, signalling me to abandon my inquiry, which I did. The Hacketts scoured the forest for Ammoniac but found nothing save for a few drops of blood. Lindenhurst, several pints of blood lighter after the knife attack, ordered everyone back to Hackett Manor where we were met by Thelma and Madame Hackett.

With a rag to his ravaged face, Lindenhurst revealed my treacherous desertion to the Nodds' side and the attempt at his life that followed.

"It seems we must, at last, bid goodbye to our esteemed guests," Madame Hackett said, inspecting Lindenhurst's great wound with something more like disappointment than concern.

"We are only too happy to depart," the Colonel assured her.

"You misunderstand," Madame said cheerily, "You are of no more potential value. Your campaign serves only as competition."

Guns were raised.

"Your cold heart was apparent on sight," the Colonel said to Madame. "But cold blood? Well, yes, I suppose I can see that now too."

Thelma and I were restrained as Lindenhurst drew an ornamental pistol from his vest and levelled it at the Colonel's head.

Just when the piece seemed prime to fire, a Manx fluttered out of the night sky and landed on the gun's golden hammer. It had a note affixed to a harness around its breast. Another Manx landed on the edge of Lindenhurst's barrel, directing it off-target.

"What's this parlour trick?" he demanded.

"Ah, news from the Strait. About time Billingsly turned over the right stone. I trust he'll be embarrassed at the time passed."

I watched in awe as the Colonel calmly took the Manx in his hand, removed the note, and let the birds flutter into the forest. The Colonel had not batted an eye, not let fall one bead of sweat, not stammered one syllable in his speech.

"Read it aloud," Madame ordered.

The Colonel straightened his posture for oration.

"I hope this note finds you all well and in good health. I am beside myself with embarrassment for the length of time I've taken. The answer is simple beyond measure. Notice first the seal at the top of the riddle."

Thelma and I wriggled our way closer to the note, as did our would-be murderers. The Colonel continued amid this preposterous scene.

"A signet that bears the image of an infant swan, or a *cygnet*. Ebbing has instructed us that homophones are in play. Below that, observe the script reading recto. Invert the page and you will find spelled out, with the very same script, the word verso. The ambigram indicates that antonyms or opposites are in play. There is no missing page as we previously thought, the entirety of information is at our command. See here the original riddle."

at the Treble of the *fare see*
Caught at the point where the *rite* and *vial* Joyless, and the ships find Less, where the Lord comes to Instill on Lakes of white Columns so grand
Deaf *dyes* a *mail, knew* and Drink
Predator to *hymn* and be Silent to the Remain of the Daughter
Single within your Buried and *meat* the Part
the Active you will have Divided at the Pro of Future Pulling Many

"Once the capitalized words have been rendered their opposite, and those italicized translated to their homophonic brother, it reads as such."

at the *bass* of the Fair Sea
threw the point where the Right and Vile *merry*, and the ships find *more,*
where the *serf* comes to *wrest* on *isles* of white *rows* so grand
hear Dies a Male, New and *pour*
prey to Him and be *aloud* to the *alter* of the *son*
dual within your *mined* and Meet the *whole*
the *idle* you will have *one*
at the anti of yore kneading sole

"Here, we must again find the homophones of the antonyms and the antonyms of the homophones. Doing so, we reveal the message's ultimate form."

at the base of the dark land
through the point where the false and good marry,
and the ships find moor,
where the surf comes to rest on aisles of white rose so grand
here lives a female old and poor
pray to her and be allowed to the altar of the sun
duel within your mind and avoid the hole
the idol you will have won
at the ante of your needing soul

"Allow me to include an important revelation before my solution to the riddle. Our dear friend Ebbing was indeed poisoned. The development being that he was eliminated by not one, but two separate barbiturates, both expensive and difficult to acquire. Each would have soundly done the job on its own and persons utilizing such advanced materials would certainly be skilled and proficient, leading me to believe he was in fact killed by two separate, and indeed very capable, offenders. As for the location of the Sphinx, I am leaving tonight for—"

Madame snatched the note from the Colonel's hands.

"Unhand my property!" he protested, despite the fact we were still a trigger pull away from the great beyond.

"Might as well identify us and the Nodds by name as perpetrators of the crime. I should think that is no longer revelatory for any here. As for the final resting place..." she surveyed the note. "Ah, how interesting." She sneered at the three of us, our backs to the manor, any hope of exit smothered by the line of Hacketts before us. "Lindenhurst, if you please."

"Allow me a moment," the Colonel shielded Thelma and I. "This may be wasted breath, but why may we not, all of us, including the Nodds, work together? The puddle of differences between us is certainly less than the ocean you imagine. Since treasure is what lures your hearts' steeds, allow me to point out that *cooperating will result in a greater return.* This is wasted animosity and you are all withering in the face of something that is less than that which makes it up."

Surely he didn't think she'd be swayed.

Then I saw my companion's aim: delay.

Out of the darkness behind the Hacketts descended the sight I loved most in the world: the Oxford Starladder. George drove her straight for the Hackett lawn.

"Kill them, Lindenhurst!" Madame cried impatiently just before the green earth she stood upon rose like the crest of a wave, tossing her and the rest of us asunder as the Ox plowed into the grass.

The Colonel's lance flashed first, drawing up the previously unscarred side of Lindenhurst's face causing the man to drop his cocked pistol. Our trio scrambled behind the safety of the Ox as rattan fractured and flew under the hail of Hackett gunfire. We took refuge on the exterior staircase and the Colonel called up to the Cloud Deck.

"Light us up, George!"

"Things are a bit dislodged up 'ere!" He informed us. "Be but a minute!"

"We'll be mincemeat in less time," the Colonel said.

I prepared another plea for divine intervention, be it from heaven or hell, when a tremendous volley sounded from the forest behind us. A line of rotund soldiers charged from the underbrush, Sharif in the lead.

The hateful families fired at one another with great enthusiasm. In a short time, the Nodds reached the Ox and, before we'd any say in the matter, joined us on the stairs.

A victorious yell from George sounded above and the Ox leapt to her haven in the sky with great enthusiasm, even with the substantial cargo of Nodds.

We set down at a distance greater than Hackett bullets could fly, but close enough that the Colonel could keep an eye on the mansion with his telescope.

The Colonel, the Newlyweds and I holed up in the map room for a bit of privacy from the Nodds on deck while we decided what to do next. I hugged the Newlyweds tightly then told my tale to them and the Colonel. I left out George's involvement in my abduction, but revealed all else as it had happened. The Hacketts' snake pit, Elmhurst eating raw meat, the Nodd kidnapping, the horrific family tradition, my rescue by Ammoniac, the corpse of Javellisant, and Sharif's journal of the Ox that had fallen into Hackett hands.

"Wonder if they had a go at it?" George said.

"I suppose this could be called an attempt," the Colonel said darkly, looking through his eyeglass. He passed the device to the rest of us.

Laborers were crawling all across the roof of the Hackett barn, ripping away shingles and timber with vigor. From below was birthed a distorted, nightmare version of the Oxford Starladder: a black, patchwork envelope married to a jagged basket by mismatched cordage. It was nowhere near as large as the Ox, and certainly nowhere near as beautiful.

There was only one thing the Hacketts had that we hadn't: an immediate destination. The freak balloon, after several shaky false starts, picked a southward wind, and rode it away from the manor.

The central staircase vibrated as Sharif's significant mass bounded down it.

"Have you seen? They're off in a balloon of their own creation!"

"We've seen," I told him.

"Set us aloft!" he shouted.

"Us?" the Colonel said.

Sharif faced the Colonel with firm resolve.

"My first tour upon this craft was through false identity. Now it has been earned by timely intervention on the field of battle. Or do you deny me that merit?"

"We are grateful for the turn of events—" the Colonel began, but Sharif interrupted.

"But not grateful enough to show it!"

"Calm yourself, Mister Sharif," the Colonel returned evenly.

"Colonel, may I point out I am putting forward a request. *The Hacketts* would give no such courtesy. Were *the Hacketts* in this predicament, they might see fit to mention they've twenty armed men aboard your craft, and that violent commandeering of said craft could come at the mere order of the man in charge. In this case, me. But I make no order. I make a request: to be repaid for our part in your escape. There are many who seek the Sphinx. Do you believe that even *if* you arrive at its hiding place, you shall do so exclusively?"

"Prepare yourself, for I'm about to speak bluntly. I distrust and despise the Hacketts."

"As do I."

"I feel similarly about the House of Nodd."

Sharif's eyes darkened but he said nothing. The Colonel went on.

"I believe your hatred for the family upon whose property we still reside will rule over all else, perhaps endangering my ship and her crew. Furthermore, you kidnapped my coadjutor. Lucky for you, she wasn't harmed, otherwise we wouldn't be enjoying a conversation as pleasant as this."

"Whose bones lay in your cave?" I said. "I touched a skull."

"A Hackett who once strayed too close to our home."

"You are vile," I charged.

"The bones of Nodds are upon their property as well. Captured, tortured, left for dead. Didn't go into the garden house, did you? It holds no tools to till the earth but a pit of serpents. There lie the bones of many a Nodd, so before you lecture me on the single skull you found in our home, understand this is a war that has carried on much longer than your involvement." Sharif faced the Colonel. "I will never deny my correct opinion of the Hacketts. But I am afraid I must now insist. We will be traveling on the Ox, that is a certainty. Whether or not you accept our help is the only issue at hand. Make for the Hackett balloon," Sharif ordered as he returned for the stairs.

"Passengers do not dictate this vehicle's movements," the Colonel said.

"But the Hacketts have the destination! They've their own balloon!" Sharif thundered.

"We'll not play mimic to that crime against engineering," the

Colonel said firmly. "We'll come about the riddle's answer honorably, and no matter the distance, we'll overtake them. I've confidence in our brain trust just as I've confidence in our steed."

Sharif must have sensed the Colonel's immovability on the subject, for though he did so with the temperament of a toddler denied a lollipop, he quit our company without another word.

"Must I live the rest of my days forced to suspect every neck-scarred, potbellied butterball to be a kinsman of the Nodds?" the Colonel complained loudly. "A caucus of disreputable thieves now reside in our home. Let's be quick about our work."

"At the base of the dark land," I offered up the riddle.

"I pray it's not the Caribbean," the Colonel said. "On our last visit, I stepped off with a Santero's daughter for what was considered an inappropriate amount of time. He didn't have the finances to serve a decent goat stew, but a generous bounty on my head was no issue."

"Some call Africa the Dark Continent," Thelma suggested.

"Ziro often called it that," I confirmed. "He thought 'The Dark Continent' to be an untapped market and had even spoken of traveling there after Switzerland."

"Let's have Africa, shall we?" the Colonel said. George pulled forth roll after roll of exquisitely detailed, incredibly illustrated maps. Here was the world, drawn on paper before me. "Some I've commissioned with surveys done by my own eye, while others are drawn by my very hand." I did not doubt this last point, as many nude women could be found lounging in the surf off the coast of Madagascar, or giggling shyly behind a Baltic mountain range. Some squares had been shaded by charcoal and labelled *terra incognita* and *mare incognitum.*

"What do these mean?" I asked.

"Ah. Unknown land and unknown sea. We have the costal borders and perhaps the general lay of rivers, but a good deal of these areas are untouched and unexplored. What a shame it will be when the mazes are all fully solved, the darkest recesses uniformly lit."

"Isn't that the aim of exploration?"

"In part, but it will be a shame when all's finished. In the meantime, there's fun yet to be had."

The Colonel smoothed out a map showing the entirety of the African continent.

"The base, a' course," Thelma pointed to the southern tip of Africa. "*Through the point where the false and good marry, and the ships find moor.* That'll be the coastline."

"False Bay." I jabbed the map.

"Here is False Bay, and here it marries the good." His finger identified a peninsular outcropping on the west side of the bay. "The Cape of Good Hope! My God, that was obvious."

"*Where the surf comes to rest on aisles of white rose so grand, here lives a female old and poor,*" I continued the riddle.

"There you have it," the Colonel said. "We fly for Cape Colony to visit every garden that bears white rose and inquire therewith until we locate a penny-starved blue hair." He made for the Cloud Deck.

"And the rest of the riddle," I said, "specifically the part about losing one's soul?"

"Don't read too deeply into things," was his unsatisfactory response.

The Newlyweds looked at one another with concern.

"He's got the look to him," George said.

"Aye," Thelma agreed.

"What look might that be?" I asked.

"The Colonel can become quite… dedicated when closing in on an aim," Thelma said. "It'll be wise to steel yourself now. Whatever relationship you hold will soon be strained."

Chapter Thirty-One

Sights as chilling as the Spectre were rare, but I found one in Madame Hackett, watching our party depart from a corner window of the mansion. Her portrait was so cold, I gathered my arms up for warmth. Her look was not one of concern, but competition. The half-smirk said she was willing to let every departed man die in pursuit of their goal, and asked if we were willing to risk the same?

I disliked the labeling of anyone as evil. The word ended conversation instead of inspiring it. Insight into perpetrators of nefarious deeds caused discomfort, examination of one's self. The use of an evil label was damn near cowardly in my book. But how else was I to describe the merciless matriarch so careless with the lives of her men? Her son even.

Elmhurst.

He was for the noose! In the flurry of kidnapping and death I'd forgotten the captive prince.

I altered our course, diverting the Ox towards Maulgate, immediately inviting the wrath of Sharif.

"What's this?"

"I've a quick appointment at Maulgate, then we can continue."

"We don't have the time," he protested. "I won't allow—"

"None are as fast as the Ox," the Colonel said from behind us. "Certainly not an imitation constructed in haste. Whatever happens, we have the Oxford Starladder, and they have not. I half expect to find their wreckage scattered upon some wind-battered coastline. What is your business at Maulgate?" he asked me.

"We must free Elmhurst."

"Out of the question!" Sharif bellowed. "It will delay us unnecessarily and, furthermore, it will strengthen the opposition. All the better for our cause that one of the Hacketts is locked away."

"But he's to be hanged!" I protested.

"We should be so lucky," Sharif said.

A substantial cannon report came from within Maulgate's crumbling walls and a speedy black ball flew mercifully wide of our position.

"Perhaps the Derringer Sisters have improved their calibre!" I jested in the face of great peril.

"Please, Bee, leave wit for desperate spinsters and men without saleable skill," the Colonel said as he flew the Ox back a touch and set us down, hopefully out of cannon range.

Warden Cain came running from the prison, a worn rifle held high over his head in a battle charge. When he recognised our group, he lowered his weapon and collapsed in a fit of tears. It seemed his unenviable fortunes hadn't much improved. The wall around Elmhurst's window was blackened, the one good set of bars at Maulgate scattered into the yard below.

"Hello there, Warden," the Colonel called out. "What's the meaning of your aggression? We're as harmless as ever."

"I thought you to be the Hacketts," he wailed, inconsolable and nearly incomprehensible. "An explosion rocks the prison. Then they land a terrible flying machine not unlike yours in my yard and make off with Elmhurst Hackett."

"The Hackett abomination," the Colonel said with supreme irritation, "could hardly be *more* unlike the Ox. But I'm sorry for your troubles."

"Two prisoners now! Two prisoners now have escaped my care this very year." Warden Cain mumbled something about cricket statistics as his tears soaked into the arid ground. "I must be tied somehow to the hapless Job of the Bible by direct bloodline."

"Chin up, Warden," the Colonel called down. "We pursue Christopher yet. Smart money's on our finding him. Good day."

With that said, the Colonel tipped his hat then signalled George to take us skyward once more. George took a wide berth around the prison to avoid any cannon-minding guards that hadn't yet gotten word of our innocence.

"That's all you offer him?" I said to the Colonel with surprise.

"I assist where I am able, as much as I am able, but presently I have work to do and my thoughts and actions are so dedicated."

"Look there!" I pointed to a clearing below where a burgundy figure lay crumpled on the ground. It was the Nodd gunpowder engineer. Surely Sharif would make no complaint in acquiring one of his own, and yet I'm almost certain I heard him groan in impatience as we set down.

"Step aside." Sharif pushed through the gathered crowd of Nodds. "Let me through to my daughter."

"Daughter?" I exclaimed.

Sharif pulled away the scarf and keffiyeh to reveal a beautiful young woman, perhaps a bit older than I. Her face was covered in soot and even burned in one place.

"They took him... in a balloon," she said in a daze. "They took Elmhurst."

"Mihri! What have you done?" Sharif shook the dazed girl.

"That's enough, ya brute!" Thelma smacked him aside. "I'm giving her the Hare, dear," she said to me. "It's got the softest bed aboard." George and Thelma began to help her up the stairs. The girl's pretty, narrow eyes flashed at me with anger, and then she fell from consciousness.

"Giving me a look like that," I said, "while I've just seen to her rescue!"

"She'll have plenty to answer for, I'm sure," the Colonel noted. "Now if all will please climb aboard, we have yet one more stop to make."

"I forbid it!" Sharif snarled.

"Would that our craft was powered by your ill manners and hatred, Sharif, we might never touch dirt again. Alas it is not, and a resupply in London is essential."

"Resupply?" Sharif asked indignantly.

"Fuel for the burner, foodstuffs for the expanded crew, expansive in their own right, casks of water for crossing the largest desert in the world, and I do believe I've run out of Lord Kimber's Shoe Tonic." The Colonel brushed his dry mustache as he took us skyward.

I felt a tug at the basket as we grazed a tall oak, as if the dastardly forest meant to drag us down forever. I wished it many a woodpecker and termite.

The Colonel marked no celebration of our much-desired departure; perched at the south-facing side of the Cloud Deck, his gaze was focused on our destination, the continent in between a mere formality of travel.

-PART SIX-

SAHARA

Chapter Thirty-Two

"That's it, dear. Get it down the neck," Thelma said with encouragement.

Mihri dutifully swallowed a spoonful of castor oil, always Thelma's first prescribed tonic for any ailment on the Ox.

"Good show." Thelma took the empty spoon from Mihri and left the two of us with a steaming pot of rose petal tea. Mihri had requested an audience with me. Alone.

The girl's injuries from the explosion at Maulgate were bad, but worse was her illness from inhaling the fumes of so much gunpowder and chemicals during the preparation. It was Sharif's stolen papers on nitroglycerine that had finally seen her reach success. Billingsly, I think, would have been proud.

"Could you check outside?" she asked me from the bed.

I cracked the door and was face to face with an eavesdropping Abbas. He grunted angrily and waddled off to the Digesting Frog. The Nodds were beside themselves at the idea that one of their own had helped free a Hackett. I now knew the Arabic words for treason, betrayal, and spineless dog.

"We are alone, now," I said, returning to my seat on the small chest the Colonel had given me the first night.

Curiosity did not remove my lack of approbation for the girl before me. I disliked her for her beauty, for spying on me, for not helping me when I had been kidnapped, for her closeness to Elmhurst...

"I apologise for rendering you no aid when my uncles brought you to our home against your will. I attempted to break Elmhurst out that very night, but my mixture failed to ignite. When I returned home, you had already gone. I went back to work on my powders, correcting the previous night's mistakes."

I'd been prepared for a verbal battle. I hadn't expected an apology.

"Why do you help the Hacketts?" I asked carefully.

"I mean to help only Elmhurst… we are in love."

My heart sank. Elmhurst and Mihri were prince and princess of warring clans and had somehow forged a secret love despite the obstacles. How could I hold a candle to a romance as grand as that?

"I have felt threatened by you," Mihri said. "You are very beautiful, and I thought perhaps Elmhurst would forget about me."

I tried not to laugh. Was this a ploy to win my favor? I'll not disparage my appearance, but to compare myself to the beauty before me… I searched her eyes for any hints of flattery. There were none. Elmhurst was hers and she his, and no part of that was a personal affront to me. I sighed, realizing I would be denied hatred of this girl. The hostility would have felt good, but to what end?

"I often find myself with a choice," I began slowly, "then look back later and regret not making the choice I knew to be correct. In this instance, I will not be so foolish. If you should wish it, I'd like to be friends."

"I'd like nothing more." Mihri gave a radiant smile.

"I was fond of Elmhurst. It's a bit embarrassing now."

"Please don't be ashamed. He can be charming without effort. He can also be careless with it."

"Let's leave it then," I said, as my face could grow no redder. "You seem rather good-hearted for a Nodd. Oh. I didn't mean to disparage—"

"My family is not blameless in our reputation. I love them, but I often disagree." I noticed her neck was unscarred. "I do not seek the Sphinx. Neither does Elmhurst. You may not believe it, but neither of us shares the treasure lust of our family. Ending the practice entirely seems unlikely, but we've at least tried to stop the killing."

"Were you at Batavia?" I whispered.

"I was. I'm ashamed I couldn't deter my family's attack on the Valirovs' ship, the Hacketts waiting on shore… It is the only time our two clans have worked in agency, and the result was a slaughter. As you've pledged your friendship to me, I pledge to you that I have no desire for that infernal stone. I wish only to be with Elmhurst and to see peace between our families."

I nodded in a flush of camaraderie. A girl my own age that had suffered and still held admirable goals. We understood one another. We could help one another.

"Did you know Christopher?" I asked, pouring her some of the rose petal tea.

"Yes!" she said. "A friend of Elmhurst's. You know him as well?"

"He's the man our captain is after. What can you tell of him?"

"I cannot claim affection, that is certain. I should have said he and Elmhurst *were* friends, until Christopher left him in Maulgate to hang. If your captain seeks vengeance, I wouldn't think worse of him."

A cascade of furnace heat blew in through the open window, stirring Mihri's long black hair. Together, we stared out the window at the impossible stretch of nothing before us.

"It's the foolhardy or the brave that attempt to cross this place," Mihri said.

I tried to see the desert before us as anything but unlimited, and failed. The danger suddenly felt much more real.

"So long as we come out the other end, I'm happy to play the part of either."

Chapter Thirty-Three

While they couldn't be considered athletes by any definition I knew of, our new passengers had the smell of well-exercised men. Going anywhere on the Ox meant pushing through stairwells and hallways crowded with heaps of Nodd that grunted and stepped aside. Sharif had secured their transport but knew the situation was delicate, and had told his kinsman to be as polite and unobtrusive as possible. Food for twenty-five saw George and me in the kitchen quite often, working with a constantly dwindling supply of ingredients. We were soon forced to get creative, serving dishes like rice with raspberry jam, lentils with raspberry jam, and eventually, raspberry jam with raspberry jam. It seemed our stock of berry preserves was bottomless. Ditto Thelma's supply of castor oil, much to Mihri's daily dismay.

A sisterhood was easily born between the three of us ladies, and we spent many hours together in the Nimble Hare while Mihri recovered. Thelma would cut my hair short while I recalled my circus days, from the lows of Ziro's abuse to the literal heights of the trapeze (that were quite humbled once one called the Ox home).

Mihri kept pace with her own tales of growing up as a Nodd. Relatives who went in search of treasure and never returned. Her refusal to have her throat cut. The first time she saw Elmhurst.

"He was buying a wheel of cheddar, and looking very handsome while he did it."

Thelma shared the main points of what she called "a particularly eventful winter" in the days of her youth in which she'd started as a governess' handmaid, and by spring, had become a genuine spice smuggler. In certain Scottish villages, one could still hear awed speech about *The Cinnamon Queen of Aberdeen.*

I've no interest in dismissal of a gender. Bad men were so because they were bad, not because they were men. But there is a harmony that can only be achieved in company that is exclusively female. These were some of the finest moments of camaraderie I'd ever experienced, put into sharp relief by the deterioration of our situation at large.

Most affected by our predicament, rather surprisingly, was the Colonel. Passing time in the presence of the Colonel, one could easily mistake him as infallible. Answers for any and all problems seemed to come without effort and always with style. But no longer. It was true he had conquered deserts before, but never with such a large crew to support and never with such astoundingly uncooperative weather. The wind had abandoned us days into our crossing—another bundle upon the fire of worry that had begun to consume the Colonel's mind.

Following a relaxing morning with Thelma and Mihri, I checked our captain's condition. He never strayed far from the map room or the Cloud Deck, even in the heat of midday, intent on pristine navigation. I found him on deck.

"Stay below, Bee," was how he greeted me, gin and tonic in one hand, sun-bleached umbrella in the other. He'd been disguised in liquor for some time, and I hadn't seen him sleep for days.

"How about a bit of water, Colonel?"

He shook his head.

"Our drums are light. Tonic's good for malaria and it's into that contemptable disease's bosom we now fly. At least we would if we could get some blasted wind! This devil's sandbox has none of the charm of the Gobi!"

Here was a man who lived his days darting from the shadow of one falling foot to another, and doing so with tremendous success. But now there were several feet at once, and his pace was handicapped by the ball and chain of a slothy, resource-depleting family. This endeavour didn't allow for the expert evasion he was used to practicing, and it was dragging him down. In his desperation, he'd latched onto a concrete goal. Finding Christopher was all that mattered. The level of dedication someone like the Colonel could apply to a task was frightening, and meant the rest of us were in for a terrifying ride seemingly without cessation.

I joined him at the railing and he shifted the umbrella to shade me. We watched the world together, just as we'd done approaching Antwerp. But this was no Belgian countryside. Look into the desert too long and you'd go mad. Countless wandering lines in the thin sand, traced by winds that had left long ago. Rocks, stones, pebbles, boulders—all baked dull by the sun, strewn meaninglessly across an edgeless plane. There were no plants, certainly no animals, no indicators of any life, direction, or time. I reaffirmed my grip on the railing, hypnotized by the immense nothing that surrounded us.

"You could've chosen anything else or nothing to take from your previous life. Why the magic lantern?"

"The Spectre."

"You've a name for the instrument?"

"Not the instrument. One of its slides. An image of a smiling ghoul. It reminds me of my mother."

The Colonel drank his gin and tonic.

"It's the expression," I said.

"Your mother never smiled?"

"That's all she did. But never with the gesture's proper intention. She would tell me..." The umbrella's shadow began to feel quite outmatched. "She said I was unwanted. Both before my birth and after. She would say this to me… and she would smile."

The gin and tonic was steady.

"All are visitors in life, even family. We decide who may stay. Some are meant to be forgotten but for the lessons they enhance us with. No relationship is wasted time." The glass raised into the darkness and returned empty.

I stood alongside the Colonel for what might have been a minute or an hour. I know only I was guided below deck by the firm hands of George. He brought me to the dining room, a place I hadn't been since Thelma's tour of the Ox. The rarely used room was full up with Nodds. Thelma entered behind George and forced me to drink a glass of water.

"Go ahead, Sharif," she said.

Sharif unrolled a map of Northern Africa and spoke to the gathering.

"While he can't be blamed for the lack of wind, the Colonel's direct path has found us marooned. Our supply of the essentials is becoming dire. We've reached a critical point in our geography. One path leads west," his finger slid left. "While civilization there may be scant, we could likely find a resupply of water, food, and perhaps even fuel. The other path, the one we now follow," his finger pushed deeper into the Sahara, featureless even on the detailed map. "Continues straight south, several more days' journey even *if* the wind cooperates. We'll die on this southern path. It must be the west." He looked to George and Thelma.

They nodded solemnly.

"You talk of mutiny," I said to Sharif. "And you go along with it?" I charged the Newlyweds.

"Everything is as he's just said," George told me. "The Colonel's gone a bit mad in the sun. He can't see our predicament, he can only see Christopher."

"The man's traded liquor for sleep," Sharif said. "In his eyes is madness—"

"I know!" I cut him off. I stared at the rattan below my feet for some time. "If we must go west then let's get to it."

We climbed back into the oven above.

I presented our case thoughtfully and clearly to our captain. He feigned consideration before positioning himself by the controls and drawing his rapier.

"Avast mutineers! I'm this ship's captain! I set her course!"

Abbas advanced with a coat rack. The Colonel speedily deflected his attack, spilling the encroaching Nodd onto the breakfast table, shattering it with enthusiasm.

"There now!" I chastised the Colonel. "See what you've done? Where will you drink your morning coffee?"

"The coffee's long gone, acrobat."

"Your gin then?"

His eyes went wide in concern. Our lives were expendable, but a comfortable setting to imbibe his liquid breakfast rendered him to shock.

Guns were drawn from Nodd belts.

The Colonel stood straighter than ever, cradling the orbed compass in one hand, rapier at the ready.

"If I'm to die, I'll die at the helm."

My hair blew across my face. I brushed it aside with annoyance and then recognized our salvation.

"Wind!" I cried.

A generous wind had rushed into our lane of altitude, carrying us quickly south. All were temporarily distracted. The Colonel capitalized on the stupor, swirling his rapier into a tornado of steel that forced us would-be mutineers below deck. He was tenacious in his defence, blocking both staircases with the deck's great leather chairs. Hamzah nearly had a clear shot until he was blanketed by animal skins from the cold weather chest. The blinded man fired anyway, very nearly missing the envelope above. Sharif shouted at the men to holster their damned pistols.

I retrieved several sounding balloons from the Bulkhead, and we discovered the south wind to be the only one blowing. Soon it made less sense to backtrack as it did to go forward. The stubborn Colonel had gotten his way.

The fortuitous winds continued through the night and into the next day. So great was our breezy fortune some of the Nodds began to deny ever having doubted the Colonel.

The next day, the winds left entirely.

Three days after that, our water was depleted. The Nodds ravaged the nursery, sucking the water-heavy succulents and bromeliads dry. While the frenzied mode of consumption was uncouth, I gratefully shared a stalk of aloe vera with Basir.

Our captain, that man who ascribed intense significance to the last meal of the day with near religious import, called all down to the Bulkhead, where he served up the last of the rattan berries.

"A soldier's supper for myself, seeing as I'm the cause of our predicament." He bowed slightly and returned to the Cloud Deck.

Perhaps he felt guilt at damning us all or maybe his instinct to survive briefly outranked the obsession to find Christopher, but some sanity had returned to his voice. It was anyone's guess how long it would last.

After they failed for the hundredth time to catch and eat Jasper, the Nodds finished the berries and reignited talk of mutiny. I tried to explain that an overthrow of the Colonel would no longer do us any good. When it came to doomed ships, the desert had no opinion of the captain's name.

Mihri's frail figure stepped down the spiral staircase. The Sahara's relentless heat had begun to thwart her initially successful recovery. The rest of us struggled to survive the sweltering days in full health, so I could not imagine the difficulty of the experience while recovering from gunpowder poisoning. She gestured weakly to the window.

"There's something outside."

I would've thought the thin line of brown on the horizon a mirage, except all saw the same thing. A forest. Water. *The end of the desert.* We would make it after all. The Colonel's stock with the Nodds soared again, but it wasn't to last. The Ox shuttered, lurching up and down in rough jitters, tossing us about the spiral staircase as we raced to the Cloud Deck.

"Our fuel is spent," came the Colonel's rasping voice as he wrestled with the burner.

Having dropped all the ballasts long ago, we could do nothing to slow the basket as she fell towards the ground, where we learned the Sahara had saved it's cruelest trick for last.

There was water here, but not in useful pools or streams. The bounty of the rainy season had been sucked up by the greedy earth, and the world below us was one of mud.

I looked again at the brown band on the horizon. Salvation was in sight but out of reach. The trees were few and almost entirely dead, but it looked a crowded jungle compared with the terrain we'd just crossed.

As if the death sentence of muck below wasn't bad enough, our fate was made even more hellish with a field of open sores in the earth that belched scalding air in huge invisible pillars.

Each time one of these expulsions would find the Ox, she'd lurch to and fro so that several of the Nodds were sick over the side. After being tossed around for what felt like an eternity, the Ox landed hard, sinking deep into the black mud.

She was entombed, likely never to rise again.

Chapter Thirty-Four

Of all the potential deaths I'd imagined our Saharan crossing might bring, I hadn't guessed it to come by swamp.

We'd been stuck for two days, meaning it had been three since anyone had had a drop of water. Efforts led by the Newlyweds to dig us out of the desert's muddy clutch had been yet unsuccessful. Of course, we'd still be without fuel even *if* the Ox was unstuck, but it was something to work at.

The Nodds were entirely useless, Mihri included, though she had the excuse of grave illness. Day and night, the squat treasure hunters slept in the shade of the Digesting Frog or crawled around for crumbs in the kitchen. They longed for their subterranean habitat of London and made no attempt to hide it. Cowards they were, Sharif worst of all, keeping his kin around him as a buffer to us and any call for assistance we might be foolish enough to make. As our likelihood of survival dwindled, we made no calls at all.

I had taken rest, or more accurately, fainted in the bulkhead, when I was awoken by Thelma grabbing a new shovel.

"Sorry, dear. Lost another one to the muck. Didn't mean to wake you."

"Any sign of the Colonel?" I asked. Thelma shook her head.

Our captain had ventured away from the basket almost immediately following our abrupt landing and there'd been no sign of him since.

I got to my feet.

"Rest a while longer," Thelma said.

"I may have only an ounce of strength left, but I'll not let it go to waste."

We stepped into the heat of the desert made worse by bursts of sweltering air from the gaping vents that surrounded us. I started to walk in the direction of the dead forest.

"Beatrix. Where ya going?" George called after me.

I could not summon the strength of a response, but no further questions followed. The calm of the condemned had settled upon us all. Finding a way out began to occupy less time on the mind, giving way to thoughts of how best to spend one's remaining hours.

I wandered the wasteland of fire and mud, plagued by thoughts of the darkest effect until my mind was not my own.

Damn the Hacketts and Nodds for their rapaciousness. Damn San Miguel for his perversion of power. Damn Mihri and Elmhurst and their found love. Damn Ziro for his temper and the Mirrors for allowing it. Damn Warden Cain for his terrible luck and Billingsly for not solving the riddle more quickly. Damn George and Thelma and their inability to dig us out. Damn Ebbing for dangling the Sphinx and Christopher for drawing us towards it. And the Colonel. Damn him most of all. The man who had rescued me from a frayed tightrope only to desert me on one much higher up.

The Sahara did a bang up impression of the magic lantern. Fiendish figures rose in the geysers of steam: Ziro and his whip, Lindenhurst and his pistol, the Mirrors and their daggers, the Spectre and his razor teeth. The grinning skeleton opened wide and I fell to my knees, ready to be received. All became but light and shadow until the shape of a great beast, larger than the world, swallowed me up entirely.

Chapter Thirty-Five

Something struck my head.

I awoke in the Ox's library, a wet cloth smelling of juniper berries upon my forehead. The Ox shook and another book fell off the shelf above. I shielded my face and pushed my wearied mind to make sense of things.

Had my walk through the wasteland been a dream? What about the great beast? Perhaps we'd never flown into that horrible desert at all and I'd find the pleasant shores of Gibraltar outside. I dragged my dehydrated body towards the window and felt the Sahara before I saw it, a big heat even in the dead of night. The Ox was stuck in the same bit of mud, except... except it seemed to have slid a few metres. How was this possible?

The floor-shaking shifts began again at intervals matched by rallying cries somewhere outside.

I staggered down the spiral staircase, my body in full revolt over the unexplained lack of water.

I foolishly imagined seeing the entire Nodd family, shackled to the Ox, pulling in long-overdue cooperation. As ludicrous an idea this was, I could think of no other force great enough to make the Ox tremble. The Nodds were outside, but they were motionless, standing in a line to observe some other spectacle. The entire bloomin' family had been born tired.

But the Newlyweds stood there too. I pushed past them all to bear witness for myself.

There in the mud, bound by thick leather straps to the Ox, was an elephant.

Further off in the mud, bound to the elephant, was the Colonel.

"Heave, old boy, heave," the Colonel cried in a hoarse voice as he pulled on the beast's restraints.

I moved to join them but was pulled back by George.

"Don't step there, love," he said softly. "That's ground that doesn't let go."

"But we must pull them out," I argued.

"We've tried," Thelma said weakly. "They are lost." She buried her head in George's neck and cried silently. The two of them were caked in mud up to the waist and looked to have aged thirty years each. How long they must have tried to save the Colonel from his suffocating fate, all while I rested on the Ox.

"I have energy yet!" I shouted. I pulled free of George's grip and trudged my way to the Colonel. If not for my lightness, I may not have made it more than three steps so eager was the muck. The elephant regarded me with a tired eye as I passed. This was the beast of shadow I'd seen, all the more huge and impressive without the blur of delirium. "Colonel, you must get out of this mud," I told him, as if it was the absence of the idea that held him in place.

"Ahoy, Bee," he said. "Mind you don't let it get past your ankles."

Both the Colonel and his elephant were sunk in all the way to their chests.

"No," I said. "This can't be the end. We've so much more to do."

"Who said anything about the end?" he grunted. "Onward!"

The Colonel pulled forward an inch. The elephant did the same... and so did the Ox.

"There. *Now* we are spent," the Colonel reached back and stroked the elephant's trunk. "Good show, good show."

Only then did I see that the doomed pair pulled not in the direction of the forest, but towards a large air vent.

"Demonstrate to me your ability for arithmetic and add things up," the Colonel said, wiping priceless sweat from his brow.

"The envelope!" I called out, lurching ridiculously through the muck. "Damn you bystanders, drag the damned envelope!"

The Newlyweds moved quickest, but even the Nodds must have realized this was our only chance for salvation, and they all put hands on the huge red canvas and pulled toward the vent.

While the elephant had its trunk, and therefore several minutes before asphyxiation, the Colonel was now up to his shoulders in the shifting black muck.

"Your haste is appreciated," he called.

The yawning hole expelled a furnace blast of air before we'd reached it. I did not know when the next would come but guessed the Colonel wouldn't last if we missed it. The ground under our feet trembled.

"Bring it across!" I shouted from my spot at the base of the balloon. Sharif tugged weakly at the canvas. "Shove aside." I pushed him out of the way and dragged the lip of the balloon across the hole just as a volcanic blast of heat shot like an invisible cannonball from the earth. My fingers were singed and I was tossed backwards by several metres.

The envelope sprang into life, snapping to form with a loud crack. The Ox jarred from its spot and jumped skyward. I feared we'd lost the craft, but the weight of a mud-lodged elephant was enough to both arrest the Ox's progress and free the elephant. The last ball on the chain, the Colonel, was easily plucked from his situation as well. The force of the blast had ripped a hole in the envelope, and encouraged by the weight of the elephant, the Ox descended onto the hard-packed earth.

Thelma and George rushed to the Colonel, both in tears at his miraculous escape. Some of the Nodds were in tears as well, congratulating one another on their fine work.

"Mind the envelope!" I shouted. Our exhausted and starved bodies were beginning to fail outright, accolades could be assigned later if we lived to assign them.

George helped the Colonel into the bulkhead.

"I think he's a broken rib or two, shoulder's out of its spot as well."

"Beatrix!" Mihri had just enough strength to push the sewing basket out the Nimble Hare's window.

Thelma and I wasted no time in sewing a great patch onto the again-flat envelope, double stitching our double stitching. The Nodds too wasted no time in returning to the Digesting Frog, where they cleaned their guns in case we ran into any Hacketts south of the Sahara.

"If they've taken our same path, they've long since perished and your work is done," the Colonel chastised their foolishness, a mere bandage around his midsection to hold his ribs together. "Let's have it then!" He yelped as George used a karate blow to put his shoulder back into place. "Ship shape, thank you George."

The Colonel exited the Ox, untied the elephant, and led it back in the direction of the skeletal forest. Using his penknife, he cut a notch into the elephant's ear, so small I doubt it was even felt by the great animal. He did the same with his own ear, producing a wound much more substantial on the smaller anatomy. Then he slapped the beast's rear, and it lumbered forward on a path of hard earth.

Thelma shooed the Colonel aboard the Ox as George and I finished positioning the canvas.

"Why did you do that?" I asked the Colonel once I'd made the Cloud Deck.

He put a cloth to his bleeding ear.

"So we'll recognise one another."

The Earth spoke, the balloon inflated, and all were forced to the floor. The Ox rose so quickly to such a tremendous height that my next breath drew only half as much air.

"Breathe carefully," the Colonel rasped. "The air is… rather thin… this high up."

His face doubled, then tripled, then vanished with the rest.

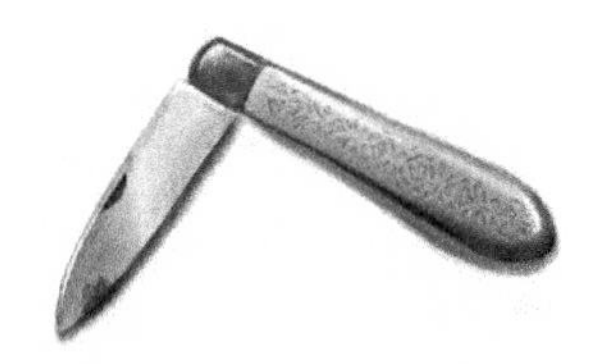

Chapter Thirty-Six

Ode to Water
The French worship wine
The Germans, their beer
But the idol that is mine
Brings far greater cheer
Friend to those on fire
Home to fish and otter
Of it I'll never tire
Cheers to my dear friend water

I was no Wordsworth, but the poem came free and honest after my first glass of water.

All had become unconscious at our apex, even the Colonel. Luckily enough, however, he had awoken in time to guide the falling Ox south, landing us near the house of a nomad. We had reached the Sahel, a less arid part of the African savannah that arrested the progress of the Sahara with a small but important tree line roamed by an earmarked elephant we owed our lives to.

The nomad let us drink our fill from his well, and refused to accept any payment or barter in return. He further offered us an edible grass called cram-cram and directions to the nearby town of Agadez. The Colonel said he would accept only if the man agreed to attend an early dinner on the Ox.

"You wish an organised supper, even at this moment?" I asked as the the Newlyweds set tables on the Cloud Deck.

"Good lord, woman, a sound dinner is the reward for another day lived! What sort of nitwit allows that to pass by?"

For a moment, our captain was his old self again. An ambassador of civility in the worst conditions.

Taste was scarce in the cram-cram, but the Colonel did as well as he could, producing a respectable soup and salad.

"Allow me the rare, acceptable toast with water. Drink hearty, thanks to our man in Agadez." He clapped the nomad on the shoulder, and the man looked quite overcome to suddenly be the guest of honor at a dinner atop a flying machine. We drank our water and ate our cram-cram with tremendous gratitude. The Colonel was quite eager as well to add the strain of grass to the poor Nursery, which had been almost entirely wiped out by the desert, and the scavenging of our crew.

After dinner, the Nodds fled to a bar at the edge of Agadez that overflowed with the sweet, blueish smoke of hookahs. They kept a sharp eye on the Ox, should we try to depart without them. Sharif seemed to linger a moment longer on the Ox, perhaps considering opening an invitation to Mihri, who the family continued to shun for her cardinal sin of freeing Elmhurst. But ultimately, he trotted off without her.

Having witnessed the rebuke, the Newlyweds stepped in.

"We're off to the market to barter for resupply, dearie," Thelma said. "If you're feelin' up to it—"

"Yes, please!" Mihri nearly jumped at the opportunity to escape her confinement. The sustenance of the cram-cram, although meagre, had seen some of the colour return to her cheeks, and so Thelma allowed it.

Fuel for the Ox, a touch trickier than general supply, fell to the Colonel and I. We walked with Mihri and the Newlyweds into the city, then parted ways in the shadow of a tremendous mosque several stories high. Agadez had previously been occupied by the Ottoman Empire but had since taken to French Colonialism. I heard many different languages and saw many different skin colours as we walked. The busy town actually reminded me of Antwerp, with its large market of vendors shouting as they traded for this or that. Instead of heavy horse traffic, there was the less-fatal, peaceful traffic of cloaked desert dwellers, and instead of the pervasive scent of fish, the streets were hung with the sweetish smell of ginger.

"I must say, I immediately prefer Agadez to Antwerp," I said.

"Both top tier municipalities to be sure. Like Antwerp, Agadez can be quite fun with the right precaution."

"You've been here before?"

"I've been several places, in fact. The thing to remember with cities of transient journeyman and merchants, is that their inhabitants are loyal only to their homeland, often several countries away. We haven't even the gentle conscience of nationalism to encourage good manners, meaning we must ourselves avoid all proposals of moral compromise and the light-fingered denizens around us."

I wondered what someone like the Colonel could possibly consider a moral compromise as we sat outside at a French café that cornered the main square. The Colonel removed his John Bull, home to a sprig of cram-cram in honor of our desert host. With the sun descending beyond the bulbous silhouette of the grand mosque, I enjoyed a brief moment of peace: we had survived.

I looked longingly at the food and drink of other customers, for we had no currency except for the Colonel's charm. Luckily this was a currency accepted by waitresses the world round and we soon drew the prettiest one to our table.

"May I assume by your sublime silk scarf that you are from Lyon?" The Colonel asked the woman, a more classic beauty with some age about her.

"No," she lit up, "but my ancestors are. This scarf was a gift, and I've long hoped to go there someday!"

"The *true* City of Light in my humble opinion, and not that *other* French city, an overcrowded slum of opium dens and burned baguettes."

The woman laughed freely, and I rolled my eyes. How long until she would find herself thoroughly exercised, with a story of romance the other waitresses would balk at, and a Derringer fresh in her hand?

The Colonel continued his artform. "The artisans of Lyon would perish before burning bread, something tells me the bakers of this establishment are similarly skilled. Alas, we've journeyed a substantial distance and find our coin purse quite empty."

"I think we've a few end of day items I can plate for you. Some coffee as well?"

The Colonel hung his head in supplicate gratitude.

"Two cups would fortify our reckless belief in human kindness."

The waitress disappeared into the café and returned with two coffees and a spread of pastries I quickly set upon. Despite the Colonel's noble efforts with the desert grass, the croissants and cakes felt like the first food I'd had in weeks. During my undignified consumption, the Colonel drew the woman in lightly by her elbow and they spoke rapidly in French. I had nearly cleared the plate by the time she walked off.

"The buying power of a skilled gadabout," I said with a mouthful of pastry.

"The Hacketts have unsurprisingly poisoned the well."

"They came through Agadez?"

"They did indeed, and it seems they had very bountiful winds passing across the desert. Half a day's time can make all the difference as weather is concerned. The Hacketts filled their stores and left an epic novel of unpaid bills, including at this very café. Luckily, our scarfed ally senses our merit. She knows a trader who can have fuel here tomorrow."

The Colonel emptied all of our table's sugar into his coffee, the watch on his wrist sliding with each movement as all of us had lost a good deal of weight crossing the desert.

"Colonel, we've just slipped the noose. Surely we've bought a few days to return to health, or to reconsider our travels altogether. Don't you see you nearly killed us all?"

"Saved us as well, didn't I? Bee, need I remind you the criminal known as Christopher is still at large and the Hacketts may be closing in on the Sphinx as I finish this very sentence. The tick of the clock still speaks our pace."

"You sound like Sharif! Is finding this criminal worth getting yourself killed? You were mad in that desert. I hardly recognised you."

"Such a disposition was necessary to see us across." Our speech was leading to an argument, as it had done so many times lately. I missed the jovial Colonel of Switzerland or even Belgium—one unpoisoned by progress in his pursuit of Christopher. "I wouldn't advise choosing the Sahel as your point of departure from the Ox, but you are free to make that decision at any time."

"So that's it? Join your suicidal folly or walk home?"

"That is precisely it. This is no instance of me being cruel. It is rather your mettle being tested and failing. The waters are rough, but what are we to do? Flee back to our port of call? I can think of nothing less enticing. I demand a life that's extraordinary. I would've thought you of similar mind."

"You hunt this man like an animal, for what? Money? Revenge? Or is it the Sphinx you're really after? If so, you're no better than those warring families!"

"You would do well to keep silent regarding matters you do not understand."

"Help me understand then. Tell me *something*. I am your friend, James."

"You are a stowaway! I've had those before. At least the others had manners and kept their concerns their own." He faltered with the words only slightly, but that was a great deal for him. He didn't mean these things. He couldn't.

"What is it you flee from?" I asked desperately. "Are you tethered to nothing and no one? You search the globe hoping to unearth some value. Is it in the folds of a flowering tulip or the bodice of some stolen woman?"

"Am I really to receive a lecture on fleeing responsibility and connection from *you*? The girl who fled to the circus, then fled the circus. Where else is there for you to go? Nothing flies higher than the Ox, I'm afraid. You are at long last trapped, young acrobat. That is why you expel your problems unto me. Well take them back. I do not want them. Humanity is drowning in an ocean of their own problems. It is not within my desire nor my ability to save them all. There will be no more wedding surprises or books in chimneys. Our rivals now possess the privilege of air travel. They have a head start and a focused purpose. I predict we approach a peak of unspeakable violence, but with speed, we may lessen or avoid it all together." He stood from the table. "Now if you'll excuse me, I must go secure the transaction I've made for our fuel." He began to leave then doubled back. "Heavens I despise all this glucose. Twists an already winding mood." He drank his coffee in one motion then set the cup down with such force the saucer below cracked in half.

Chapter Thirty-Seven

Consumed by frustrated anger, I stormed about the empty Ox, kicking all I came across: the rattling magnet on the Cloud Deck, a stack of periodicals in the library, a freshly-potted plant of cram-cram in the Nursery, a bundle of rattan in the Bulkhead. This final victim slid down the wall, landing hard on a lumpy blanket that grunted in pain. I froze. A corner of powder blue cloak stuck out from under the disturbed blanket.

I considered a scream, but spoke softly instead.

"Ammoniac?"

A whisper of a man slid from the disrupted rattan. So wasted was he that I might have failed to recognize him were it not for the telltale cloak, tented in places by juts of bone and joint. His mouth was stained red from surviving exclusively on the powdered dragon's blood of the rattan berries. I fetched some water, which brought some relief to his face, but I knew it wasn't nearly enough. The man needed significant medical attention, immediately.

I pulled the Flemish skeleton onto my shoulders and found he weighed almost nothing. My stride was hardly altered as I made for Agadez, and the last slivers of sunlight were swallowed by the horizon.

To know a city only in daylight hours is to know it only in part. Most towns reveal their true energy only when the commerce of the main avenues is shuttered and priorities have shifted to personal pursuits of entertainment and pleasure.

My calls for aid were answered with closed windows and locked doors. I'm almost sure Sharif and his kinsmen must have heard me, but they did nothing.

Ammoniac's weight, insignificant at first, now pressed upon me. I collapsed in an alley, careful to keep my cargo's head from hitting the stone.

A shadow spilled down the alley, weaving back and forth in drunkenness. Had salvation arrived at the perfect time?

"Hello?" I called out. "Hello, can you help me?"

The drunk, incredibly top-heavy, somehow stayed vertical as he stumbled forward. As his features came into view, I beheld a pinstriped suit, epaulette shoulders, and a whip-adorned belt. With the unluckiest eyes in the Sahel, I watched Ziro's face emerge from shadow.

We stared at one another for a long while. Then he hiccupped.

"I don't believe it," he slurred. Then he said it again, laughing this time. "I don't believe it! The loose thread that's unravelled my brilliant circus, supine in an African back alley, with a dead assassin I sent to kill her long ago."

He succumbed to a wave of laughter and finally fell down.

"Here is the most fateful meeting either of us will've ever had." Ziro squinted and pointed a shaky finger at the body next to me. "Who've you got there? Ammoniac or Javellisant?"

"Ammoniac," I choked. "Javellisant's dead."

"Beatrix! I didn't think you had it in you."

"I didn't kill Javellisant. Ziro, please, if you can claim to bear a conscience—"

"There it is." He crawled to his feet and began to creep forward. "The insolent tone that left my life. I've longed to hear it again so *I* could be the one to silence it forever. You cost me *everything*. Your defection gave the others ideas. Ideas they never would have had otherwise. Without my controllers—" He kicked at Ammoniac's foot. "—I couldn't stem the flow. They're all gone now."

"Jacques? And the Fräulein?" The names escaped my mouth before I could cover it.

"Why, yes." Ziro's eyes flared even hotter. "The last of the jugglers escaped only last night. Sure he's not dead?" He kicked Ammoniac's foot again. "I suppose he's delivered you after all. You and I will rebuild the company, and you'll work off your debt to me for the rest of your miserable life. You won't know the comfort of an employee. You'll be a slave. But first, I believe you're owed something from Switzerland." He removed the whip from his belt.

I deflected the first blow, and the second. The third curled round my back and snapped the skin, spilling me to the stone below. Through the gap in arms held over my face I saw the whip coil for another strike.

I've no belief in guardian angels, and even if they exist, I doubt they work in nothing more than suspendered trousers. But this was the uniform of the seraphim that fell from an apartment window above.

The Colonel's bare feet landed nimbly, and he wrenched the whip from Ziro's hand. Ziro turned to face him, and there was no chance of immediate understanding. The ringleader, drunk in a foreign land, who was first forced to reconcile meeting me by chance in an alley, now beheld a gentleman in white pants and suspenders the color of cram-cram, clutching his beloved tool of dominance, wearing an expression of panicked anger.

"Avert your eyes, child," the Colonel said.

I did, and heard, but did not feel, the crack of the whip.

Chapter Thirty-Eight

The door to the Digesting Frog was closed. No surprise there, as the Nodds liked to sleep in. Mihri had been returned back to her healing roost in in the Nimble Hare, and through the open door of the Intriguing Mongooses, I could see George reading a book aloud to Thelma while she knit, a pair of steaming teacups between them. Most was as it had been, but not all.

As I grasped the rail of the spiral staircase, a chill ran up my arm and into my heart. The Ox now had a resident ghost. Somewhere down below, in the Bulkhead, was Ammoniac. His infected bullet wounds obtained in the Hackett forest had been treated by a doctor in Agadez. The Colonel granted him passage and even offered him the Ostentatious Mantis for recuperation, but the mute chose to return to the Bulkhead instead.

Odd too, was the Colonel himself.

I am convinced the flock of Manx and their behaviours were directly tied to the Colonel's state of mind. It was one of the most curious things I'd ever witnessed. The captain said he didn't go in for auspices, but I think he was rattled by the fact that the animals were a direct indicator of himself, and he sought to obfuscate that connection. When he felt cheeky and roguish, these constituted the majority of time, the Manx were the same, chasing one another in fast and twisting spirals around the basket. They nipped at guests on the Cloud Deck and even stole things from the bedrooms that were usually then stolen from the nests by Jasper. If the Colonel was drunk or despondent, the birds stayed inside their fold, one or two dropping down as cruciform anchors to pluck fruit from a passing tree. When the captain had been away from his ship for too long, the birds became restless and favoured a slow looping procession that haloed the craft. I had learned to check the animals' behaviour in the morning for a preview of the unreadable man.

This morning however, as we left Agadez on healthy winds we'd needed so desperately over the Sahara, the traitorous birds disclosed nothing. Some ambled about the nests around the basket, some swooped and dived out in the clouds, and others peered at me from the shadow of their roost. Our captain's state was without precedent.

The Colonel had been quiet since our encounter with Ziro, arms locked aft in his pose of contemplation. Instead of gamely dancing with a problem that could be battered with tightly focused intellect—he was genuinely confused. I found him inside the Nursery, repotting the disrupted sprigs of cram-cram. For the first time since I'd met him, he bore a look of dislocation.

"I'm about to put the kettle on. Can I bring you some coffee?" I asked.

He stared at me, long enough for a wayward Manx to circle the basket twice, then nodded.

I brewed the drinks and returned, sitting in the warm dirt below one of the Dutch windows to feel the once-familiar touch of earth as I sipped my tea.

"What is this space for?" I asked.

He shrugged.

"For whatever we find. When the last planter is filled, I usually set course for The Hearth."

"What is that?"

"My home."

These words shocked me, perhaps more than they should have, but it was hard to imagine the Colonel residing anywhere as common as the ground.

"I would love to see it someday."

"You would be most welcome," he agreed, pruning the cram-cram.

"The Manx have been acting strangely," I said, trying to draw him out again.

"Have they?" he said distantly.

"Colonel! What has put you in such a state?"

"Why, it has been you, Bee."

It sounded as if he'd arrived at this conclusion academically, surprised at why my involvement would produce such a result.

"Me?"

"It's strange. I have of course had guests before, but their affairs were always separate from mine. I feel as if we are more intertwined."

"You're almost ready to admit us friends," I joked.

"Yes, that may be it."

"Colonel, why do you do this?"

He sat on a windowsill, idly drinking his coffee.

"I once read the words of a treasure hunter asked a similar question. Why bound so carelessly, over and over again, after things that never satisfy? He said that artefacts are collected voices from the past that shout, *Here! Here is the best of us. It is what we value, what we wish to live on.* The bones of ancient lizards that dwarf the largest living mammal. The entombed remains of godlike rulers thousands of years old. Paintings of pure ecstasy created with nothing more than hair, pigment, canvas, and often, poverty. The past can be held in your grasp and in that small moment, a connection is created. A conversation takes place over hundreds or thousands of years. That was Ebbing's answer. But it is not mine. I seek my brother."

I fumbled with his words.

"Christopher is your sibling?" I expelled.

"He is. As is the maid you saw me with at Lord Chartish's. As is Billingsly. As are fifteen others."

"You've been locating your siblings all this time? But... Billingsly is rather dark-skinned compared to you."

"My mother held no prejudice about nationality when it came to copulation, and she'd a wandering spirit, just as I do. So, her progeny are spread the world round. Nineteen of us total, and so it is nineteen cubes of sugar that pass into my drink. I adore cream, but will have none of it until I've found the last sibling. That is Christopher. I may not share Ebbing's reasons principally, but I do not disagree with them either. He was an explorer disguised as a treasure merchant. 'To leave better than found' was his operating credo. It is possible to travel widely and with great enthusiasm and leave not ruin and rubbish, but seeds." He turned to me fully. "Our wake must be frothy with good will, otherwise what's the god damned point? These actions are far too grandiose for self-fulfillment alone. I seek Christopher because in a world of dispersal and disarray, to *collect*, is an absurd yet noble act of revolution."

No matter the greases we'd had in the past, always I had believed there was good in the Colonel. He had nothing to prove to me of course, but it was a great comfort to know a noble purpose lay beneath all the gallivanting and mischief, and my spirit to locate Christopher was enlivened.

"Thank you for considering me worthy of your confidence," I said.

"And you for your interest in it. Now then..." He drained his cup of coffee. "What say we find the blasted Sphinx, find my wayward brother, and leave this predicament for the halls of memory."

"I say yes."

Chapter Thirty-Nine

The remainder of our journey above Africa was mercifully uneventful. I was napping in the Nimble Hare's bed, my feet at Mihri's head and hers at mine, when I was awoken by a chilled costal mist invading our window. The Ox had arrived at the Cape of Africa at last. Mihri and I looked at one another, her complexion fully radiant now that she'd returned to health. We bounded to the Cloud Deck, where all eyes were already scouring the coastline below for a garden of white rose.

The Colonel found False Bay easily enough, but we glided amongst its shores for nearly a day without success. I wanted very much to be the one to spot the garden. To be the hero of the day. I was not.

"There it is!" Sharif announced.

My eternal shame was mitigated by excitement of the discovery, then fear as Sharif attempted to steer the Ox straight for the target, nearly dashing us upon the sea-sprayed rocks.

The Colonel corrected our fatal course and we drew nearer to the garden. An old woman came into view, walking amongst the flowers. This was the riddle incarnate! An aged female amongst aisles of brilliant white roses that were most grand indeed! Ebbing hadn't falsified the riddle, and my estimation that we might actually find the Sphinx doubled many times over.

But something was wrong. Closer now, I could see the old woman was not nurturing her crop, but destroying it. She was clipping each rose and tossing it into a freshly dug hole before casting salt upon the earth.

"Something is awry," the Colonel said.

The woman raked a final heap of dirt atop the picked roses and collapsed to the ground.

"It's an ambush!" Hamzah shouted, drawing his pistol.

"This is no ambush, you boob," the Colonel said, unmoved. "She is overwhelmed. Sharif, your family experienced all at once can be rather intimidating. I think it prudent if some remain with the Ox." He landed on Cape soil and we disembarked, leaving the roundish gang to loiter on the Ox, weapons at the ready.

On our approach of the fallen woman, she rolled over to face us, dissolving any suspense about her mortal status. The Colonel crouched low and removed his John Bull. She pulled him close, and I thought for a second they would kiss. But she studied his eyes instead.

"Treating this as the game it is, aren't you? I hoped someone like you would come." Her head lolled back. As the concealing shawl fell aside, we could see she had been badly beaten.

"My word," the Colonel said. He picked up her delicate form and made for the quaint house that flanked the garden.

George treated the old woman's wounds as best he could, shooing away Thelma and her well-intentioned spoon of castor oil. We allowed the old woman to rest, despite repeated protests from the Nodds.

"Lindenhurst Hackett will have the Sphinx!" Sharif announced, the rest of the Nodds bristling behind him. "This is sabotage! Treason!"

"Persist in the matter and I'll be forced to make the situation unpleasant," the Colonel said, blocking the door. "She'll speak when ready."

A staring contest ensued before Sharif stormed off mumbling something about superior numbers. The situation with the Nodds had always been an awkward one. They had forced their way aboard the Ox in Britain, but the journey across the African Continent had been without incident, partly because our lives had been equally threatened by the terrain at large. But now, polite exchanges were becoming terser, and compromise seemed to draw further and further away.

The Colonel and I rejoined the Newlyweds inside. The cottage was simple and uncluttered. Everything was in twos: a pair of sun hats, a double bed, place settings for two.

"You there," the old woman gestured for the Colonel.

He kneeled at her bedside.

"Noel. Is he dead?"

It took me a moment to recall Noel as being Ebbing's first name.

"He is, I'm afraid," the Colonel said. He presented the two pieces of Ebbing's cane I'd forgotten about entirely.

The old woman nodded and accepted them.

"In Belgium?"

"Yes."

"I told him Antwerp was dangerous." She lingered on the thought a moment, then rotated the cane pieces thoughtfully in her hand. "Always taking a beating for his mischiefs, he was. At least we look more the couple now," she said of her ruinous appearance.

"You're Grace Ebbing," the Colonel said with whispered reverence.

Grace Ebbing nodded.

"Noel and I constructed the riddles together, you see. These days, he would execute them alone, as I'm not as mobile as I once was. He did love the Belgians and their chocolate."

"I am greatly sorry for your loss," the Colonel said. "Allow me to say if this riddle has been the last, it has also been the best."

"Thank you," she said. "The man who came alone... red of hair..." she began.

"His name is Christopher," the Colonel said with great interest.

"He is the one that's done this to me," Grace said.

The Colonel recoiled.

"Surely the Hacketts— "

"The men with tattoos of a viper?"

"The same."

"They offered me no assistance, but the lone man is guilty of my condition. You see, there was another riddle to solve. The Sphinx is not here in Cape Colony."

I shared a glance with Thelma. Had we come all this way for nothing?

"The man you call Christopher had no interest in another riddle. I refused to disclose anything at first, but he assaulted me. After some time, I had to tell him. The Hacketts came only last night. I could not resist their inquiries either. As soon as I'd the strength, I began to pick my garden bare for I can withstand no more."

"No further harm will come to you." The Colonel looked positively sick, face as white as his John Bull.

"The place you seek is far in the ocean, southeast of here. A place called Xibalba. You will find it on no map. Noel and I came upon it in our younger, more adventurous days. If you are unlucky enough to find it, you will understand why we've christened it with the name of an underworld. The Sphinx waits in a cave at the centre of the island. Bring me some parchment."

The Colonel produced some, and she scratched out coordinates. The Colonel looked at the numbers and smiled.

"This will put it amongst the most isolated places on earth. *Positively brilliant.*"

"You see the humour where others did not. Those Russians, the Valirovs, tried to find it some time ago. I do not know if they were successful, but Noel sold the riddle again anyway. He had me make several more copies of the riddle, thought it a terrific laugh to pit the covetous against one another. I think Noel would've liked you to find it." She took a single white rose from a vase at her bedside and handed it to the Colonel. "Now I'd like to rest if I may."

"Of course." The Colonel backed away and we began to leave.

"And I'd like to speak with the young lady. Alone."

I looked to the others for an explanation, but they seemed just as confused.

The door closed and the hut was silent.

"Sit with me, Lovely, sit with me," Grace Ebbing cooed in the candlelight. "Forgive my curiosity. The couple has one another, and your friend has his fair share I imagine. He's of no relation, is he?"

"No," I said. Unprompted, I continued to speak, for the frail woman exuded trustworthiness. "We have carved, with great effort and trial, what I take to be a powerful friendship. Perhaps that sounds insubstantial."

"Not in the least," she smiled. "Your captain is a man of dedication, but your ears may still be receptive. What do you think I've to say of the Sphinx?"

"You'll say something like… treasure is not treasure."

She closed her eyes and nodded.

"The treasure you seek will transmute as often as you find it. A compass will always change direction as time moves on. What is of capital import is what that compass is set by. I hope to have given you that knowledge, and not simply a shimmering jewel."

"And you have," I breathed, endeavouring to communicate as much sincerity as possible.

"You carry a weight," she said plainly.

With almost no hesitation, I confided in her.

"My mother... I was unwanted before my birth and after. She reminded me of that often."

"And your father?"

"I didn't know him."

Her eyes softened, but to my great appreciation, never showed pity.

"There is a practice in gardening known as deadheading. Removing dead parts of a flower in order to encourage blooming. Perhaps more appropriate, abscission is when the organism sheds the dead part on its own. Like all things, there is a season for it. I believe your season is now." Grace Ebbing studied my face up and down then settled on my eyes. "You've got hellfire in you." A mischievous grin found her. "I had that too. So I've got one last piece of advice." She closed her eyes and lay back to rest. "Leave the past to itself, and go get the god damned Sphinx."

Chapter Forty

The Colonel strode alongside the ruined garden in his thinking position while Sharif tailed him like a bothersome little dog.

"We must leave immediately," Sharif declared, fist gaveling into his palm.

"This has gone far enough," the Colonel said. "Our journey ends here on the Cape."

"What in blazes are you talking about?" Sharif hissed in alarm, and I must admit the Colonel's words shocked me too.

"I've endangered my crew enough for a lifetime. I believed it was for honourable reasons, but how can I claim that now? Christopher is prosecutably vile, a scoundrel of the worst order."

The Newlyweds looked down. They too knew Christopher to be the Colonel's brother. He'd travelled all this way for a thief who had lain violent hands upon an old woman.

"That old woman was in league with Ebbing! She knew the dangers of such an engagement," Sharif persisted.

"She may well have, yes. That does not make right what was done to her."

"We're going to that island, Colonel."

"You may charter any number of boats for the task."

"We've come too far to deviate, and time is of capital importance." Sharif's chubby hand went to his pistol, and the rest of the Nodds followed suit.

"Enough!" I announced. "While his manner is uncouth, Sharif is right. This ship must sail to her final destination."

All looked a touch startled by my determination.

"We will prepare for departure." Sharif stated and walked to the Ox.

The Colonel turned to the Newlyweds and me. "If you all wish it, we can slip these bonds. The wherewithal to overcome Nodds in broad daylight, especially given the flimsy constitution of their character and meager calibre of their ornamental pea shooters, is no doubt possessed by us."

"It's Xibalba for me," I said.

"Bee, if I may advise—"

"You may not," I interrupted. "I value your input, but in this case my mind is made up. Yes, we've danced with death many times on the way. All the more reason to see things through. Not for the Sphinx, but for you to get your man, be him sound of heart or not."

The Colonel's arms folded behind his back.

"I cannot abandon Grace Ebbing in her condition. She is not yet safely escaped from her injuries."

"George and I will tend to her," Thelma said.

"Oh, but you must come," I protested.

Thelma took my face in her hands.

"Beatrix, there was a time I would've, but that was in another life."

"You've had another life?"

"Anyone that's reached my age has had at least one other life. Death waits on that island. But if you must go, then you must. Just mind to keep each other safe." She hugged the Colonel. "Won't you, James?"

"Aye."

"Keep yer head on a swivel." George winked at me.

I hugged them tight. George and the Colonel shared a salute, and the Newlyweds returned to Grace Ebbing.

The Colonel turned to me.

"You and I alone shall chaperone these dastardly butterballs to the gates of hell. I do not doubt your courage, but in all our journeying we've hardly strayed from the meridians. Now we fly straight east, into the rising sun and the underworld itself. Crossing the Rubicon doesn't begin to tell it."

"Let us find a good curtain for this production and return to tell the tale."

For the first time since I'd been granted passage, the Colonel and I grasped hands in a binding handshake.

We flew for Xibalba.

The sunlight reflected off the brilliant ocean so that the Ox's shadow was painted on a cloud above, and we passed into it like a key into a keyhole, course set for oblivion.

Chapter Forty-One

At long last, the Colonel and I were in total harmony. Our goals and our path had been fully revealed, and a spirit of oneness and camaraderie had found us as a result.

Inversely, Sharif had been growing increasingly mad in direct relation to the Sphinx's proximity. Much like the Colonel passing through the Sahara, the head of the Nodds was irrational, hostile, and purely bad mannered.

"Surely if we fly much farther our coordinates will be polar!" he shrieked one morning, attempting to wrestle control from the Colonel.

The captain employed some feat of silky combat that saw Sharif spilled flat onto the Cloud Deck.

"I cannot vouch for the validity of the coordinates, but I can attest that we shall meet their point exactly. Compose yourself and evacuate my presence." There was steel in the command, and Sharif left us alone.

The Colonel had been taking a tremendous brow beating from the Nodds as to whether we were headed in the right direction and why we hadn't reached our destination yet. The swiftest craft on earth apparently not swift enough.

"How did the Starladder come to be?" I asked, nearing the conclusion of my sewing project beneath a table on deck. The abundance of down time in our African crossing had made up for my initial slow progress.

"It was rather simple. I needed getting around and so conceived of a craft that would match my level of patience for travel, which is low. The grounds at Oxford University were not as curated as they could have been, so there was my open window. The two green thumbs I acquired at birth were put to work. My deftness with horticulture earned me lessons with four professors who became fast chuckaboos as I immersed myself in their respective fields: structural engineering, aeronautical theory, the chemistry of natural and artificial fuel, and poetry."

"Poetry?" I asked, nearly missing a stitch.

"Do you think my success to women is due entirely to a smart tailor? One must be fluent in the language of love if one desires its carnal fruits."

I exhaled at the wolfish admission but let it pass. I sought to know the man after all, not change him.

"No professor worth including as an advisor would leave his post at the first call of a flora-crowned man. And they have a natural distrust, almost disdain, for non-alumni. But I was persistent and creative in my strategy for knowledge acquisition, and with my residence, the flowers on campus bloomed like never before. Garden pests were identified and eradicated, and plants I alone knew to be mildly poisonous were mailed to Cambridge per the Oxford dean's wishes.

"With this motherlode of flourishing greenery, so too blossomed my knowledge on the desired subjects. And, bit by bit, so too grew what would come to be the craft we now travel upon. I was the sole labourer, riveting the slats, battening the rattan, and performing many other tasks whose terminology exceeded my lexicon at the time. To honour these brilliant professors, each bedroom is named after each man's personality."

"And just how does someone exhibit the traits of a digesting frog? Or an intriguing mongoose?"

"It's art, Bee. Don't overthink it."

"Alright. Let's talk of you then."

"I do not find that an interesting topic of conversation."

"But you yourself would admit that you are in rare form. Surely this period of transition or uncertainty is worth discussing."

"Hmm," he thought aloud, twirling the white rose between his fingers. "I have lately done much contemplating in the presence of others. Normally I try to do all my thinking beforehand, allowing for freer thought in the present. But the recent events of our journey have put even a mind as limber as mine to the test. I've rather enjoyed being an open book."

This had been an open book?

He clapped his hands, then put one on my shoulder.

"How truly wonderful it has been to travel with you, Bee."

"Colonel." I ran the last stitch in my project and nervously handed over my work. "I've made something for you."

"My word, for me?" he said, truly stunned.

I watched anxiously as he let the flag unfurl, revealing the crest I'd made for the Ox. In the centre, a Manx shearwater flew for the horizon, in its grasp a sprig of rattan. Below were the words *May the Winds Carry Us Home, but None Too Quickly*.

The Colonel had yet to say anything and my nerve began to falter.

"It is not a banner with which to charge into battle as those horrid families would have us use it. Rather a beacon, a landmark by which to set our compass. The stitching isn't as fine as Thelma's and if you find it in bad taste—"

"My dear Bee, I shall keep it all my days on this earth. You have blessed my life beyond measure. I've… I've nothing to give you."

"Colonel, you've given me enough." But he seemed unsatisfied. "I'll take the Sphinx then."

A fat raindrop shattered upon the brim of his hat. We were amongst the scuds, whispy clouds that lined mountains of cumulonimbus we flew towards.

"Have you seen it?" Sharif shouted, scrambling to the Cloud Deck.

"A storm means to take us," I said.

"No, you idiot." He pointed below the titanic storm clouds.

The Hacketts' balloon.

Beyond it, Xibalba: an island of black rock hidden deep in the bosom of a forgotten part of the ocean.

"The only good things here are the memories we come with," I said absently.

The Colonel carefully pocketed my needlepoint and manned the burner.

"Our dear Mister Beaufort would rate this a twelve on his beloved scale I think."

I recalled the sheet in the map room that ranked wind conditions. Were we really headed for hurricane forces? The Colonel's eyes stayed on the troubling clouds, as the Nodds accumulated on deck, vibrating with impatient hatred as we neared the Hacketts.

Our quick approach gave indication of the far superior engineering of the Ox, and the Hacketts' balloon's ghastly appearance confirmed it.

The jagged nest of a basket below the piecemeal envelope that would have held at most six Nodds, held two dozen Hacketts, glaring at us with weary eyes full of disgust.

"How do you fancy? Madame's puppeteer strings, traipsed down the length of the globe and still as efficient as ever." The Colonel shook his head, then raised his voice over the thickening sheets of rain. "Ahoy, Hacketts."

"Ahoy yourself, treacherous bon vivant," Lindenhurst shouted from his perch, a long scar down either cheek.

Elmhurst was at his side, and even at this distance, I could see wounds upon his wrists. He had been bound and taken against his will. I imagine the Hackett heir wasn't pleased about leaving Mihri alone and injured in a field outside Maulgate Prison.

His eyes lit up and he waved. I looked over the edge of the Ox to see Mihri waving from the window of the Nimble Hare. Seeing Elmhurst again briefly stirred the infatuation I'd originally felt for him, but I felt genuinely glad to see the two reunited, or nearly reunited anyway.

The Hacketts, thin at their own manor, now resembled the damned crew of a marooned ship. Ragged clothing hung angular with the protrusion of well-defined bones, just as I'd seen with Ammoniac in the Bulkhead. As trying as our journey had proved, how much more hellish theirs must have been without the Ox and her sound captain, even with the fortunate winds they'd enjoyed.

"How your true colours are visible amongst your finally-revealed alliance!" Lindenhurst charged the Colonel as we drew ever closer.

"Don't be an ingrate, Lindenhurst! As I have indicated and still maintain, my concern for your family quarrel would be crowded on a pinhead. It is not my affair."

"Spoken like a true Nodd," was the reply.

Sharif shoved the Colonel aside.

"Let's have it then, you bastard!" He brought forth his pistol and fired at the Hacketts. The Hacketts were quick to act, drawing their own firearms and issuing a responding volley.

Rattan chipped all around us. The Colonel let fly a string of curses as he grabbed my shoulder and we dashed to the spiral staircase.

"The damned fools!" he cried as a bullet sparked off the staircase railing.

A Nodd cried out above, stumbling to the stairs before being struck again in the back by a shot. His eyes closed, and he tumbled down the staircase.

"Good heavens," I breathed.

Loud thumps on the deck above suggested more deaths. Cries of pain came from the direction of the Hacketts' balloon and I could only assume they too suffered losses.

"It's our great fortune that they're all too stupid to aim for the envelopes," the Colonel said. "I just hope—"

The Ox lurched hard in one direction, then another. Squinting up the spiral, I could see small tears on the inside of the envelope growing into larger ones. The Hacketts had figured it out first.

"Aim for the balloon!" Sharif called out to his fellow Nodds.

"These insufferable bastards will be the end of us all," the Colonel growled. "Vault, Bee! Vault the stairs! We're headed for the drink. Can't be caught below deck when the water comes."

We climbed back on deck into total bedlam: bodies everywhere, Nodds clutching to the edge of the Ox as they traded fire with the Hacketts.

I looked over at the Hacketts' balloon where one man was struck in the head by a shot and fell into the merciless ocean below, killed many times over.

A bolt of lightning, purple and white, struck the island. We were close now and might have steered for it, but the Ox was beyond control, spiralling at a dizzying rate. The basket swung wider and wider, until it slammed into a corner of the Hacketts' basket, obliterating the inferior construction in an instant. Hacketts rained down into the raging ocean as the weight-freed balloon disappeared into the black weather above.

Our spiral was so tight, Nodds were being cast overboard with each rotation. The orientation of the horizon became indistinguishable, blurred and rounded with speed. I clutched as tight as I could to the spiral staircase and shut my eyes.

With a shock, the motion stopped. The Ox had hit the water, and the Colonel and I were sent spilling across the deck. The axis tilted in the opposite direction and I fell back into the stairs. The Colonel, already on his feet, cut some extra line from one of the envelope's straps. He affixed my waist to the stair rail.

"Stay with her," was all he got out before a surge of water wiped him, and the few remaining Nodds, clean off the deck.

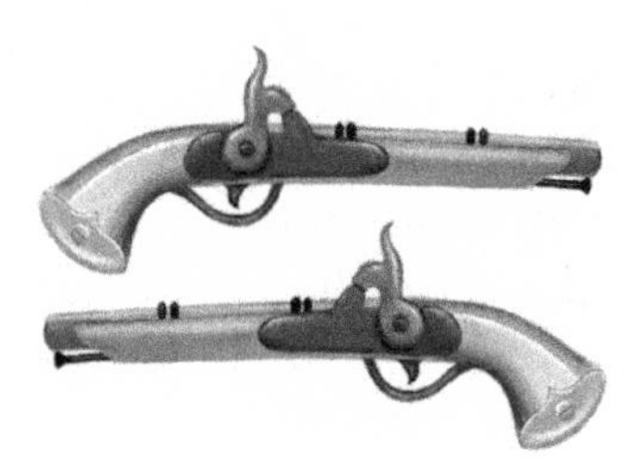

-PART SEVEN-

XIBALBA

Chapter Forty-Two

Towers of black water rose all around me. Higher and higher the Ox would climb, almost to the familiar clouds, before racing back down to a level improvised by the sea.

I know not how long I endured this horrific ride, but at length, the basket hit ground and spilled onto its side in the surf of Xibalba.

Flashes of lightning and gunfire revealed figures on the beach, shooting at one another even as they trudged out of the sea. I loosed myself from the railing and fell onto hard, wet sand. Too exhausted to move, I simply lay in the crashing waves where my body was pelted by floating objects that littered the water all along the shore. I grasped one in my hand. It was a rock. I lay amongst *floating* rocks. Had Sharif been right? Had we truly travelled to some bizarre hellscape where the waking world held no power?

A dark figure slogged out of the sea behind me. I waited for a muzzle flash but was instead greeted by a tip of the cap.

"Colonel!"

"Serendipity has found us both!" he wheezed with relief as water drained from his angled brim. Arm-in-arm, we helped each other out of the heavy surf.

"The Ox can float?" I exclaimed between deep breaths. Strange that this was my thought, but I had assumed the Ox, inherently unsealed by the material of her construction, would've taken on water immediately and sunk in less than a minute.

"Forget not our dear Sicilian friends and their fine Portuguese cork!" The Colonel slapped the bulging canvas skirt at the bottom of the Ox as we ran up the beach. "There will be time to marvel later. We must get the burner functioning and vacate this beach immediately. There's a great deal of weather about and far too much gunfire for my taste."

"I'll see to the envelope," I exclaimed and scrambled into the horizontal Ox, choking on the island air that was black not only with storm clouds, but smoke.

The Nimble Hare was empty. It looked like anything not fashioned to the basket had been washed out the window. "Mihri!" I called out. No response. I recalled then the ghost in the Bulkhead. "Ammoniac?" I cried down the stairwell. No response came, not that it would. There wasn't time for an investigation. If the Flemish ghost was still in the Bulkhead, then his survival depended on our flight as much as mine did. I found Thelma's sewing basket and stumbled back out onto the beach.

My fingers worked quickly as I weaved the heaviest thread I could find through ill-fitting patches. My sewing mentor would've thought it a crude job, but I trust she'd have understood my haste.

I tied off the last stitch and bolted back to the Cloud Deck as the Colonel tested the burner. It fired true and clear, flapping the envelope upon the sand in a rolling wave.

This finally drew the attention of the fat and skinny figures who warred further down the beach. They didn't cease their fighting, but instead moved it in our direction. The skinny ones were closer.

"Grab ahold," the Colonel said as bullet strikes spit up the sand at our feet. I wrapped my arms around the staircase and the Colonel pulled full burn.

The envelope took its form and the Ox's basket began to right itself. The Colonel and I met each other's gaze, smiling at our miraculous escape.

The fabric on his shoulder split and bloomed red.

He lost his hold on the burner and tumbled from the Cloud Deck just before it levelled out. I ran to the railing.

The Colonel sat up in the surf and met my eye just before the Hacketts beat him down with the butts of their rifles.

I reached out, foolishly, trying to get back. I could vent the envelope, but to what end? Capture awaited below in totality. I would do none any good by subjecting myself to the fate the Colonel had found to secure my escape. I let loose more flame and ascended into the dying storm above, leaving the roaming exchange of bullets behind.

Tears crowded my eyes as I struggled to steer the Ox deeper over the island. My patchworks held, but control was noticeably lessened.

With difficulty, I set the Ox down on a plateau covered on all sides by a thick mist. I wanted nothing more than to stop, to let myself breathe and allow the Colonel or the Newlyweds to see to my worries.

But they were not here. The Newlyweds were thousands of kilometres away. The Colonel was likely dead for all I knew.

I wiped the sand from my clothes and the tears from my face. Summoning some courage, I descended the stairs to see if Ammoniac or his corpse were in the Bulkhead. The kitchen and library were completely upended by the beach landing and wrecked by the projectiles that had passed through. One of the Intriguing Mongooses had suffered one such bullet and was now without its head. The Nursery was beyond repair, dirt and upended plants covering every available surface. Jasper was beside himself, running here and there to collect the windfall of objects thrown about. Last was the Bulkhead: our supplies strewn in total disorder, most crushed or ruined by water. Ammoniac's body was not amongst the wreckage.

Back on the third floor, I forced open the door of the Nimble Hare and equipped myself with one of the remaining Oriental swords, trying not to think of what I might actually have to do with the weapon. How grizzly the possibility of cutting flesh with metal seemed to me. But that was my predicament. Leaving the bedroom, I nearly stepped on my cherished magic lantern. An idea came to me then, inspired by the lion I had used at Gibraltar to accidentally capture the Jacans. Perhaps I could minimize or vanquish entirely any requirement of swordplay on my part. Next to the lantern was a dislodged roll of parchment.

Deed of Ownership as relates to The Oxford Starladder

Insomuch as a craft such as this can be owned, the following persons are hereby granted shared ownership in concert, or exclusive ownership in the case of a sole remaining listee.

Below were four names: the Colonel's, the Newlyweds', and my own.

The Colonel's name was dated the earliest, followed soon after by the Newlyweds. The date accompanying my name was the day after Chartish's party. He had felt I would prove worthy upon our immediate meeting. There wasn't time to express the flood of sentiment I experienced at this information, so I merely pocketed the parchment and made for the stairs, steeling myself with every step.

Keen flight of the Ox had eluded me at every turn. Inexperience was first responsible, but the more recent culprit was a lack of confidence. Now the choice had been made for me. With no guiding hand or whisper of advice to direct my hesitant actions, were I to do what had to be done, belief in myself would be paramount. I made the Cloud Deck and stood at the controls with resolution. I was a steward of the Ox, the proof in my pocket. Far more important, I believed it.

A Manx landed on my shoulder.

Several others hopped about my feet, until they joined the circle of their brethren forming around me. The beating of a thousand wings brought heat and noise, raising my hair in an updraught as the birds formed a kind of cyclone.

The captain of the ship was absent, perhaps no longer living: the trick at the helm had fallen to me.

I was no longer Beatrix the Acrobat. I was Bee, Captain of the Oxford Starladder.

I extended my arms, and the avian cylinder dispersed. The black birds took up their wavering ring around the envelope as I assuredly flew the Ox into the dewy sky above.

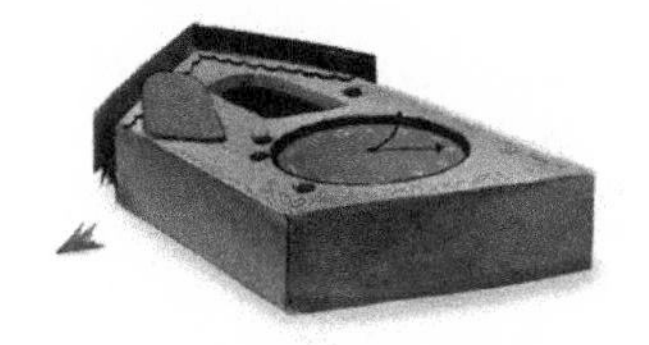

Chapter Forty-Three

No flora or fauna enlivened the desolate planes of Xibalba, all vistas were of ice and glistening black rock that shimmered strangely in places like wandering pockets of mirage. The ocean and air above suggested cold, but the tempestuous island insisted hot, leaving a robust veil of fog. A more inhospitable and impenetrable location there could not be. Ebbing had hidden his ultimate prize well.

A gunshot amid the nothing below easily pulled my attention.

Just visible through the haze, a group of slender figures hurried down a jagged hill. Roundish shapes still navigating the mountainside higher up fired at them with regularity.

Within the group of fleeing figures was one led by a rope. A prisoner. The Colonel breathed yet!

The Hacketts ran towards the mouth of a great cave, the inside of which glowed in waves of orange and red. I could not see if either Elmhurst or Mihri were amongst those still living. Had they perished in the aerial battle? Drowned in each other's arms?

It was imperative I reach the cave before the Hacketts got inside. I found and stayed within a lane of wind that took me towards it, operating the injured craft with such skill I lamented none were present to witness it. Bringing the Ox low behind the mountain that was the shell of the cave, I set the burner to a low idle so that I was just out of view.

Not knowing if my plan was supremely foolhardy or brilliant, I set about it nonetheless, withdrawing a pane of coloured glass from the magic lantern and positioning it above the burner at a tilted angle.

I opened all of the vents in the envelope, then jumped and landed my full weight upon the burner strap. The jet glowed yellow and white. The envelope shuddered violently as the flame and hot air wasted through the vents but largely stayed put. Ascension was not my aim.

The Spectre was projected onto the island's cloud ceiling, hundreds of metres long. His gaping maw would've been large enough for the Ox to fit through, his eye sockets could have comfortably sat a gaggle of Nodds. The rolling clouds gave the image such a veneer of life, that I myself, its knowing creator, was struck by a pang of fear.

Recovering, I tied the burner strap off so the flame would continue then started to roll the magnetic rock from the centre of the deck to the edge, the inset compass clanking angrily with each turn. The Manx were immediately incensed at the disruption of their hearthstone. Their agitated screeching filled my ears, reaching unbearable levels as more and more joined the cause. It gave me no pleasure to upset my recently gained friends, but all had to do their part.

The steadily drifting Ox now floated directly over the entrance to the cave. The Hacketts stood below, frozen in fear. The Spectre was working. Now for the finale.

Summoning every scrap of strength I held, I gripped the rock and heaved up. My legs burned. My back quivered. I thought of all the hard labour I'd done in the circus as leading up to this moment. The Manx were hysterical, positively screaming their sinister cries like so many vengeful demons, and my ears joined in the hurt the rest of my body felt.

I thought of the great fortune that had found my life following that night in Switzerland. Had I deserved it? It didn't matter. I would earn it now. With a Manx-like cry, I shoved the rock across the lip of the balcony and let it fall away. As the magnet plummeted to Xibalba, it pulled a vortex of black birds with it, their demonic cries magnifying in echo off the surrounding mountainsides. In the same moment, the Spectre glass burned and melted. The huge skull above shuttered as it was wreathed in flame, producing an image I shall never forget. The pane of glass shattered in an explosion of blood-red sparks. The sinister smile faded from the sky and from me in turn.

The crowd of Hacketts had dispersed, leaving a shattered magnet, a flock of disoriented seabirds, and a man bound by rope.

I set the Ox down without delay and disembarked to rejoin the Colonel.

"Lady Beatrix," he said, standing so still I thought him paralyzed. "You are, beyond all doubt, astonishing." I cut his restraints with my sword. "Legends will be told of what you've done here tonight."

"Let them be accounts instead, told by us upon our return."

We quickly anchored the Ox, made for the cave, and were ingested by the wide corridor of charred rock and pools of liquid fire.

"It is an actual underworld," I said, resolve wavering only slightly. "Did Ebbing really journey here?"

The Colonel pointed wordlessly to a headstone engraved with a message.

Hark grand explorer!

Cheers to you and yours and your successful location of the resting place of the Blue Star Sphinx. Accolade is due in this feat alone, for it is this discovery that is of the utmost importance. As an additional token of esteem, please take to heart this warning: do not seek the treasure. Men have died for it before and will continue to do so – do not number amongst them

Adventure was required to reach this point, and so you've had it. The Blue Star Sphinx is a thing. The Blue Star Sphinx is only a thing. Set your caravan by some other star and go to that place, and to the next. It is in our journey that we most fruitfully gain. If you still feel cheated, please return to Cape Colony to share a visit with my wife and me. We are honoured as hosts.

Yours,

Mr. and Mrs. Noel Ebbing

The Colonel turned to me.

"I am bound to continue. I must know if Christopher is here. The personal risk involved—"

I led the way into the furnace.

The tunnel that twisted deeper and deeper into the earth would have been darker than black were it not for a river of molten rock that flowed below our feet, visible through great fissures in the rock. Cauldrons of lava bubbled amongst jagged juts of rock that protruded all around like the teeth of an entombed fire beast. The air was so hot, it was becoming difficult to breathe. I brushed a curtain of sweat from my face and saw the Colonel had stopped.

Ahead was the largest fire vent yet, wider than the Colonel was tall. Shimmering mushrooms of scalding air belched from the spot at irregular intervals. Next to the crater of flame, charred perfectly black, was the skeleton of a man.

Chapter Forty-Four

The Colonel sank to his knees and removed his hat.

"There you have it. Christopher is at rest."

Delicately, I placed a hand on his shoulder.

"You're sure it's him?"

"There." He gestured towards an indented spot on the skull. "Took a blow to the head in his youth while trying to rob a druggist. The damned fool. Yes, this is my brother."

He reached out and took the skeleton's hand. The outer layer crumbled at the touch, revealing whitish bone beneath. The sight was ghastly but also somehow tender. The Colonel bowed his head.

"I sought my soul, but my soul I could not see. I sought my God, but my God eluded me. I sought my brother, and found all three."

I hung my head in reverence, and we let the burbling hiss of the fire below be the only sound for some time.

"We should depart," the Colonel said at last. "Lest we stay and be hanged by those who hunt us." He gently lay Christopher's hand back to the stone and walked in the direction we'd come.

I did not move.

Just beyond the hole of fire, there was a bend in the cave. Surely this was the sepulchre which held the Sphinx.

"We've made it here. I'll see you have the Sphinx," I said.

"Step away, Bee. I have no wish to possess that infernal gem."

"But we've come all this way!"

"As did he." The Colonel nodded at Christopher's remains. "Do not join him."

This cut through my blinding greed. What a ghoul I had become. Standing at the bones of this man's brother and I argued to possess the same fate. Tears found my eyes.

"I'm sorry."

He wiped away a tear from my cheek even as it evaporated in the heat.

"Dry your eyes. We're not meant to die in this place."

"Aha! They're here!" A voice echoed.

The cave flooded with Hacketts *and* Nodds. Shoulder to shoulder. The last armistice between these families had seen the eradication of the Valirovs. What would it produce now?

"That's the criminal then?" Sharif said of the skeleton.

"It would seem so," the Colonel returned, disclosing nothing of their true relation. "You may fight over the prize yourselves. We have no wish for it."

I nodded to him in agreement. We began to push through the crowd until a strong hand arrested me. It was Lindenhurst's.

"Stay. Stay and be of use." He tossed me back towards the hole of fire.

The Colonel set at him but was restrained by a litany of sabre tips and gun barrels pointed at his throat.

"Put him against the wall." Lindenhurst gestured, and his men obeyed.

Elmhurst and Mihri were amongst the crowd. Elmhurst had his sword at the Colonel's throat but gave me a slight, reassuring nod.

"Jump, Beatrix." Sharif pointed to the rear of the cave. "And bring me the Sphinx."

"Let me be the one to jump," the Colonel announced. Lindenhurst delivered a blow to his jaw and bade Sharif to go on.

"Make the jump or I'll run him through," Sharif said to me with cold simplicity.

"Let me do it." Mihri stepped forward.

Elmhurst gave a start and his blade nearly punctured the Colonel's throat. Sharif threw his daughter into the arms of some Hacketts, who held her tight.

"Mind your grip," he bellowed at them then turned to me with eyes blazing. "There will be no more volunteers! This is your last chance. *Jump.*"

The Colonel shook his head at me, but what else could I do?

I imagined I was back at Chartish Manor, just before my triumphant performance on the chandelier.

"Now!" Lindenhurst thundered. He brought his sword down like a guillotine, forcing me to vacate my position. I ran hard and leapt at the burning rim of the gash. The heat was so tremendous I thought I'd fallen in, but then I tumbled onto the opposite landing of rock.

"Your blouse!" Mihri cried.

I swatted out a flame threatening to engulf my shirt, several windmills already charred black.

"Well done," Sharif called eagerly. "Go on then."

I left behind the cabal of murderers and walked into a chamber at the end of the cave, the lair of the Blue Star Sphinx. The room's dimensions flexed with the lick of the flames behind me.

There was only one object in the room, and it was no Blue Star Sphinx.

Chapter Forty-Five

I emerged from the chamber, laughing.

"What's this?" Sharif shouted? "Toss it over."

"There is no Sphinx," I said.

All were silent for a moment. Even Elmhurst and Mihri looked a bit crestfallen. The Colonel alone smirked at the news.

"No," Lindenhurst growled. "It must—"

An enraged Sharif pushed past him, spit flying from his lips as he ran to the edge of the hole.

"You lie! *You lie*!"

"Come and see for yourself then."

"There! What have you got there?" He pointed at my hands.

I let unfurl what I'd found: the lupine crested flag of the Valirovs.

"It seems we're not the first ones here."

Sharif turned slowly to the Hacketts.

"You fools. You god damned fools."

Lindenhurst stepped forward.

"If you've something to say, then say it, Sharif Nodd!"

"You laid waste to the Valirovs!"

"As we agreed," Lindenhurst said.

"Their ship was wrecked at sea! The Sphinx cannot be found at the bottom of the ocean. It is lost forever!"

"If you wish my blood, then come try it!" Lindenhurst bellowed.

Sharif knocked aside Lindenhurst's drawn blade and began to pummel him. The truce was dissolved. Nodd and Hackett once again turned on one another, and in such close quarters, the quarrel was much more fatal.

Elmhurst swept his sword across the others pointed at the Colonel's neck then parried the attacking Nodds.

"Beatrix!" Mihri beckoned me, freed from her Hackett captors cut down by bullet and steel.

I leapt but had not the running start as before. My feet made the burning edge opposite. Mihri grasped my hands and pulled me forward, then put out the flame upon my blouse.

War filled the cave.

Screams of men pierced by swords were drowned out by eruptions of gunfire. Blood and smoke became our atmosphere.

Lindenhurst and Sharif each had their hands around the other's throat, edging closer and closer to the lava hole. Sharif was a substantial man, but Lindenhurst's strength was the more. The fatal dance ended as Lindenhurst swung Sharif near the hole the moment a great furnace blast arose. Sharif was engulfed in the searing heat. He set aflame immediately and fell screaming into the inferno below.

I shielded Mihri from the grizzly scene as best I could, but it was already played out. She trembled terribly as we darted through the carnage until we reached the rear of the scuffle where Elmhurst and the Colonel battled Nodd and Hackett alike.

"My father, he's gone," Mihri cried into Elmhurst's chest.

A roar of rage from Lindenhurst echoed above all else.

"They've murdered Sharif! Nodds! Fight us no more. We have a common enemy." Those left directed their rage towards us, failing to notice as Lindenhurst jabbed his blade into the back of several Nodds.

The pursuit was on, the four of us running appropriately like the dickens through the hellish tunnel, avoiding the pitfalls of orange and yellow as bullets sparked the rock above our heads.

We reached the mouth of the cave. The Ox waited only some distance across the flat rock. But it was far enough. Our pursuers' guns would find us in the unobstructed setting.

Beyond the anchored basket, arose a line of men, guns raised. They were not Nodds nor Hacketts. These men were sailors.

"Angels from on high and, by God, they are Sicilian!" the Colonel cried.

At the centre of the line, Billingsly and the cork merchant Augostino beckoned for us to drop to the ground. We did.

"Fire!" Augostino shouted.

All fired in unison except Billingsly, who hadn't heard the order and delivered his shot a second later.

The murderous mob behind us thinned but returned fire.

Gun smoke mixed with the fog of Xibalba and clouded the field of battle.

I crawled in the direction of the Ox, past fragments of the shattered magnet and the Valirovs' compass. The oft-kicked instrument had finally fractured following its plummet from the Ox. Inside shone something... blue.

I scooped up the compass just as the Colonel pulled me to the Ox.

The walls splintered around us in the crossfire of both factions, then the basket lurched at a sharp angle.

"One of our anchors has been severed," the Colonel shouted.

"What about the other—" I began but was cut off as the other anchor line was split by bullet or blade, and the increasingly vermiculate Ox rushed skyward as if to save its own wicker hide.

We raced to the Cloud Deck to regain control of the Ox as she twisted wildly away from the battle.

"It would seem we're in for a rough landing," the Colonel said as any heat we applied passed through the holes in the slowly withering balloon. We were caught in the windy draught of a valley inlet, and soon sped through the narrow gorge that ended at a mountainside.

It was our Swiss predicament all over again, soon to become much worse.

The click of a pistol's hammer spun me around. Lindenhurst Hackett stepped from the perimeter staircase.

"I saw you pick it up. Give it to me!" Lindenhurst hollered madly beneath matted, bloody hair. "Give it to me!"

Swirls of gray snow danced about the scarred madman, the mountain growing ever closer behind him. Some of the particulate found my tongue, but it was not snow. And that was no mountain. The Colonel recognized it as well, and although the Ox had travelled far and wide, I could tell by the look on his face that it had never before flown into a volcano.

Lindenhurst moved his aim from me to the Colonel.

"Last chance."

"Alright," I cried. I tossed Lindenhurst the compass. He cracked it like an egg upon his knee and withdrew the Blue Star Sphinx.

The volcano's heat drew us up the incline until we passed the crest and the direct heat of the lava sent the Ox's already struggling envelope into hysterics. The Manx, trailing the Ox like a kite tail, now veered away from the volcano, their home and her captains passed into a place they could not follow.

Lindenhurst clutched the treasure tight to his chest, his smile satisfied and insane. He'd nothing left to gain, but fired his pistol at us anyway. The lilting Ox saw him miss to the right, then the left. With errors on both sides, the bastard zeroed in, sight lined up perfectly with the Colonel's chest.

Then his eyes went wide, the gun and the Sphinx dropped from his slack grip.

He turned around to face an assailant revealing two daggers in his back. Ammoniac hugged Lindenhurst and stumbled the two of them to the edge of the deck.

Ammoniac looked directly at me, then fulfilled an obligation he'd given himself in the forests of London: he leaned backwards, spilling himself and his brother's killer into the molten earth below.

I witnessed the sacrifice through dizzy eyes as the Ox spun worse and worse, trapped in a torrent of hot air over the very centre of the volcano. The air was so hot that were the envelope not riddled with tears, I think we'd have been lifted straight to the moon. The strained holes tore themselves larger and larger, and we began a spinning descent into the hellfire below.

The Colonel picked up the Sphinx.

"To die for a possession, even one as beautiful as that, is a shame," I shouted above the roar of the volcano.

"You may have yet provided our deliverance," the Colonel said. "You are talented as an acrobat. We shall see if you are skilled as a seamstress as well." He dropped the Sphinx into a pocket and withdrew the flag I'd sewn for the Ox. He beckoned me to the railing of the Cloud Deck. "Grab ahold!" I joined him, and noticed he waited a precious moment longer, allowing Jasper to scamper onto one of his boots.

"Onward!" he cried.

We leapt into the blazing oblivion, my arms firmly grasping his waist, his hands firmly grasping the flag overhead. We fell in a sickening drop until a joust of hot air speared us. Our skin was singed, but the flag snapped taught and we were carried aloft. The Ox hit the lava with a mighty splash and, encouraged by the hydrogen in the Bulkhead, was immediately engulfed in licks of all-consuming flame.

That magnificent craft had one gift yet to give. From the heat of her fire, our flag was pushed even higher.

As we flew towards the lip of the volcano, we were permitted to witness the Oxford Starladder sink into the lake of fire. How many countless treasures, *true* treasures, burned within her? The wonderfully strange taxidermic stewards of the bedrooms, the cracked fox tureen and sturdy china cups that had delivered a thousand instances of sustenance, San Miguel's kitchen-relegated sword, a stockpile of Derringers that would never find a wooed woman's hands, the countless hand-sketched maps and catalogues of plantlife, the walls lined with Jasper's treasures of minutiae, arrows and bullet holes from one-too-many close shaves, and the nests of generations of loyal seabirds whose progeny eagerly awaited our uncertain deliverance at the edge of the caldera. Even as I weighed all this in my heart, far more was lost to the flames.

"A worthy steed," the Colonel said.

A rare tear sizzled on his cheek.

We were being cooked alive. My grip upon the Colonel was failing, and he could feel it.

"Just a touch longer, Bee. Hold tight for God and Country and that which truly matters!"

I blew at one of my sleeves that had caught fire.

"Legs aloft!" he shouted. We lifted four smoking shoes as high as strained muscle would allow and landed, knife edge on the crater, our momentum charitably propelling us outward to spill down the long decline of charred earth.

We came at long last to rest upon the warm shelves of slate below: burned, injured, and homeless, but very much alive.

Chapter Forty-Six

"Pumice! What a specimen!"

Billingsly eagerly collected floating rock from the surf while we took coffee on Augostino's ship.

The Colonel poured an entire saucer of milk into his brew. The dairy had been acquired in Cape Colony, while Augostino and Billingsly searched for the garden of white roses. They'd been waved down by the Newlyweds, informed of Xibalba's location, and raced to the scene with what turned out to be first-rate timing.

"Back on dairy, James?" Billingsly asked as he climbed aboard, pockets overflowing with the buoyant stones.

"My search now ended. I shall resume my preferred method of drinking coffee. Truth be told, I despise sugar. Granulated balderdash that makes the body ill. Leave it to the ants and honeybees, I say. At last, I imbibe." He drank down his entire cup.

Empirically, I felt I knew the Colonel even less than when I'd met him, and for the first time, I didn't mind. He was a reliable friend, and that was knowledge enough. The Nodds and Hacketts were another matter entirely.

Death had visited their families in a devastating way, but if they mourned, it was in a way invisible to me. Fathers, sons, uncles, nephews, even grandfathers and grandchildren lay where we'd gathered them on the shore of Xibalba. The family trees had been substantially cut, from the deepest roots to the highest branches, yet there were no tears. Unbelievably, some still made to bicker under their Sicilian captors.

With most of the elder generation gone, Elmhurst and Mihri were finally able to helm their families. Their relationship was announced, and although no applause greeted the news, they received no challenge in leadership. Elmhurst limped towards our coffee table, as his leg had been shot clean through outside the cave.

"Cheer up, son," the Colonel poured him a cup. "Four and four may be gone but five and three still equal eight. More importantly, what'll you do with the British authorities?"

"Perhaps the sum of Hackett deaths on this island will satisfy them. I've no intention of re-incarceration. With Christopher gone, Warden Cain soon may find himself sacked."

"It'll be the best thing to ever happen to the man," the Colonel said.

Wounds treated, coffee drunk, there was grim work to be done.

The first joint endeavor for the Hacketts and Nodds was a sour one indeed: graves for the dead. Even with help from Augostino and his sailors, the task took nearly all the day. So it was, that after Mihri asked the Colonel for his services as an orator, the eulogy began with a backdrop of sunset's warm hues settling on a horizon of blue ocean.

"I despise an extinguished life. All who died on this island saw this world we inhabit in their own way. Many worlds were erased here. I will recite now words from one of the many men more eloquent than I, John Donne. '*No man is an island, Entire of itself, Every man is a piece of the continent, A part of the main. If a clod be washed away by the sea, Europe is the less. Any man's death diminishes me, Because I am involved in mankind, And therefore never send to know for whom the bell tolls; It tolls for thee.*'"

The Colonel gestured to the remaining Nodds, who had been given a skipper, and the remaining Hacketts, who had been given oars.

"I've left you just enough fat to fry yourselves in should you wish it. You can fight to the death and leave more European bones on this tragic island, or you can make your way home, together. The thorn of the Sphinx has been removed. Allow the wound to heal, or do not. I care no longer.

"Disgust is an invaluable tool we all possess. It keeps us from drinking diseased water, from eating spoiled food. It is our primal body keeping us from harm. Well I must say that I am disgusted by unnecessary death. I do not decry the constraints of mortality, but I do decry visiting others to that end prematurely. I am disgusted by this inane rivalry based upon greed without end. There are few things that aggravate me worse than the man who seeks more water even after his thirst is slaked. What remains of your families should like to see you again I think, even without the bounty of the Sphinx. I advise you listen to your Prince and Princess, for they alone amongst you have sense."

He stepped down from the rocky pulpit and addressed Elmhurst and Mihri.

"Are you sure you won't travel back with Augostino? He assures me it is no trouble."

"We've a great deal of mending to do in our families," Mihri said. "Both within, and beyond." She took Elmhurst's hand. "Your division of the boat and oars is correct. Our first challenge of unity."

"Should we make it back, we'll look in on the Valriovs. Some must remain," Elmhurst said, nodding solemly to me.

They looked so right, standing hand in hand, and peace actually seemed possible for the devastated families if they wished it.

I hugged them both. What I once thought was love for Elmhurst and what I know was dislike for Mihri, both settled to a friendship I hoped to stoke for many years to come. The pair walked hand in hand to the boat and oars, and quieted an argument brewing between the men. Reconciliation would be a hard bet, but if any were to bring it about, it was the Prince and Princess.

Christopher's bones were laid into a coffin fashioned from the remainder of the Hacketts' basket that had washed ashore. The Colonel and Billingsly stood with the coffin for some time. Then Billingsly walked over to my place on the beach.

"He'd like you to see him off. Wait here just a moment, please."

Billingsly shouted to Augostino, who was readying his ship for our departure. The cork merchant climbed below deck for a second, then reappeared to toss Billingsly a bottle of brandy. Billingsly handed it to me.

"Off you go," he said gently.

I approached the Colonel, seated beside the open coffin.

"Though his character proved unsavoury, I must credit my departed brother with intelligence. Christopher solved Ebbing's riddle and travelled the length of the African continent by land faster than us, and he did so alone. When I say he was bright, you will understand it is not simply sibling pride. Do you believe in an afterlife, Bee?"

"I... I don't know."

"When you've lived amongst the clouds as long as I, a place only slightly more wonderful isn't that difficult to imagine. I cannot claim Christopher a saint. Without making pardons, I believe he was troubled and desperate. That can shade any man's soul after a time. If there is some future plane we are all travelled to, I hope he finds a kind place there, for he surely found none here."

"I've no doubt he has gone to that better place."

"Provided past deeds, future intentions, and overall merit are not taken into consideration for admission, he very well could have." The Colonel smiled at me below the smart moustache. "Now, for a bit of accounting. When you gifted me my flag, I offered the Sphinx in return. I still find it a lopsided deal for you, but if you wish it, the Sphinx is yours."

He produced the cursed jewel from inside his vest, hidden from the Hacketts and Nodds lest it rile them up again, and handed it to me. All but the two of us thought it lost to sea. I studied the thing, its face frozen in an alluring expression that was at once wicked, innocent, and sad. It was heavy and smooth, and very, very beautiful.

"It is common," the Colonel said.

"Colonel," I protested. "You may have opinions on the treasure, but I can hardly agree that it is common."

"It has the power to make men kill. It's the most common thing in the world." He looked at me seriously. "My dear consociate Bee, sometimes the most essential duty of a treasure hunter is to bury what he finds even deeper. Many do not have this will. You and I together have achieved this victory, so I cannot decide its fate without your consultation and blessing. If you desire it, the object is yours, and I will never question you about it again. In the case you do not desire it, I have an alternative suggestion."

Months ago, before the Colonel and the Newlyweds and the Ox, I wince to think what I would've done for an object *half* as precious as the Sphinx. It held immense value, value which could grant the owner many freedoms. But that was a previous life. Now I had these freedoms. The freedom to travel, the freedom to associate with those I liked, the freedom to pursue my interests independent of the order or opinion of others. I had no use for an ornament that the Colonel correctly said had the power only to make men kill. I'd kept the magic lantern and the Spectre because ownership gave me a feeling of power. But I was beyond that now. I no longer needed to control something to hold dominion over it.

I handed the Sphinx back.

"Do with it as you see fit."

The Colonel nodded his thanks. He tilted Christopher's skull back so the jaw opened and placed the Sphinx inside. In that moment, it was struck by a dying ray of the nearly set sun. Red sunlight scattered through the blue of the Sphinx, giving the burned skeleton a lively violet glow. This was no phantasmagoria—it was real, and I was relieved when the Colonel affixed the coffin's lid and nailed it down.

"If the piece truly is a heart scarab, and if heart scarabs hold any power whatsoever, it will take one as supreme as the Blue Star Sphinx to vindicate Christopher. Now then, would you be so kind as to help me set him afloat?"

Together we pushed the coffin through the surf until its weight was taken by the water. Then the Colonel climbed atop.

"My dear Bee, it is now I will bid you *adieu* until we are to meet again."

"What do you mean?"

"I'm afraid the final internment will be private. A brother of mine deserves more from me than a general eulogy focused on Hacketts and Nodds. I hope you don't think it presumptuous, but I ask two favours before we part." He pulled an envelope from his vest pocket. "Where do you intend to go?"

I'd given this no thought.

"London, perhaps? I'd like to see it true."

The Colonel nodded in approval and handed me the letter. "The Newlyweds will help you back safely, and you them, I am sure. Please open the letter upon your return."

"You're setting off alone? Floating upon a coffin? Colonel, you'll die."

The Colonel shook his head and rapped his knuckles atop the coffin.

"It's come from the Hacketts, true, but this is sound English oak! A more seaworthy lumber you'll not soon find."

"But you've lost so much."

"Ebbing perished in the service of his chosen passion, Christopher had the power to prevent the fate that found him, and as for the Ox... she passed into retirement as ceremonial kindling to a fire mountain!"

"Colonel..." I faltered, bringing about my confession at last. "All our time together, I've sought to know you. I don't know whether I do or not."

"I am afforded the pleasure of a great many people in my life because I will it so. We are friends, Bee, in the most undiluted and plainly honest definition available, and I endeavor to earn your future company." He took Grace Ebbing's white rose from his hat and placed it in my hand. He'd somehow kept the flower firm and healthy despite the time passed. The Colonel's energy was evergreen. "It has been, at all times, a pleasure." The coffin was taken up in the receding water, and the Colonel floated away with a tip of his John Bull.

"Colonel!" I called out.

"Nobody likes a prolongued goodbye."

"The second favour."

"Ah yes. The liquor!"

I hurled the forgotten bottle with all my strength, and my aim was true. The Colonel pulled the cork out with his teeth and spit it into the ocean.

"Onward, dear Bee! Onward!" He took a long pull from the bottle and floated upon his brother's coffin into the mists of the sea, a halo of Manx keeping company from above.

-PART EIGHT-

THE HEARTH

Chapter Forty-Seven

Several weeks after departing Xibalba, the Newlyweds and I arrived in London. They assembled for me a chest similar to those given to the Derringer Sisters, and we tearfully parted. They reminded me to read my letter and expressed a hope we would meet soon again.

I read the letter, then began to build a life.

I slept indoors. I ate regular meals. I found employment as a baker's assistant. The work was sometimes dull, but I never shunned a new skill, and my employer possessed no whip. With the tale of the Sphinx told, life returned to its calm pace. Safety became less of a rare luxury. My bed stayed in one place. I played snooker and drank tea with regularity.

The life I'd lead with the Colonel had been one of extremes, sometimes in the negative: close acquaintance with murderers; descents into madness over the sands of Africa; a frail old woman, battered and abused; deceit and greed and betrayal and death. All had been present. I knew not if the Colonel was even alive. A journey of a hundred leagues before he'd touch shoreline, with a coffin for a ship and nothing but bourbon for company? Dubious. If any could manage it though, surely it was the Colonel.

But of course there were terrific heights as well: the tease of adventure that pulled from within the ribs; unpredictable cuisine linked only by loving preparation even if it was no more than desert grass; lightening the burden of souls we met on the road; the Ox, enchanting, elegant, and the closest thing I'd ever had to a home; travelling alongside a utilitarian couple that defined love; and a philandering dandy whose greatest rival could be as deadly and organized as motivated families of means, or as seemingly unremarkable as a common pack rat.

I boarded a train and slept, awaking some time later to the emerald quilt-work of British countryside speeding by my window. I'd a decision to make.

I withdrew the Colonel's note, stamped with CJB in yellow wax, and read it for the hundredth time.

Dearest sibling,

I pray this form letter defies its nature, and is of some interest. We call different countries home, we wear different shades of skin, and we no doubt come from different fathers, but we are, family. Some of you I knew in my youth, some of you I hadn't met until delivering this letter, in either case you are hereby invited to a dinner at my property in Galloway, Scotland. The time and place are included below. Fear no annual obligation of dreary small talk. This is a one-time gathering, never to be repeated. Your attendance would honour the event, and is requested with the utmost enthusiasm. Should you require funds for travel, please write to the address.

Yours in relation,
Colonel James Bacchus
The Hearth
7 Lynne Way
Galloway, Scotland

~~~

Addendum:

Bee,

You have found yourself caught in my familial trawl. I sense you may have been seeking a tribe, even as I endeavoured to assemble my own. Should you wish it, my home is yours, whenever desired.

If you see fit to attend this dinner, and I hope you do, please see yourself arrived earlier in the day at Country Haberdashery and Tailor, located in the same town of Galloway.

The conductor announced Galloway.

Stasis in London was comfortable and not without promise. The largest city in the world at my disposal.
~~~

Travel was… well, travel. I recalled a rare bit of nostalgia from the Colonel, unlocked with a bit of jenever as we'd been drifting above Spain.

"To cross Prague's Charles Bridge in a day's dusk, as fall gives way to winter and a light frost grows upon the bridge's statues, giving their eyes a mischievous glint. To glide an arm's length above the Mediterranean at dawn as the world warms to summer, the scent of toasted almonds and Winter Daphne dancing in the air to lure sailors to the fertile shores. To crest the Temple City of Cambodia at absolutely any time of year, day or night. I have drunk the golden sunlight of Africa and been sung to sleep in fields of diamond snow to the tune of Alpine angels. And the clouds. Fellow travellers that give the sky definition. The noctilucent, glowing icily only at night in the fleeting moment when the sun is below the horizon but some light remains. The stratus, those wonderfully lazy buffers that spread a sprawling carpet for the sky. The mighty cumulonimbus, toiling to reach the heavens and gifting us the artistry of their efforts. The best the world has to offer is not delivered by want alone. One must leave the comfort of the familiar and reach, sometimes into darkness. Think I'm being verbose? Well that's because I am, of course. But these experiences demand the extent of my vocabulary and even then, any wordage falls far short of how those days and nights truly felt."

I left the station. Friendly townspeople guided me to the haberdashery that bore a simple sign reading *Tailor*. I knocked, having no idea what to expect.

The door was answered...

"Thelma!"

"I'm so glad you came, dearie." Her hug briefly relieved me of breath.

"How are you and George? The Colonel. Is he alright? Is he alive?"

"None are in mortal peril. Do come inside, we mustn't be late." She stepped aside for me to enter.

The cozy shop was crowded with the loveliest dresses I'd ever laid eyes on.

"Go ahead," she smiled. "Have a look around."

I did, laying eye and fingertip upon the finest fabrics, the richest colours, and the smartest stitching to ever pass under a needle. The Queens of the world could do no better.

Amongst the dizzying array of finery, one dress stood out. It was the perfect shade of a lavender, and the collar was clean, without the lace and frills of some of the more ornamental numbers. I took stock of the details and stepped backwards, delivering Thelma a look of disbelief. She only smiled.

Stitched into the dress were patterns of flowers. Dandelions, a chocolate daisy, an Osiria rose, a snowdrop, bluebells, Chinese wisteria, the humble cram-cram, a brilliant white rose, and petals of every colour that formed the rainbow of my travels.

"Would you like to try it on?" Thelma asked.

I was speechless, but Thelma knew my answer. She helped me into the lavender wonder and as a sword in its scabbard or a bird in its nest, no place was loose or tight.

"The man knows dimensions by sight I'll give him that," Thelma said, admiring the fit.

"It's the Colonel's commission?" I found my voice at last.

"His idea, his stitching," Thelma scratched a few spots on the embroidery that may have been slightly below her pristine standard. "It is a gift from his heart and hand."

"I... I don't know what to say."

"Yer sayin' it already," she admired me, fighting back tears, then adopted a more dutiful disposition. "Shall we?"

We stepped from the shop and found George waiting with a coach. He wore a top hat.

"If I'm to play butler, I figured I'd best look the part."

"You look dashing," I said.

He extended a hand and delivered me into the coach. Then he saw to Thelma. They shared smiling eyes that must have looked the same the day they met. I estimate that in the history of the world, perhaps six pairs of true soulmates have ever found one another, and I'd the fortune to know one of them. I rode in the harmony of love.

George soon turned down a pretty lane of homes. The modest cottages were largely uniform, and I wondered which could be the Hearth.

A bevy of coachmen chatted pleasantly amongst themselves on the side of the road, smoking and laughing as they did so. Each tipped his cap to Thelma and I as we stepped from George's coach onto the cobblestones that led through the most handsome garden I'd ever come across.

Our path was beset with citrus trees of every kind, branches crowded with fragrant ornaments of yellow and orange, green globes of yet ripe pumpkins and squash crowded delicacies like pineapples and mangoes I'd previously seen only in books. *Scottish mangoes.* Tangles of peppers and chillies neighbored vines of plump tomatoes atop a carpet of wintergreen, the leaves just starting to chequer red. I guessed only the Colonel's touch, or detailed instruction in his absence, could keep such a range of vegetation alive in the inconsiderate climate of Scotland. Each plant grew robust and healthy, not a weed to be found. Two calico cats, lazing at opposite corners of the garden were likely responsible for the absence of animal pests, save for an excessively crafty packrat I spied darting away with a sprig of rosemary amongst hedgerows of herbs.

Although I could see my feet carrying me forward, I must insist I floated through that most improbable of gardens, straight across the doorframe of the house, where waited the most impressive display of all.

Flowers.

By my estimation, all of them.

Tiered rows of tulips like a stadium of pretty spectators, hanging baskets of orchids looking exotic and alien, arrangements of roses in frozen explosions of blazing red and whispering pink. Old favorites and unfamiliar curiosities too numerous to list. A mecca of flora.

"Impressive, even for him, innit?" George said.

"Breathtaking," I agreed.

George introduced me into a large dining room where a group of seventeen men and women chatted happily in several different languages. My top-hatted escort left me with Billingsly and the maid from Chartish's estate, then excused himself to finish some preparations.

"I recall your talent well," the maid said with a glow. "I don't think any present that night will have soon forgotten it."

"I hope you've found employment in a place other than Chartish Manor."

"My dear, bolstered by my brother's generous gift of currency and your brash performance, I quit the very same night."

"How are your experiments going, Billingsly?" I shouted.

"My what? Oh, experiments! Absolutely marvellous! Haven't had a fire in the lab for weeks now."

I met each of the Colonel's siblings, all of whom promised to be very interesting, exceptionalism proving a common trait amongst them.

"Ladies and gentlemen, please take your seats at the table, dinner is about to begin," George announced.

All seemed to know their seat at the broad table, and easily filtered into waiting chairs. I alone was left standing, wondering where my place was. Had my attendance been overlooked?

Thelma emerged from behind a kitchen door, carrying a tray of delectable cuisine. She wore a splendid evening gown that flowed in her hasty wake. George hurried off to help, and with their efforts, every centimetre of the wood was quickly covered in food and drink.

Then, from the kitchen, emerged the Colonel.

Preparing enough to feed an army hadn't affected his manner of dress: a brilliant orange Tiger Lily blazing in the breast pocket of a tweed suit. His combed hair was surprisingly visible, the usual John Bull must have been for traveling. The last detail I noticed was the face upon his watch, finally correct as a grandfather clock elsewhere in the house struck eight o'clock.

His eyes found me. He nodded and smiled. I've no idea if I even smiled back so overwhelmed was I with contentedness. Somehow, through unimaginable fortune, I'd found the Colonel and his Ox. Against improbable odds we'd bested adversaries, solved mysteries, forged a friendship, survived a journey to hell and back. And although neither of us had gotten perhaps what we believed we deserved, we had both arrived at this place and seemed not dissatisfied.

The host pulled a chair I'd failed to notice next to Billingsly and beckoned me forward. I took it and nuzzled between support on all sides, a banquet of food before me.

The Colonel stood at the head of the table and raised a glass.

Through the window behind, I watched the play of Manx shearwaters, hopping from perch to perch atop folded red canvas, bundles of freshly cut rattan, and a flag bearing the crest of our family.

About the Author

Patrick was born in Wisconsin, grew up in Illinois, and now lives in California, practicing the alchemy of writing: coffee turns into words, words turn into money, money turns back into coffee. Repeat until dead.

For more, please visit Patrick online at:
Personal Website: www.PartickCanningBooks.com
Publisher Website: www.EvolvedPub.com/PCanning
Goodreads: Partick Canning
Twitter: @CanningWrites
Facebook: www.Facebook.com/Patrick.Canning
Instagram: www.Instagram.com/catpanning

More from Evolved Publishing

We offer great books across multiple genres, featuring hiqh-quality editing (which we believe is second-to-none) and fantastic covers.

As a hybrid small press, your support as loyal readers is so important to us, and we have strived, with tireless dedication and sheer determination, to deliver on the promise of our motto:
QUALITY IS PRIORITY #1!

Please check out all of our great books,
which you can find at this link:
www.EvolvedPub.com/Catalog/

Thank you!